SOUR LAKE, TEXAS

Jon Plaut

MINERVA PRESS

LONDON
MONTREUX   LOS ANGELES   SYDNEY

SOUR LAKE, TEXAS

Copyright © Jon Plaut 1998

ISBN 1 86106 849 2

First Published 1998 by
MINERVA PRESS
195 Knightsbridge
London SW7 1RE

2nd Impression 1998

Printed in Great Britain for Minerva Press

SOUR LAKE, TEXAS

To my wife Anne,
who is my inspiration and support, and my industrial and
environmental colleagues, who provided a place for me to
personally and professionally grow. The story and characters of
this book are entirely fictitious and a product of my
imagination.

About the Author

Jon Plaut lives in the United States. He has an engineering and legal background and is the retired director of Environmental Quality for a multinational corporation. Mr. Plaut was appointed to the Joint Public Advisory Committee of the NAFTA Environmental commission by President Clinton in 1994. He teaches environmental policy at the Pennsylvania State University and writes and lectures extensively in the United States. He and his wife Anne are long-time residents of Summit, New Jersey, and have three sons.

Contents

Author's Note

This journal fragment by Dan Straus was found in the back of a desk drawer in his office after he left American Industrial, Inc., for Stanford University. The journal was written in the year before the events of this book started to unfold. It sheds some light, perhaps, on his strivings. The last entry is in November 1994.

Dan's Journal

August 9, 1994

It's funny how thoughts converge. I am sitting in this little vest-pocket park. Cal's Park, next to Cal's Way, a shaded walkway, bestowed with flowers, leading to Central Avenue on one end and a parking lot at the other, in nearby Westfield, where I like to stroll and shop. Who Cal was (local hero, revolutionary war minuteman, merchant, mayor?) I don't know.

For a few months, now, I've found it a particularly contemplative suburban oasis in which to scribble in my Journal. Sitting here today, on the wooden bench, with its little plaque to the mysterious Cal, I find myself thinking about the more recent works of V.S. Naipaul, the Trinidadian/ Indian/ English writer. Naipaul has challenged my imagination with single-line thoughts or sentences spoken to the reader which he then at first simply and then comprehensively expands to profound elucidation. In his books about colonialism he expresses a subtlety of thought and communication which particularly speaks to me.

Why? Because that type of expanding elucidation (although probably not so profound) happens in my head, too, and often.

Take today. I am sitting in Cal's Park thinking about this beautiful, young, Hispanic woman I have seen several times on the street, and just seen as I write this.

She is lovely-looking – tall, long, black hair, which she wears to each side, and an angled, sensuous face off a Velazquez painting. She has large, rounded breasts, which seem to want to break out of their restraints, and a pert rear end set up high on long legs. Her clothes are chic and she dresses to emphasize her endowments, as does her regal posture and bearing. She is a friendly, young woman, talking to the many acquaintances she passes as she strolls during her lunch hour. Indeed, she has begun nodding or greeting me with a smile and hello, which I return, when she passes me upon my shaded bench. Her voice is melodious with the islands, but her English is quite good.

I doubt we will ever really meet, but I find myself thinking about her beautiful body. My thoughts are erotic. My features may remain a pleasant mask, when I see her, but she is putting me in inner tumult.

I am not a stalker, but today I went to my shady spot hoping I would see her. She occupied my thoughts in bed last night after my wife and I said good night. I literally put myself to sleep thinking of her.

Now, what does this all mean, I ask myself. I have problems in my marriage – lots of anger and tension. But we have two wonderful young children! What the hell is going on in my mind, my loins, my inner life? What does this mean for my future? Am I destined to this apparently frustrating sexual turmoil as I grow older?

A prisoner in the house of love, Anaïs Nin wrote. Am I such a prisoner? I sincerely hope not because I do not want such strife, as my searching apparently brings me. I am not strong enough to disregard the feelings of others in pursuit of my sexual ego. I will just cause pain if I gratify my lust – and I will be the first and the last to feel that pain, I think.

What if this beautiful, Latin, young woman were to pursue me for a mere dalliance? Whom am I kidding? Wouldn't I eagerly succumb! But then my mind plays back on my thoughts, redigesting them. What if I met a woman who truly met my needs and satisfied my cravings? Could I walk away from that; from my marriage, my children and my history?

How much does my sexuality dominate my pursuit of what is good for me? While on the surface, job, career, family, public good predominate, underneath that is not what seems to impel me at all. The veneer of society and responsibility just covers the lusting heart. Jimmy Carter was right after all!

I think, next week, I'll alter my routine and sit in this lovely park at a different time. No use tempting fate. Or giving my desire the chance to triumph over my better nature.

September 23, 1994

I have this great fear that my life will be a stereotype. I suppose everyone worries about that. My dad used to say that the secret is to find out what is yourself because you could not 'to thine own self be true' until you knew yourself.

I know I do something useful. If environmental advocacy isn't useful, particularly in a big chemical company, then what is? I've got a wife and two terrific, little kids, but still I feel I'm living this stereotype of rising Jewish boy in the suburbs. Stupid, because it's someone else's stereotype, not mine, yet it dogs me.

One of the most devastating books I've read in a long time is John Updike's short stories collected about a theme, *The Maple Stories*. The theme is the dissolution of a marriage and personal disintegration, with all the resultant cruelty and pathos. Updike takes the casual and deliberate hedonism of a marriage unglued and makes it so personal and unnerving. At least, for me, who worries that this is beginning to happen in my marriage.

The corrosive effect of the breakdown of caring for another (that's real hedonism to me) is horrifying in *The Maple Stories*. While I do care about my marriage, and particularly about my wife's well-being, as well as my daughters (everyone cares about their children, don't they?), and, in fact, try and act in a caring manner, the yelling and discord is more than I seem to be able sometimes to bear. We must work harder at our mutual caring, and stop assigning blame!

To some extent these thoughts came to me as part of the special day today is.

It is Rosh Hashanah – the Jewish New Year and I am at my bench in my little park, increasingly my way station in Westfield.

Rosh Hashanah is always hard for me. I am a Jew and proud of it, but there they all are today at the traditional synagogue, while I sit in my little park, my way station, with my beliefs and doubts, worrying about our future.

October 4, 1994

Ten days since I last wrote. I miss my journal when I don't write in it. That doesn't say I'm particularly egotistic or infatuated with my thoughts, I don't think. Because I miss the theater, too, when I don't go for a while. And I have to be in the process of reading a book or I guiltily feel I'm wasting my time.

All that has to be a legacy from my parents who were culture doers – writing, going to museums, plays and movies, and always reading up a storm. I joined their book club when I was thirteen as a sort of Bar Mitzvah present.

As very modern, non-believing Jews, they did believe in the cultural education and admission to Judaism that my Bar Mitzvah signified, and to seal the bargain they asked me if I wanted to read *Lust for Life* and participate in the discussion group with them. As a stammerer, emerging from that painful affliction in adolescence and now thinking more like an adult, I was overjoyed. From then on I was a fully accepted part of that adult group.

The only art form I really added culturally to the arsenal imbibed from my parents in terms of appreciation was classical music. Somehow they missed that, although my father was a real student of musical theater (Gershwin, Cole, Rodgers and Hart, etc.) and did sometimes listen to opera on the radio.

But the dedication I feel to switching on classical music along with *The New York Times* in the morning is a ritual they did not experience. Incidentally, while I have that one newspaper I buy everywhere, my dad read at least four each day – *The Tribune*, *The Post*, *The Brooklyn Eagle* and of course the *Times*, and sometimes *The World Telegram*, too. If they were still available, I probably would emulate him there. But only *The Post* and *The News* survive, besides the *Times* and *The Post* particularly is a disgrace, a rag, a shameful, libelous, scandalous blast on journalism, which cares not how wrong it gets the story or whom it defames.

Anyway, it's been ten days since I last wrote, so today is Yom Kippur – the day for fasting and atonement for religious Jews and for rethinking and restating for liberal Jews like me.

I have been rethinking. I feel something's coming, as Stephen Sondheim wrote, in *West Side Story*. I don't know what but I want to be ready for it. My life seems on the verge of expanding, of growing, of changing. To a large extent I feel as I did in adolescence and ceasing to stammer – on the verge of a new life. But what?

I want my family to share in it. For my wife and I to get over these hard personal times. To not only, do something extraordinarily good, but with growth and change in it for me and for those with whom my life is so intertwined.

I feel a renewal, a refreshment, a breeze of excitement this Yom Kippur. I will respond with love and new, intellectual vigor in my striving for something better. Does that sound hopelessly idealistic? Anyway, that's my New Year resolution.

October 5, 1994

Yesterday I was optimistically writing about a renewal for me. And I do feel optimistic although not Pollyannish.

I have always thought the calendar New Year should be celebrated in September. The Jewish holidays have it right! When kids go back to school, when Summer's heat is renewed by Fall's freshness (or in Spring in the Southern hemisphere), that is the right time for the New Year to start. At the Fall equinox. To celebrate at the Winter or Summer solstice is not, for me, when renewal begins, the accident of Christ's birth, if he was then, in fact, born, notwithstanding.

I've had two great renewals in my life. The first I've already mentioned occurred between about twelve and fifteen years of age, when I stopped stammering.

I had a bad stammer, so bad that I often couldn't speak, particularly in school. A bright kid frustrated by being unable to achieve? Growing up in a home with great expectations and the resultant pressure? Some physiological cause? I don't know, nor did anyone else, but the stammer was a great burden, which often rendered me helpless, and perhaps a little more sympathetic to the underdog than most kids.

I suppose I always knew in my thought processes that the stammer would go away, as it so often does, but I didn't see when, and my gut ached from the rejection I felt. When the stammer terminated, and after, I didn't know why. I just discovered in adolescence increased confidence, greater intellectuality supporting athletic ability, which my peers respected, and increased comfort in myself. And, also, and I realize this is not such a little 'and', my developing sexuality gave me a drive and self-awareness, which I believe made me believe in myself.

The second renewal occurred a few years later, at Michigan State.

I was a good student – actually academics were always easy for me. I was still considered a good athlete, even at college level, developing out of adolescence an easy talent other young men respected and sought in me. My ability to talk and think (no stammer, thank you) attracted smart, pretty girls to me and me to them. I found that nothing charmed a girl more than good talk. Chatting her up became a skill I perfected. I was really good at what is now called 'relating' and my driving sexuality won for me whatever I could not otherwise gain.

I did not exercise my intellect, verbal and athletic ability, and sexuality for power, however, but for approval. I was still so desirous of approval.

I had a wonderful professor, Dr. Tom Foley, who urged me and my college roommate into the debating club. In that we were perhaps anomalies. Engineering students in debate. There we were, with all the poly scis and pre-laws, researching, arguing, dissecting, reasoning and orating in competition. And I was really good at it – more than that, I excelled.

Debate changed me. It put me on the road of careful thought and analysis. I began auditing what I heard and saw – putting it through an intellectual separator, which also demanded verbal analysis of the rationale perceived. Intellectually, truth and my perception and expression of it became more important to me than pleasing.

I do not believe I have yet completed this course of renewal begun in adolescence and reinforced at Michigan State. Emotionally, I am still not mature. Emotionally, I still want to please. I believe love and caring should be constant. I can't abide the anger. I don't know what I want, but I think I need to trust others more, even when they are unreasonably angry.

I am hopeful.

October 10, 1994

I am on the road doing an environmental audit in Lumberton, North Carolina. I have a slight sore throat and I guess a developing cold, so I am babying myself tonight with hot tea and honey, which I got the room service kitchen to rustle up. I will have a very early sleep, I hope.

The audit team, including myself as the leader, just had a small first-night dinner with the plant management. I begged off further discussion over drinks, although it was quite interesting and unusual, perhaps even unique, in view of the plant we are reviewing. Lumberton, North Carolina, is the home of a reservation of the Lumbar Indians, a tribe of thousands still intact in these Pinelands. The plant, where molecular sieves are made for such uses as HF gas treatment, employs eight hundred Americans of Indian descent in an intensive assembly operation.

In fact, all the employees are Lumbar Indians, with the exception of the plant manager, who is a pleasant but very out of place, red-headed and red-faced Irish chap, called, appropriately, Red.

The Indian tribe runs the plant and tolerates Red, according to Red. All the other management people are men with tribal positions, even the environmental and safety director who went to Duke and has a civil engineering degree. The plant is well run, and, in many ways, a tribute to the tribe and their constructive family (tribal) approach.

The only really disturbing issue (I doubt we are going to find any serious environmental or safety issues) is gender-related. Women have all the lower, hand-assembly jobs. Men are the managers, the heavy lifters and the maintenance people. I'm sure this reflects the tribal organization and you don't want to mess with local culture we always say, but it sure was evident on the first walk-around today.

I raised the gender subject with Red, informally, at dinner. He said that is the way it is, and it works quite well. I felt he was warning me to stay away from this issue. I heard the same thing, in an audit in Brazil recently, from a Brazilian-Portuguese plant manager who told me, when I asked about the young age of some of the lowest-level female workers, 'Okay, Yankee, but it keeps them off the streets, you know.'

I'm thinking also that this is the first time I have been even a little sick since I don't know when. I pulled some ligaments in high school, sliding into second base, and spent some time at home, until I could hobble around, but that is not sick!

I just don't get sick. But I also don't think of myself in any superman terms. Decidedly not. My childhood stammer was a searing disability, which will not allow such haughty nonsense.

I do have a friend, who I don't see much any more, who bothers me with his self-centered conceits. Maurice thinks of himself and his family as the super élite. The strange thing about Maurice is that he is a surgeon, but he clearly believes that good health is good genes and mind over negative thoughts.

I digress. What I wanted to express is my feeling of hope and optimism, but also my worry that my family and I are more vulnerable than I suspect to some danger or destruction that I can't pinpoint. I seem to anticipate disrupting change. I don't know what I'm talking about, except that I know my personal life must change to avoid an illness of spirit for me. But change how? What am I looking for, or at least waiting for?

October 17, 1994

One week has passed since my last entry. I went to the dentist this morning – but that is another story, which, maybe, I'll dwell on first.

I hate and fear all dentists.

It goes back to my childhood, I'm sure. My dentist was up a long, narrow flight of stairs from a street-level landing. I'd ride my bicycle there. In those days, before the wholesale thievery that exists today, I'd lock my bike to a lamppost and ascend those stairs to the waiting resident sadist, Dr. Simon.

I had lots of childhood cavities, which Dr. Simon would insist could be drilled and filled without painkiller. I was not the type of child to protest. Simon used to call his young nurse, Mary, in to help him (and presumably to watch me writhe and sweat in anticipation and then pain). He would always smile benignly, while he inflicted the pain. I knew he was a fake, but no one else, including my mother, seemed to notice. I think I learned to distrust the smiling veneer of personality because of Dr. Simon.

While he drilled, the good doctor liked to rub Mary's ass. She liked it too, I guess, because the ritual was repeated on each visit. God knows what they did after I left!

Anyway, that sexual play between Dr. Simon and Mary was my only diversion in the dentist's chair of torture – sort of like the function office fish tanks serve these days. Very modern and considerate of the sadistic doctor!

So, I still feel great apprehension on going to the dentist for yearly checkups, which these days pass quite without incident.

To compensate, I take a half-day for the semiannual experience, so I am sitting in my little street park again today, waiting to smile and nod at my beautiful, big-busted and tight-assed Hispanic secretary. Memories of Dr. Simon and Mary make me envision much more, if I were ever so bold as to approach her more familiarly.

I've had this realization lately that my job is sinking into the repetition of weekly plant visits, with the routine of recommendations and improvements in environmental operation no longer as satisfying to me. I know that routine maintains and produces good environmental conduct, but I'm getting less of a kick from it. Perhaps I will become like

Dr. Simon rubbing the rear end of some little Mary, to keep myself going. I hope not.

Something's got to happen to lift me out of this lethargy.

October 20, 1994

I had an amazing and frustrating luncheon today with a Congressman from New Jersey. A Democrat, Joe Marks votes liberally and is sensitive to the needs of his constituents, the lower middle class of mostly Jewish, but some of Irish, Hispanic and Black African origin of the Newark suburbs. He is very pro-education and environment. He runs with almost token opposition.

Yet, where he could afford to be a decent fellow, as well as the progressive leader he is, rather he is all ego, defensive and a true bastard. Congressman Marks is a screamer.

He didn't miss a chance to act disgruntled, blame, ridicule and even yell at his chief of staff, his press secretary and a poor young lady, who was a note-taker at the meeting. I was truly embarrassed, as were they – although Marks didn't seem to care or have a clue as to his shameful conduct.

I was there to discuss environmental issues, along with Tom Foley from Michigan State (who invited me) and a public health expert from EPA-Region 3. Seems Marks is a Michigan State graduate and is very favorable to the university, even though he represents a New Jersey district. At one point he started to berate me because I think he didn't agree with my view about NAFTA. He said he was against NAFTA but for GATT! I asked him to explain that – I was truly interested – and he said, raising his voice, that he didn't need to explain to me as I was there to brief him.

I told him I couldn't continue if he persisted in this insulting way of talking to me, and he backed off, saying it was just his way of talking and I shouldn't be so touchy. His press rep was actually cringing with hatred for this guy. Fuck him, his eyes said. What an ego.

I talked to the press representative after the lunch. A really intelligent and sweet young guy who was obviously good at his job, he told me he would leave Marks as soon as he found another good job. He – David was his name – explained that those who stayed with Marks were beaten into pulp psychologically by this maniac egoist. David explained that, no matter how good Mark's rating and constituent record, staying with him was impossible in view of his reign of terror as a boss. Those who stayed, David said, became meek subjects, cynics or, worse, alcoholics.

David told me there were many representatives like Marks in Congress. They thought of themselves as the product. When he told me that he would not leave Marks until he found a good, new job, because he needed the recommendation of this tyrant (and not to leave on his wrong side), I despaired for him.

If that is the political process – who wants it! The arrogance of this little king, and he gets away with it. It's enough to turn you into a mountain man, or an anti-government vigilante, until you remember that those people are even more dangerous bums.

Oh well. Whatever is coming for me – it's not where the environment meets politics, unless I can somehow do good without doing harm there.

November 1, 1994

When I was fourteen and still stammering slightly, but feeling a new power, maybe even a new me, emerging, I fell under the sexual spell of a rather rough, lower-class and stunning girl in my school.

I first noticed her in an assembly, when she sat almost directly in front of me. We weren't in the same classrooms because I was on the upper college preparatory track, and that was not in her scope. She had long brownish-blonde hair and a pouting, Russian face. Her bust was developed and high. And she had a splendid shape – particularly her narrow waist and beautiful legs. She probably would grow fat, as she aged, but, at fourteen, she was luscious and magnetic. I was infatuated by the sight of her.

Her name was Carolyn Dryer. At first I walked the halls between classes keeping an eye out for her. As I learned where Carolyn walked, I went out of my way – rather frantically – to see her. In not too long, she began locking in on my glance and smiling when our eyes met.

I was crazy with her shape and sexuality. I thought about her constantly, day and night.

Then, one day, I was at my book locker, after school, after a basketball game and she came down the hall toward me, swinging her body in a female teenage swagger, which said 'I know what I've got'. It was clear that she arranged this little walk for me and that I should respond, or go down as a wimp.

Without stammer, I said hello and asked her what she was doing in school so late in the afternoon. She said she was a majorette at marching practice. She said she had seen me playing basketball.

Without recounting more details of the conversation, I will only say I amazed myself with my sexual confidence and boldness, not to mention my absence of speech defect. We walked out of school together. She was very forward and, when I stopped before turning toward the bus stop, she turned, so that her hand touched my arm and her breast brushed me, and asked if I wanted to walk to the other corner and a drugstore, where we might have a Coke. I nodded and we walked and chatted. I had a tremendous hard-on, which I covered with the books I was carrying for homework that night.

She walked freely – no books – and I chatted her up. Where did I learn to do this? I had never done it before and my fantasies always went straight to sex, not plotting what I would say. It was clear to me, as we sat in the luncheonette, that talking with her in an inclusive way, while my physicalness was in view, turned her on. She felt complimented that I would actually converse with her – a lower-class girl, who was clearly on a different track from me but who, as I had demonstrated over the weeks as I sought her out, attracted me.

In later years, I found that talking, talking, talking, while sexuality developed, was a great technique. The intellectual and sexual, symbiotic effect I had on women seemed a power to emerge organically from me. My torture and turmoil over the stammering years seemed to me to be a precondition to this power. I didn't understand all this clearly with this first girl, Carolyn, nor do I now, although I have often examined it, as I have grown increasingly restless these last few months.

This power and its genesis are both realities for me and the women, including my wife, to whom I relate. My ability to easily talk and intellectualize and to naturally include the woman within that orbit in a way that compliments her, is a tremendous aphrodisiac to the sexual relationship, which I thus have the power to coax along.

It seems to me that my wife has recently grown tired of this technique and power of mine – as if it is not an organic part of my personality and character. I can't turn it on and off; it is just there. It is me. Is Gloria growing tired of me?

Is that the source of her fierce bursts of anger which so defeat me? Do I handle her tirades so poorly because I feel my confidence – my emergence from speech deficit – slipping? I don't even like to think about this.

And the end of my adolescent story. It is not so unusual. Our puppy love and attraction took hold for a while. We were briefly a number. She was so goddamned attractive and I was an athlete/ student, who was starting to be noticed. We lost our virginity to each other but, ultimately, our differences prevailed. Our eyes wandered in the adolescent dance.

November 2, 1994

The first time I went to Carolyn Dryer's apartment I was shocked by the surroundings and my boldness.

She lived above a store in a railroad flat-style apartment. It had had a fire at some earlier time and still had charred areas, albeit mostly painted over. You could still smell the fire and burnt wood. I learned early – almost as a warning – from Carolyn that her mother was a single parent. The alcoholic father 'Bastard,' as she put it, was, apparently, a petty hood and had abandoned them when she was a child. Her mother worked in a garment factory and had a gritty life of her own. I only met her once. She was a blowsy, portly faded sexpot. A tintype, I was sure, in my class consciousness, of what her daughter would become.

We went to her tiny room, empty of almost all the things I treasured – books, a TV, paintings, posters, mementos – except for a little forty-five r.p.m record player, to make love. Frank Sinatra sang *Blue Moon* over and over while we did it. She was fearless, reckless, passionate.

But we were both mainly into our own pleasure. We enjoyed the sexual relationship, as two puppies might enjoy their play, but mostly we liked being a number to our disparate friends. We never kidded ourselves, however, into thinking we loved each other or were a permanent couple.

When I say I was bold, it was not only to Carolyn or her surroundings so alien to me, an upper-class, Jewish fourteen and then fifteen-year-old, but also to my own capacity and capabilities. I was so damn sure of myself! It was like my organic change conned my old self into total congruence with the new.

My experience with adolescence was thus extraordinary. It wasn't just maturity and not stammering. I emerged from my old self physically, sexually and socially. Oh, the old Dan – steeped in family and in educational striving was still there – but internally built upon, to produce the new confident, physical and verbal Dan.

I went through a very cocky phase, which Carolyn loved, in our brief, intense, although always external, relationship. She once told me quite matter-of-factly, when I had apologized for the moralizing of one of my affected friends, who was lording his brightness over her, that I shouldn't worry, as long as she could hang on to my arm and feel my cock in her at night's end. She knocked me over with that!

Another funny thing. We never used protection (this was pre-AIDS) and she didn't get pregnant. God knows what we would have done if she had. She said she knew an abortionist, when I raised the issue. I guess she just assumed I would pay for an abortion if she was unlucky.

One night, soon after my fifteenth birthday, I begged off a party she wanted to go to, saying playing a school baseball game had worn me out. The truth was I was tiring of Carolyn and her limitations and didn't know how to break it off. She said she would go anyway with a girlfriend. Mid-evening I decided to go and found her, in a corner, making out with our muscular, star Italian catcher. I wasn't as outraged as I pretended, and used the incident as my excuse to end it. In retrospect, I believe she was as glad as I for us to split.

I never stammered again. My years of doubt and agony were over. I was the star of my confirmation class delivering the sermon on a modern Jewish interpretation of the Ten Commandments. I felt I was something special. I so deeply loved my parents, my new confidence, my life, my future.

Not until later-life events – Dr. Foley raising my intellectuality to scholarship, the courtship of my wife and then the birth of our daughters – and then my dad's death – was I to again feel such profound change.

November 27, 1994

Thanksgiving with my mom in Florida was a mixed experience, at best. The girls loved Florida – the beach, Sea World, the excitement of such warm weather in late November. But my mom witnessed an explosion of temper by Gloria, with me as the target, which was based on almost nothing, and so dispirited me.

I rallied for the sake of the holiday and because I am weak, when it comes to family conflict, but I am so sick of the irrational contentiousness. Gloria even turned to my mom that night, when I was trying to smooth it over, and asked her how she had managed to have such a paragon of temperateness, 'Such a Jesus Christ,' she said.

I had bad dreams last night. First I restlessly fell asleep to dream my dad had returned to my house from death, to be in my care. He was very infirm and unsteady of body, but sharp as a tack in mental acuity. I kept commenting on that to him, and he answered, 'What did you expect? Nothing works, but I died intact.' I was responsible for him, but in ways unspecified in the dream. I was failing him. I awoke very disturbed.

The second dream, when I forced myself back to sleep, was worse. It was the only time it has ever occurred, but once was enough. I dreamt I was at a family party and I was to make a toast – to what I know not.

My stammer had returned with a vengeance and I could not speak, no matter how hard I might try. Gloria was laughing quite hysterically, saying she sympathized – Oh, she really did – but it was funny, you know, for the perfect man and the family icon to be so humbled. I was in agony and woke up in a cold sweat, shaking. I did not go to sleep again, but went into the living room and watched *It Happened One Night* on TV.

What is my resolve? I don't know. I want to find a new path with Gloria, but what is it and how will we find it when she has so much anger.

I don't know what to do.

My confidence doesn't help me to know. I feel lost. Trying doesn't seem to help. What would my dad say? Work is not enough to get me over this. What will happen to me? To us? How will I go on in this mode? Gide wrote 'Life must go on. Life can't go on. Life goes on.' But how? In what way?

Chapter One
Prologue

1. The President

Marv Friedman was a self-made man. And a tough man, yes sir. He liked to demonstrate that to his business subordinates at the Specialty Chemicals Sector of American Industrial Inc. Formerly an accountant, with a sharp eye for fat in any budget, Marv had risen as a Jew in the chemical industry, with all its active and latent anti-Semitism, by being the hard-nosed businessman. He was short, stocky and pugnacious. He practiced giving the air of no nonsense, and he did everything in the stereotype of the know-it-all, too loud Jew.

Marv was unintentionally making that point to Dan Straus, the thirty year old corporate environmental auditor, at a meeting between the two at the company's suburban corporate office, in New Brunswick, New Jersey.

'You have to have balls in this business, Straus,' Marv said to Dan with a steely intensity.

Marv always used shock and his lustiness to make a point in his moves with subordinates. He affected the rough exterior of a drill sergeant. His staff said there was no heart of gold underneath. It was early January, 1995. They were reviewing the excursion and accident report the previous quarter at Specialty Chemical's hydrogen fluoride plant, in Sour Lake, Texas.

'The investigation by the plant and those government schmucks is over,' Marv opened. 'The chairman thinks there is more to it. Give us the answers.'

'If somebody screwed up, I want his ass,' Marv said, 'because I won't tolerate screw-ups. A fatality is a royal screw up,' he added, putting special vocal emphasis on the royal. 'But don't you think you can close that process down, whatever the freaking policy might say,' Marv continued, 'because I'll have your ass, too, if you do that. Money, money, money,' Marv was saying to Dan, 'That's what I'm interested in. You can threaten whoever and whatever you like, when you get down there, but don't think you can close it down, my corporate staff friend.' Marv concluded, 'Because that plant is a key to our production and sales and our profit.

'Profit, profit, profit,' Marv reemphasized, actually banging his fist an his desk, 'and don't you forget it, buddy boy.'

Before Dan could reply, or even blink in response to this demeaning lecture Marv came out from behind his massive desk and led the way into the adjoining conference room, where, all smiles, he welcomed his plant manager, from Sour Lake, whom Marv just called J.D., and the graying and balding environmental staff VP, Charlie Moore, who was nervously pulling at his tie and buttoned collar, as he contemplated how this all might cause some difficulty before he reached his retirement date, just two and one half years hence.

Marv waved to the group to sit down. There were no introductions. He opened aggressively with, 'Has anyone seen that legal ass-licker Cory?' Bill Cory was the company environmental lawyer assigned to the Sector.

As Marv made the inquiry, almost on cue, Bill entered the room in a three button and vested suit, looking at his watch and saying to no one in particular, 'Sorry I'm late.'

'Okay,' Marv said in his best no-nonsense manner, but also deferential to the professional corporate lawyer in his midst. 'Now let us get started. Here are my rules for this investigation,' he continued. '*One*', he almost shouted, 'no one gets in Straus's way. We want to know what happened to those crackers in Sour Lake. Straus reports to me and no one slows him down. *Two*, whoever is at fault is fired. Cory you can dress it up nice, but he is *out*. *Three*, fuck the media, no reply to them till we know what happened. You all get it.' No response was necessary or wanted.

At that point, Anne Hennessy, the young (twenty-eight year old) PR gal, entered the room, after knocking gently on the open door, smoothing her short skirt and taming back her luminous red hair as she sat. Charlie Moore liked looking at her shapely bosom, and even joked about it with Marv in private, but he kept his eyes down in this meeting. He had learned long ago that to avoid direct eye contact was often to avoid trouble, no matter what the level.

'Miss Hennessy,' Marv said focusing on the young and snappy public affairs officer he had brought into the organization from the Toronto operation, 'I want you to go down to Sour Lake with Mr. Straus and arrange for whatever he needs.' Lewd thoughts went through Charlie's mind, but he continued to keep his eyes down. After all, wasn't he the one Marv relied on to keep things humming.

Marv continued, 'And I want the families of our two dead workers treated well through the investigation, Anne, although we don't have to roll over dead on the damages process, Mr. Cory do we?'

Marv really didn't like lawyers, that was clear. He had just returned from a Chemical Manufacturers Industry Association meeting, where their monkey Washington lawyer had ridiculed his view that they ought to fight those Washington bureaucrats at every step.

'Why the fuck should we give in to those guys,' he said. 'They don't run our business. They're just busybodies, or worse, whores, out for votes.'

He took up that argument with Bill Cory now saying, 'And what are we doing in Washington these days, if we can't get them to understand the costs of totally useless community hand holding.'

Charlie thought about Marv's statement to him, a few months ago, before the accident. 'Those pricks in the Federal Government want to give all those local environmental dicks a blow job to keep them happy,' but he kept his head down.

'I want reports,' Marv said to Dan, 'and from you, too, but daily, Miss Hennessy. If we need a consultant to help on technical matters, good old Charlie here will help you out,' he added, 'but let's keep it in house and away "from the corporate moguls" [he meant the chairman, they all understood] until we know what's what.

'Any questions?' he concluded. There never was. J.D. had never spoken, nor had they been formally introduced, Dan realized later.

2. The Environmental Vice-President

Tom O'Rourke was hail-fellow-well-met. Even his severest critics agreed that he had great political skills, including antenna reading the temper of management and the times.

Tom was skilled at conciliation and working things out with his good-fellow attitude. He had led environment into a new era in the company. He was creative and fun to be with. He hung on through many crises, because he knew when to hang in the back.

Tom had been a scholar from a poor Catholic family in Staten Island, who went to RPI. He was gaga over the upper crust of society, attending and joining the local country club and fitting in. He saw himself as a success and had switched from his laborer father's popular New Dealism to become a dyed-in-the-wool Republican conservative, an individualist, as he preferred to think about it.

What survived of his parental Irish influence was his tremendous interest in people and their stories, their lives, their fates. He was famous for his interest in people, or his humanism, as his supporters put it.

Tom had a facility for hiring creative young professionals for his staff. He liked giving them their lead, as long as they didn't get him or the department in trouble. So, they had begun environmental auditing in the Seventies when it was largely unknown in other companies. Tom O'Rourke was proud to think of what they had pioneered at American Industrial and strongly believed the government was not capable of such a breakthrough.

Dan Straus was one in a string of environmental auditors who had learned the system at American. Tom had quickly become Dan's mentor, and he encouraged Dan to mentor others coming up the ladder. That was his way.

Tom liked Dan for his independence and even for his liberal leanings. He thought of himself as a mentor to these young people, and indeed he was, while he kept them in line and played the corporate political game.

Dan Straus was reviewing with Tom O'Rourke his assignment to investigate the accident and resultant fatalities at Sour Lake. 'So I'm given *carte blanche*, Tom, but Mr. Friedman really got excited about not interfering with profits. "Profits, profits, profits," he actually yelled at me.'

'Look Dan,' Tom responded, 'you'll get used to Marv – he wants you to do a good job, he really does, but he's a hard-headed businessman and wants to do his job, too, thank God, and that's make money. He's paying your salary, Dan. So you go down there, Dan,' Tom continued, 'and leave no stone unturned, but don't rattle those good old boy Texans too much, okay? And keep me informed.'

Dan squirmed. He thought of his dad joking that a major league manager – Leo Durocher – would tell a pitcher at the mound 'to make the batter hit a bad ball, but don't walk him'. But Dan nodded his assent, adding, 'By the way, Marv asked that PR gal upstairs, Anne Hennessy, to go with me and handle the press.'

'Good,' Tom responded. 'She should be a big help. Just don't let your wife get a look at who you're traveling with.' Tom chuckled.

Dan squirmed again. How much did Tom know about the uneasy state of his marriage? Was he fishing or just being conversational? And what would Gloria think about his traveling with Anne for a week. She was attractive – and sexy. Would it just provoke another argument, he thought.

'Hey, don't worry about any of that, Dan,' Tom said, reading his mind. 'I was only kidding. Just do your job,' he concluded and then added, 'and keep us out of trouble.'

There were a lot of details to take care of before going, and Dan plunged into them. This was a plum assignment, he realized, a chance to spread his wings and make something of the opportunity.

He needed not just travel arrangements and contact with the business group and arrangements with J.D., the plant manager, as to when they were coming, but reading up on the HF process – a dangerous technology, fail of peril, if a leak or emission occurred.

Dan called his doctoral professor and mentor, Tom Foley, in Chemical Engineering at Michigan State, to get his advice on how to proceed. He so admired Dr. Foley, combining engineering scholarship and debate, as he did. There was no one he trusted as much. But Dan also wanted Professor Foley's continuing approval for what he had chosen as a career, so he kept the initial description down to being sent by the company to investigate a bad accident in Texas in a company HF facility.

Tom Foley updated Dan on HF (nothing that Dan didn't know, actually) and, then, in wishing him good luck, added, 'And don't let those ambitious industry grunts down there wear you down, Dan. If you have a real problem, make sure you raise it to a level where someone with imagination and ethics, or, at least, ambition, will support you. I know the American Industrial Chairman, Tony Casey,' Foley concluded, 'he is on the engineering advisory council, as you may recall, and I can help you with this if it would be useful.'

Dan physically drew back from his telephone voice box, recalling Tom O'Rourke's admonition to stay out of trouble and quickly assured Professor Foley he would call on him if he needed him, but that was not necessary now.

3. The Public Affairs VP

H. Jeffrey Bush had been with American Industrial for about ten years. He had been brought into the company from Shell in Houston by the chairman's predecessor.

Jeffrey was a big, hulking man, who liked to quote from his experience in Vietnam ('Nam' he called it), although he had never left Saigon central headquarters, to show he was one of the men. He liked to picture himself as rough and tumble, only interested in his work, but, actually, he was an elitist, who had lived in London and Paris with the oil company, Shell, and looked down on these chemical company bozos, with their constant assessments and evaluations, and networks.

There was a story around the company about Jeffrey that, at a senior level dinner with the board, an entertainer had ridiculed him, in an otherwise genial roasting of the execs; as an upper-class snob posing as the common man. The 'H' in his name was the tip off, this comic had said. 'Who starts his name off with "H",' he said, 'but a society column wanker.'

He struck a nerve of truth, they all knew. There were lots of stories about the inside information that had had to be given to the entertainer to have successfully accomplished his witty barbs toward H. Jeffrey Bush. Many thought Jeffrey had gotten his just due, but he had, in fact, made the adaptation to the new chairman.

Anne was sitting across the desk from Jeffrey, that Friday afternoon of the meeting with Marv Friedman and Dan, nervously contemplating the trip she would begin the next morning to precede Dan to Sour Lake. Jeffrey was using his best total quality or TQ style with Anne, in a non-authoritarian, empowering discussion as to what should be accomplished.

Jeffrey rather liked the TQ mode the chairman had brought in with him from Consumer Electric. While it had resulted in a lot of downsizing, or rightsizing as Jeffrey liked to say, in staff size, including in Public Affairs, Jeffrey rather enjoyed the opportunity, the trappings of democracy, TQ brought with it in management style, since he was regularly assigned the role of moderator or facilitator at the senior management meetings. This allowed him to appear humble and witty, while he kept those bozos in line with his worldly approach. It also allowed him to ingratiate himself with the chairman, who clearly had his own problems.

'What will be your agenda on arriving this weekend?' Jeffrey amiably inquired.

'I'm going to focus on the families and the press at the start,' Anne responded, 'but also I want to find out what the lay of the land is at the plant, to assist Dan Straus in his investigation of the accident. Perhaps Bonnie Sutherland can be of some help,' she said, 'although she has had such a tough time with her mother's death in the accident. We're old friends, you know.'

Anne was a Sour Lake girl, who had gone to the University of Texas and then found her way into American Industrial, through the small Canadian operation. 'I know Dan wants to get to the root cause,' she added, recrossing her beautiful legs, as if the secrets of what took place in the Sour Lake plant were to be found between them.

Jeffrey leaned back in his chair contemplatively, his immense body dwarfing the seating space, and said, 'Give Dan every help you can, but don't let those watermelons in environmental get too friendly with the press.' Responding to Anne's quizzical look, re-crossing of her legs and smoothing back of her long hair, he said, winking, 'You know, like a watermelon – green on the outside, pink on the inside.'

Anne smiled at H. Jeffrey Bush's old style business perception. She had her marching orders. She also had her own views and dreams.

4. The General Counsel

Horace G. Carpenter had been in his New Brunswick office since 7.00 AM when his limousine driver brought him from the back country of Westchester County, New York. Horace rose every morning at 5.00 AM. If he was going to the office, he was out by six. He never woke his wife, whose heavily drugged sleep of escape from him, in the next room, would not have allowed such an action anyway. They had tacitly agreed years before to a separation in place. It suited Horace. 'I am a tight ass, white bread that is, gentlemen', he told his lawyers, 'and you better be the same or you will be on the street.'

Horace G. Carpenter was a Harvard Law graduate and had been a middle management partner for one of the big Wall Street firms. When it became his perception that the Jews of the upper partners were not going to let him progress further, he joined American Industrial in their top legal job. His wife's connections had helped. He liked his job a lot, actually. One hundred lawyers under him, the chance to be the sage to a bunch of management dimwits. Tough cases could always be farmed out to his previous New York City firm, which now catered to him for his business. Yes, sir, Horace often thought, but never said, he had certainly outsmarted those Jew boys.

Now Bill Cory one of the young Rutgers lawyers he had hired, was sitting with Horace, in that little, cozy alcove, with Raphael prints on the walls around their small, circular conference table. Horace was telling Bill that he should keep Dan Straus tied to a high ethical plain during this investigation.

'Do you think he wouldn't be?' Bill asked. 'He seems like a straight guy to me.'

'I'm not saying he's not,' Horace underlined, 'but your job is to insist on the highest integrity in the investigation, without the cutting of ethical corners. These guys sometimes try.'

Bill Cory didn't get it, obviously, but that is as far as Horace dared go. 'And besides,' he added, 'as good a man as Dan Straus appears to be, he is going to be dealing with a bunch of red dirt, good old boys down there, who don't know which way their cocks point.'

Horace was considered lovable by his lawyers, at least officially, for his colorful language and mixed metaphors. So Bill just wrote it off as one of those crazy *non sequiturs* from this apparently brilliant and powerful legal force in his career. Indeed, he assured Horace that he would keep close tabs on Dan's assessment of things. He indicated he would fly down to join Dan on the close out, if useful.

It did not escape Bill that this really sexy Anne Hennessy would be down there. God how he would like to crawl in the sack with her!

But the General Counsel was not through. He played a card and used the incident to draw himself closer to the chairman. He briefed Tony Casey first on what was to happen over the next few weeks in Sour Lake and who was involved. As he suspected, the chairman suggested that he wanted to briefly meet with Horace and Dan Straus, just before he left for the weekend in the company helicopter for Greenbriar, golfing with the other Chairman. 'We are supporting young Governor George Bush, in Texas, in his exploration of a bid for the Presidency,' the chairman noted.

5. Vice President – Human Relations

Paul Atkinson had seen it all. When he was just a cub manager from Sour Lake in American Industrial, he had come to the attention of the then corporate VP, Hal Shorter, of what was then more mundanely known as 'personnel'.

Paul had organized the defeat of the aggressive chemical workers' union at the Sour Lake HF plant in the Seventies, although they were back trying to organize the plant workers again.

Paul hated the workers. They were a pain in the ass with their goddamned unions. He did his job for the chairman and the management, career pathing the key managers and spreading TQ. And he had overseen the census reduction of American by thirty per cent over the past three years, keeping the chairman out front in profits and leadership. But he hated 'the fucking unions and their workers', although he didn't show it to them. He had no compunctions about screwing organized labor at any turn.

'Shit,' Paul told the chairman, 'I think Jack Welsh at GE has got it right – nuke the workers and keep the plants.' Paul was a champion of more with less through automation and TQ. He was anti-employee, anti-worker. Behind his back he was referred to as 'unpersonnel'. The chairman made good use of him.

The chairman knows how good we make him look, Paul thought, as he interviewed a high performance work group from synthetic fibers plant, that had been organized a few years before to make total quality (TQ) savings.

'We are working with our unions,' Paul told the workers, 'as partners, to be globally competitive. We value your contribution.' He added, 'It is essential to the further progress that we be partners and all make sacrifices.'

The twelve men and women shifted uneasily in their seats in the conference room, as they awaited the Specialty Chemicals President, Marv Friedman, to give them their awards. They knew Paul's reputation as anti-union, but they hoped the increasing productivity of their plant would save them from the downsizing going on all over their industry. What they didn't know was that Marv and Paul had already planned reductions at the plant. Paul admired those business leaders who could cut workers and increase profits. 'Shit,' he reasoned to his management friends, 'how else can we compete with the god damned Asians?'

When the recognition ceremony was over – the chairman had briefly stopped to congratulate the workers on their TQ contribution – Marv drew Paul aside saying, 'You heard that that environmental kid is going down to Sour Lake to see what happened?'

'Yeah,' Paul replied.

'The chairman is going to see him today, before he goes; I'm sending a PR gal, Anne Hennessy, with him to grease the skid,' Marv said.

Paul smiled, but said nothing immediately in reply. Years ago Paul had arranged for a liaison between the old VP Hal Shorter, and a cute, buxom, good old Texas gal, at the plant, Beatrice Sutherland, who gave Hal a really good time during that start-up year, whenever he journeyed down from New Jersey. Paul himself had become somewhat involved with her after Hal. It gave Paul a little heartburn, once in a while, when he remembered that woman, because she and her daughter were still in the plant.

He smiled because Beatrice was killed in the accident, so now the past could not come back to haunt them. The arrangement was now permanently in the past, he thought. It couldn't come back.

'I wish them good luck,' Paul finally said, 'and I'll be interested in the results.'

6. The Manager and the Worker

Anne sat at her desk that Friday afternoon and thought about Bonnie Sutherland and her mother, Beatrice. They had not been a close mother and daughter. Bonnie was too rebellious, and, besides, in those days she had disapproved of her mother's hard drinking and sexual activity. Now Beatrice was dead in the accident they were to investigate. All the intimations were that something was not right at Sour Lake. Was her friend, Bonnie, still at the plant, the key?

The fact that neither Beatrice nor Bonnie apparently would live without sex for more than a night or two didn't bother her. She was much the same, wasn't she? But Beatrice's drinking was more than Bonnie or she could take, when they were together in those earlier, heady days.

Anne thought about Beatrice bringing Bonnie up as a single mother in Sour Lake. She had guts, no doubt about that. When Anne's parents died in a fiery crash of their car with a Semi, Anne, as a teenager, had lived with a cousin in Sour Lake, but Bonnie and her mother became her focus.

Bonnie was as wild and restless as she, and Beatrice provided enough cover for them to roam and party, but still get through their high school years intact. Anne had gone to the University of Texas, under the influence and sponsorship of her mother's wealthy brother back East, who recognized her gifts and felt responsible for her, as long as she didn't invade his family life, she often bitterly thought.

When Beatrice realized that Bonnie (and for that matter Anne) as teenagers had something special going on upstairs, to complement what Texans would call 'sweet poontang' downstairs, she used her wiles to assure Bonnie's chance. Anne didn't know how, but Beatrice had helped Bonnie, with her beauty and brains, win a special scholarship from American Industrial to get her to UT and then keep her at Sour Lake as a chemist.

Since she had been working for Marv Friedman and Specialty, Anne had been kept away from the Sour Lake plant. Especially with the history of labor problems, Anne understood that it was better for her – as well as for the company – to focus elsewhere. But this was different. Three dead workers, with one, Bonnie Sutherland's mom, known so well to her. She would talk to Bonnie, who, in high school, used to go to Houston and sell herself and her sweet Texas body (as Bonnie used to say) at the Warwick Hotel to visiting executives of the oil companies.

Anne wondered whether anyone at the Corporate Office at American Industrial in New Jersey realized what a tragedy the gas leak and deaths were to a town like Sour Lake. Hell, these shits hardly understood the impact of Bhopal, Anne thought, no less a few dead at one of their plants, in a remote Texas town, Sour Lake.

Well, she would do whatever she could for the company and the town, and she really would help Dan Straus every way she could. She liked Dan. She respected his quiet, intellectual tenacity. 'It's a hard job being an environmental auditor,' she had told Jeff Bush and Horace Carpenter, 'and I'll help him all I can.'

They all knew Carpenter was an anti-Semite, the Harvard snob, but that was his problem. Anne had known Jews at UT, as both teachers and fellow students. She had no problem and she was sure Dan had none working with her, although at the Christmas party Anne had felt distrust in Dan's wife, when they had chatted about loving New York City. So many American Industrial executives hated the variety of the city, but not Dan or Gloria, as New Yorkers (or Jews for that matter). And Anne liked the fun of Manhattan, too.

She had told Gloria that the city 'reminded her of Austin, only more so'. She meant it in terms of music and diversity, but she thought Gloria, looking at her and reading her obvious sexuality, read it as her love of the available men and bars. And that was not so far from the truth – New York City allowed her a certain weekend anonymity to boldly drink and fuck, which Beatrice would have appreciated.

7. The Chairman

Anton Casey, the American Industrial chairman for about four years now, scratched, the back of his hands, then smoothed back the silver hair, where it came neatly to conclusion on his thick, wrinkled neck. As a matter of fact, Tony scratched a lot, although less these days, since he started taking Prozac on a regular basis.

Tony Casey was the eighth and last child of immigrant Irish parents. He was the only son and a lot had been expected of him. Well, goddamn it, he had not failed. He had steered his way through Holy Cross outside Boston on an athletic scholarship for football, and then, when he was injured in his junior year, refocused himself on financial management and moved up the corporate ladder.

By the time Tony reached American Industrial he was legendary in his ability to focus a company around increasing profit. And recently he had discovered total quality as the newest tool of the 'Sun King Arsenal', he liked to think of it. What he meant by that, he recently explained, at a Harvard Graduate School of Business seminar, was 'get the attention and fealty of your top managers, and make them into leaders, focused on making the numbers (primarily profit), and you can't fail. It ain't rocket science,' he liked to say, 'just letting people know they will walk the plank, if they don't pay strict attention and make the financial objectives.'

Tony was not adverse to firing his top management brethren. 'Anyone for that matter,' he told HGSB, 'to get what I want.' 'The chairman can learn from the military,' he added, 'by requiring fast action and complete disclosure. On the other hand, if my leaders do what we agree must be done, I reward them.'

The chairman's wife had been a woman of youthful ardor, and for him, convenience. Tony Casey often thought of her as a modern incarnation of a mail-order bride.

When Casey had been on the rise, he had met her on a Trans European flight. She was a stewardess, very pretty and quite saucy. They had had a great time in Paris together over the long weekend, and he started arranging to see her. There was never much to her upstairs, but she was attractive and had been finished in her manners by the airline training, to take advantage of her optimism and politeness. He had little time for more than that and so he married this sturdy Catholic girl, from a good family in the

Midwest. She took in her stride his ambition, his travel (how could she not) and his success.

Now she had returned to the religious zeal of her parents. She was not confused by contemporary family life or the modern business world – she took her rewards as due her. She did not have the intellectual acumen to realize that she was not a modern women. In fact, she did not want to be. She did realize that the chairman was not always faithful, but she accepted that as the price she paid for the comforts of this world. She was focused these days, Tony Casey often ruefully told her, on the next life.

Tony thought of himself in Messianic terms at American Industrial and in business generally. And that was the image he quite liked generally. Sort of an industrial George Patton, single-mindedly pursuing profits. But there was a lot of pressure to succeed, he admitted, which made a mess of his stomach and his head. His mood swings were kept under better control these days with the Prozac. As a matter of fact, he was thinking, as he scratched again, I've got to see old Doc MacDonald today or tomorrow and get a checkup to renew the long-term prescription.

Tony jumped up and buzzed one of his secretaries to come in. He preferred the younger one. She could be one of his daughters and he liked her spunk. 'Miss Lazorri,' he said to her, rather formally, 'I understand Anne Hennessy of Public Affairs is going to Sour Lake with Dan Straus of the environmental group.'

I know Straus well enough, he thought, and I trust him, especially since our meeting this afternoon. 'Straus will be governed by the facts and that's all I ask of him,' he had said to Horace Carpenter, after the brief meeting. That SOB lawyer, Carpenter, was always manipulating everyone to his own advantage, and he gave Jews a hard time, Casey knew.

Casey disapproved of anti-Semitism, as he disapproved of all social or class prejudice or pretense. Money is democratic, he often thought.

'God, I hate lawyers,' the chairman told Miss Lazorri. 'And who the hell is this Hennessy gal? I want my employees to know I care for them,' he said to the secretary. 'Tell Bush what I said and ask him if she is up to it. Tell him I hold *him* accountable,' he added. Tony did not like Bush, but he tolerated him, as long as he kept his nose clean.

He smiled now at Miss Lazorri. 'Connie, how is that boyfriend of yours?'

'Okay,' she replied, looking the boss straight in the eye as she knew he liked.

'When are you going to marry him?' he chided. Tony couldn't get over the new morality which let these kids live together without guilt.

He had rarely slept with another woman, besides his wife, until the last few years. She was a pain in the backside these days with her daily masses and excessive adoration of the Virgin Mary. 'Let's call a spade a spade,' he told her recently, in the loud voice he used too often at home. 'You are becoming a religious fanatic.'

His hand darted back to the hairlines which he had patted. 'Oh, Connie, make an appointment for me with Doc MacDonald at the clinic, before I grab the helicopter for West Virginia,' he concluded, as he rushed out to his next appointment. 'And did my wife remember to put my golf clubs in the car they sent over for my bags?' A little spot on the back of his wrist really itched. Fuckin' nerves, he thought.

8. The Corporate Environmental Auditor

Dan Straus drove the Garden State South. The day was finally over and his weekend promised respite on Long Beach Island, before the week would begin with Sunday afternoon's trip to Sour Lake, Texas. Dan loved to drive, and he found it especially relaxing to drive and think. After he graduated from Michigan State, he used to drive back to see Gloria, who was a year behind him. People always complained that Michigan State was eighty miles from nowhere and nowhere was Central Michigan, but Dan had loved that drive and State's remoteness. The drive gave him time to mentally recapitulate, summarize, rationalize and even forgive, where that was necessary, he thought.

That last thought – forgiving Gloria for whatever her most recent doubt or distrust – brought him to a nagging worry. Gloria had been wary of Anne Hennessy when she met her at the Christmas party. I mean the girl is a knockout, he thought. And Gloria has sized her up as bright and ambitious too. What would that spark ignite, when he told her he would be in Texas with Anne all week? And yet he must tell her because he always strove for directness, even when it hurt, and because it would be deadly for Gloria to find out some other way!

Their marriage was troubled by his traveling and her jealousy. He wasn't sure whether they shared a love strong enough to overcome their difficulties and their increasingly bitter arguments. Frequently they had been having arguments which ended in her great anger and yelling and his stony silence. They were on the rocks, he thought, and Dan found he was increasingly impatient with Gloria, even though he thought he still loved her.

God knows this was an exciting assignment, and out of the ordinary for an environmental auditor. He would do his best, and that was damn good, he knew. And he would try to stay away from the political problems he smelled all over the upper management in this one. Dan turned from the Garden State South to the Jersey shore. He and Gloria were going to work on the house and just walk on the beach on this prematurely warm, winter day. The girls would love it, although little Jessica would complain about missing Brownie Scout games. He needed the time with Gloria, of that he was sure.

★

January 18, 1995

Professor Tom Foley
237 Sackett Building
Michigan State University
Lansing, Michigan

Dear Tom,
As I mentioned on the phone, I have been assigned an environmental and safety audit job, at a plant in Eastern Texas, which distills HF from feedstock and then unloads it for distribution. The plant had a release with a number of fatalities. I'm not sure of the load-off dependability – how could it have gotten so screwed up, but I guess I will find out. I know, don't prejudge, don't prejudge!

I have been working on my thesis outline in the number of areas we discussed. I am excited by the fact that I can complete the work using my industrial experience. I have developed a number of strands relating to industry diligence being very positive on the environment, once the environment is taken up as an industry interest under the banner of quality. I will send you summary drafts of these new ideas (for me), thesis strands, as you call them, for the Ph.D. committee.

You were nice to inquire about my personal unhappiness. I guess Gloria and I just have more problems than most. I'm sure all the traveling I do contributes to the problem, but I don't feel especially guilty about that.

What I do worry about is how much I dislike the Specialty Chemicals Division President. I know your advice is to keep personal feelings out of the job – just perform professionally as you always say – but it is hard with this aggressive, self-centered, obnoxiously opinionated bird.

The fact that we are of the same religion makes it worse for me, because I keep seeing my cultured and humanistic father shaking his head in disbelief over this stereotypical Jewish business gorilla, and his complete abandonment of his soul to the making of profit. 'Money, money, money,' he said to me the other day, in describing his business goal.

In the Threepenny Opera they sing derisively, 'the bulging pocket makes the easy life.' That's all this guy wants, and all he wants you to want. Perhaps they – successful businessmen – are all like that – perhaps we are all like that, but I would hope not. Anyway, working for him makes me uneasy.

While I know I must pursue my own course and not be distracted by personal likes and dislikes, if I am to do something worthwhile in industry in the environment, I cannot help but despise this self-important capitalist invention, who would be better suited to be a hotel manager, oiling his way about while brutalizing the clerks and housekeepers who serve his economic interest. For he has all the characteristics of the old time – the public-be-damned industrialist, but dressed up in modern business clothes and powdered to hide his rapacious nature.

(His) Friedman's operations have publicly embraced a responsible environmental attitude, but everyone in the company knows he cares only for profit. We saw a case recently where his general manager for his tiling business acted unethically and encouraged illegal conduct in disposal methods to save money, and thus enlarge profit. When confronted with the conduct, Friedman dismissed the manager and claimed his dedication to good environmental management. We all know the truth because Friedman says it all the time, 'get the profit out'. I once saw him throw his wallet to the floor and dramatically stamp on it at a meeting, and say, red-faced, 'Fuck the ethics, get the profits.'

I'm for profit because it generates the wealth to make social and environmental progress. But such rapaciousness will give us all a bad name in the end, not to mention a bad taste in the mouth, now, for me.

I hope I can stay clear of him. The chairman's interest gives me the chance to get the job done with or without him, and I intend to do just that.

Your response that profit is at least a measurable and visible target may be true, and that the desire for power may be more hidden among other corporate leaders – and something to be more careful about when dealing with those guys. But I have a great personal repulsion to this aggressive, obnoxious Jewish

*business leader, which shows, I'm sure. I am glad the
chairman's involved in this.*
Thanks for all your continued help.
Yours,
Dan Straus

Chapter Two

Sour Lake

Dan was floating over the clouds on his way to Houston from Newark Airport. Then it would be on to Sour Lake. On his laptop was the process diagram for the Sour Lake Hydrofluoric Acid Process.

Dan did what all good environmental auditors do – he tried to master the general flow of the plant before he had his first overall tour. Then, while the plant manager and he trooped around, looking at the layout, and the plant manager gave an overview of what they were looking at, he would be able to make mental notes and compile his first round of questions and impressions. That technique placed him ahead of the auditing curve – it placed him in control.

There is a general misconception about technology, Dan thought. It was not a new idea. It had been drummed into him at Michigan State by Dr. Foley. 'You can't understand the problems of a process or a technology,' Foley would say, 'without an analysis of the weak points. And you can't find the weak points,' he would add, 'without visual inspection. First understand the process,' Foley would say, 'then walk the process.'

That would be how he would start on Monday, walking the process.

Questions filled his mind. Did he have an accurate understanding of the Sour Lake plant? How many changes had taken place since it was designed? The weakest link was generally the truck and rail loading, where the human element would be most involved. That is where the rupture emission had occurred? What were the written procedures? The training? The past history? What were the informal, unwritten procedures, that every plant had?

What was Beatrice Sutherland, who worked in the shipping office, doing out there during truck loading? One of the other two fatalities, a Jon LaFlate, was only twenty and the apprentice or helper on the loading station. Why wasn't he wearing the protective equipment? The third was a vehicle operator, a Carlos Gonzales, on the road adjacent to the plant, who apparently received no warning or medical help. Just died! So quickly! How could events have rushed forward with no control or warning from the loading operation?

The plant was scheduled for mothballing in twenty-four to thirty-six months in favor of a new facility yet to be built in Mexico. Was the training pursued, attended, taken seriously in view of the future closing? Did the plant manager take the risks of HF seriously? In view of the closing, was upkeep maintained or considered a source of extra profit?

Dan would interview all the plant people involved. First he would walk the plant with J.D. Hutchinson, the plant manager, in the morning, after he learned the lay of the land with Anne that night. He would sleep on what he thought he knew and what Anne told him.

Dan switched on the headset. The movie was *Disclosure*. It occurred to him, as he dozed off, that Anne resembled Demi Moore, but was a redhead.

★

Anne was speaking across the darkened lounge table top of the Liberty, Texas, Holiday Inn, a few miles from Sour Lake down US 90. 'I spoke to the families of all three victims. I'm sure we will have a lawsuit from Carlos Gonzales' mother. I don't think there is a father living there, and she speaks little English. Carlos was only eighteen. No one in the family seems to understand how a cloud of the material, whisking overhead, could cause immediate death.' She paused. Dan remained silent. He was taking in information. 'I got the feeling that he was a wild but nice kid,' she said.

'Was there an alarm at the plant when the line ruptured?' Dan asked.

'Yes,' she replied, 'a loud horn which the neighbors know means an emergency, but the Gonzales' family weren't immediate neighbors and I don't get the idea this kid would have responded to a warning anyway. I've asked for a copy of the coroner's report on Gonzales.'

Dan noticed that the few other men in the Holiday Inn lounge were focused on Anne. No wonder, he thought. She looked just absolutely terrific in her Levis and sweater, hair swept back. She made his blood boil, but he had no intention of going that way, even if she wanted to. This would be strictly business.

'The apprentice operator, Jon LaFlate,' she continued, 'was only working for us for three weeks, but he had done a few of these truck loadings before. His family is in a complete state of shock. They are Louisiana Cajun, very family and work-oriented, but not particularly in the mainstream.' Dan looked inquisitive, so she added, 'The Cajuns stay to themselves here except for work which is usually menial. They are not what we would call upwardly mobile, but they are very steady, industrious workers. They are sort of the backwoods people you see in East Texas, but straightforward and honest too. I don't know what the kid knew about the job or emergencies. That's for you to find out.' She stopped there and sipped her glass of wine.

'And the other fatality,' Dan prompted, thinking again how gorgeous this woman was.

'Beatrice Sutherland has worked in the plant for years,' Anne went on. 'I don't know what she was doing out there by the truck. The family is small, just her daughter, Bonnie, at the plant, who is very upset, and a few cousins in the area,' she continued. 'There is a certain fatalism there, which I don't understand. You know, I know Beatrice's daughter, Bonnie, quite well, from growing up here, and she is gritty. I think she will be okay, but she is asking the same question I ask you – what was her mother, Beatrice, doing out there?' she said emphatically to Dan.

He liked this woman. He knew she was purposely repeating the names so he would more quickly grow familiar with them. She had an appealing directness.

'Did you see *Disclosure*?' he asked her. 'You look like Demi Moore at times.'

'Well, thanks,' she replied. 'Actually I saw it on the plane coming down here.'

'So did I,' he responded.

'I won't trap you in any sexual harassment, I promise,' she said and smiled, coloring oh so slightly. 'I thought the movie never made it clear why she would entrap him,' she said, adding, 'what did they care what Michael Douglas thought? It would have been better if she were more a lecher or a psycho, like that Glenn Close character, or was simply seeking revenge. I kept thinking, she is so beautiful and sexy, why couldn't they both just enjoy it. Michael Douglas seemed quite the nerd, didn't he?' she asked.

Anne and Dan were now making direct eye contact, until he cast his gaze down at his drink. He didn't know it then, but that was a trick the two fast girls – Anne and Bonnie – liked to use in the old high schooldays in Sour Lake. There was a pause. Dan searched for his next topic.

'Tell me about the press. Is there anything I should know?' Anne took a little note pad from her pocketbook. She explained: *The Beaumont Texan* carried the story with front page banner headlines, when the leak occurred last month, as did the Houston and Dallas papers, although on an inside page. The *Texan* has stayed with the story with pictures on the first page and follow-up stories on the causes of the accident and the families since. They pretty much have bought the unfortunate accident theory and the plant people, including J.D., are congratulating themselves on handling the press well.' She added parenthetically, with a change of voice to a lower tone, 'I think Marv Friedman has congratulated them for that, as well.

'Sour Lake has only a few thousand people in the immediate area,' she continued, 'but the *Beaumont Texan* is independent, goes back to the Civil War, and covers the town. Lately there has been interest in the Newhouse syndicate to buy it, but so far the paper remains family-owned. This is a proud area – East Texas – rich in history, and oil and gas, at one time, but it is not like the rest of Texas. More southern in the society sticking together against the outside.

'The Carpenter family members – the owners of the newspaper – live in Beaumont,' she said, 'and they are rock-ribbed Dallas Republican, but the editor, Joe Wiseman, is a crusader and a Democrat. He lives in Sour Lake.

'One way this is Texas,' she added. 'Unlikes tolerate each other and make room and use each other in this state.

Joe Wiseman has been accepted as one of their own. Maybe because he distinguishes them.

'Wiseman is Columbia University Journalism. His wife, Sarah Cohen, a Sour Lake girl – a Jewish girl – was real smart, escaped and went to school at Columbia, only to return with some new blood – Joe – for East Texas,' she said. 'Sarah's very special. Always was. You'll see. Her father was the editor of the *Texan* before Joe and he passed it on to Joe to the Carpenters' great relief.

'So far we can't complain about the coverage,' she concluded, 'but I hear Joe is thinking about an investigatory story if a more detailed, explanation is not forthcoming. He knows someone from the Corporate office is coming down to look into the operations and we may be able to convince him that we mean business as much as he does, in terms of a thorough going assessment,' she said.

'How does he know that?' Dan asked.

'Sour Lake is a small town in East Texas,' she replied matter-of-factly, rolling her eyes. 'Nothing goes unnoticed here.

'I spoke to Sarah yesterday (I've known her all my life) and she asked if we would like to come to dinner,' she said. 'We means you and me. She means it socially, believe me, but Joe probably suggested it. It does fit into my idea of how you could meet the press,' Anne continued, 'so I accepted for later in the week, dependent on your schedule...'

'Okay,' Dan said. 'I'm perfectly happy to rely on your expertise and experience in Sour Lake. But let me see how things go. And how is J.D. taking all of this?'

'I heard J.D. was quite shook up at first,' she said. 'He never had anything close to a fatality in the plant before and he's been the plant manager for over fifteen years. But yesterday,' she continued, 'he was quite philosophical, although he is also defensively talking to me about the appropriation request he has had pending with Charlie Moore for eighteen months on upgrading continuous monitoring and safety for the operation. J.D. says Charlie treats it as J.D. covering his ass. I don't know what that all means technically, but it sure doesn't help from a PR standpoint, if it gets out, and, as I said, everything eventually gets out here, if it's not solved.

'Actually,' she continued, 'J.D. is talking about retiring or being bought off, but I don't know if that is what we want right now. He is a strange cracker, there is something fanatical I can't quite put my finger on, but I'll let you make up your own mind about him.'

The waitress, with the low-cut midriff and larger than life breasts and stumpy legs, halted their conversation with a question about drink refills. Dan looked down, somehow quite embarrassed. Anne gave her the stare, right between the eyes. She stared back, and they seemed to engage in a Sour Lake female staring contest.

Anne ordered two more glasses of wine, which she signed for.

The staring provoked Dan to ask, 'Do you know her?'

'I do,' she said. 'She was a cheerleader and beauty queen in high school, and dumb as a post. I don't think she quite recognizes me, although she's trying,' she added. 'They do age quickly here.'

They drank their wine in silence for a while amid the leers of the males populating the motel bar. 'There's one other nagging matter,' Anne said, 'and that's Ray Gapt's record keeping, or rather lack of it. Ray is the plant environmental coordinator. The shipping and receiving records required his sign off for inventory purposes, but

Ray's main job in the environmental arena was management of the hazardous waste of the plant, according to J.D. J.D. says the records aren't right, but it's not important because Ray is so well connected, through the old boy network to the regulators. What J.D. says was important was the way the loading job was done by Jon LaFlate because that's what killed them all. That's for you to look at, I guess,' she said, 'although I don't see how it all adds up to any more than we currently know.'

'I don't see either,' Dan responded mildly, but his antennae were up. Assertiveness and denial always aroused his auditor's instincts.

'I'll nose around.

'By the way,' Anne added, 'J.D. and Beatrice Sutherland were a real hot item for a short time, according to plant rumor. I don't get that either. What would Beatrice ever have seen in that cracker? Bonnie hates the guy, but, as the plant chemist, she has to work with him almost every day.'

At about 10.00 PM Anne asked Dan how tired he was, and Dan said, 'Not very.'

'Good,' Anne said, 'because this would be a good time to drive you around Sour Lake for an hour to give you the lay of the land. You can see every nook and cranny of the tour in an hour.'

All heads turned to watch Anne and Dan leave.

★

Anne explained as they drove:

'Sour Lake is a little oil and gas town, of about two thousand Texas folk, northeast of Houston and west of Beaumont, in the part of Texas known as East Texas. Splayed along North-South State Route 326, it has seen better days, much better days. The Sour Lake name has to do with early gas deposits. There was a lot of money made here. The best times have passed. Nevertheless, it is a proud town that goes back into the early history of Texas.'

Dan observed that, like many smaller towns in the south, the main drag, Route 326, was a country road, populated with fast-food shops, gas stations, a few honky-tonk bars and then an elementary school at the south end. On a Sunday night the cars slowly rolled along with teenage boys, and the not so young, honking at each other. There appeared to be lots of beer drinking in the cars.

Dan wanted to ask Anne if she had been a part of this scene, but he didn't. His attention was diverted by the towers at the east end of Highway 105, which bisected the town and crossed Route 326. On 105 were two large refineries and gas storage plants. Pumping wells were everywhere. The towers signaled the rise of the American Industrial HF Plant. Aging and somewhat rusted-looking from the road, the plant was all lit up and obviously chugging away.

Anne reading Dan's thought, said, 'Texas OSHA finished here after the accident and left a clean report. So they started up again.'

'Good,' Dan responded, remembering his instructions, not to impede production, from Marv Friedman. 'I expected the plant to be operating by now. I'd rather see it in operation, if the truth be known,' he said.

Anne asked if Dan wanted to go in and just ride around.

'Yes,' Dan said, 'as long as it doesn't look like I'm being sneaky.'

'That's okay,' she answered. 'They all know you're here tonight and with me. They would be surprised if you didn't come. J.D. asked me if I would take you in tonight. I said only if you wanted to.

'They expect me to sleep with you tonight, and turn you into a good old boy,' she said smiling. She smoothed her beautiful hair back. It was an attractive mannerism on her part, he thought, and opened her up to his frankness.

'But you don't expect that?' he said, in response, his calm voice belying his astonishment at her directness.

'No,' she answered, 'I just wanted you to know the way people think here.'

'Probably anywhere,' he responded. 'Just not spoken out so directly.'

Anne felt herself trusting this handsome Eastern, Jewish, professional auditor, and she wondered at the integrity and ease of his manner.

*

They entered the plant. The gate guard did not ask who he was, when he saw Anne's company identification tag. He either didn't want to know or did know! It was about 10.30 PM. They stuck to the main roads. Anne was quiet, letting Dan absorb the structures in the harsh illumination of night-time production.

Dan noticed that there was a small squad of black and Mexican men sweeping and generally cleaning up. He was sure that that was for his benefit tomorrow. He was used to that. There was a joke among environmental auditors that plants were always the cleanest and most tidy when they entered. And hey, that was not all bad. At least then they fixed them up, he thought.

When they approached the truck and railcar loading platform, Anne asked, 'Do you want to stop?'

'No,' he said. 'I want the first time I walk it to be with the plant manager.'

But there was a unit not in his layout drawings as he remembered, at which he asked Anne to stop. 'What's this?' Dan asked, in front of a short column and a lot of control equipment lying on the ground just by the truck loading station. There were two Mexican workers pounding in stakes around it, as they spoke.

'I don't know,' Anne answered. 'But Bonnie told me there was some new exciting work for her going on in the plant, which they were afraid was going to be permanently mothballed – maybe this is it.'

Dan nodded and waved his hand as if to say go on. 'Probably nothing,' he said.

'I think J.D. wanted it gone,' she said, 'but maybe Bonnie wanted to keep it there covered for you to notice the cleanup.'

They circled around the outside of the property on a perimeter dirt road. A car sat on the other side of the fence, with a young couple going at it. 'Lots of lovers and quail hunters out here,' Anne said.

Dan noticed a lot of fairly new equipment piled up by the fence in one area. 'Maybe it's time to quit,' Dan said. 'I'm about worn out. You've been really helpful,' he added, 'and I'm looking forward to tomorrow.'

She smiled her nicest Texas smile and they sped back to the Holiday Inn in Liberty, Anne waving at the guard, without even a slow-down, as they exited from the plant.

At the Inn they said a quick good night and rather formally and oddly, Dan thought, shook hands in the elevator, as she exited for the second floor. He was on the third.

When he got to his room, Dan undressed and in his pajamas called Gloria. They talked about her day – she had just watched *Thérèse Raquin* on Masterpiece Theater, about infidelity, she said, but she didn't make more of it than that. 'Kate Nelligan was wonderful,' she said. He didn't mention Anne at all, just saying that he had had a brief tour of the town and plant by car and was very tired.

They said, 'I love you', as they did every night, to reaffirm their most binding reality, whether he was home or not, and good-bye. He switched off the light and was asleep almost immediately.

★

By 8.30 AM J.D. and Dan were walking the property. They had had their coffee and were trooping about. J.D. was a crusty guy, but he knew that Dan's mission came from the top and he must be nice to him and appear open.

'Whatever you want to see, you know, just point like a bird dog and we'll go that way,' J.D. said.

Dan smiled. 'I hope I'm as smart and reliable as those wonderful dogs, J.D. Let's just walk around, ending up at the truck loading area,' Dan said. At this point, he would let J.D. steer him, compliantly looking at whatever J.D. wished him to view.

And so, for the next hour, they looked, at least briefly, at every area, arriving finally at the truck loading. 'I'll want to talk to the supervisors and operators,' Dan said. 'But what is your general impression of what happened, J.D.?'

Dan knew, as an experienced auditor, that J.D. was waiting, planning, anticipating the chance to give his version of the events leading to the fatalities. The best practice was always to ask early and get it out of the way.

They were standing by the outlet valve for truck loading, which was marked by a placard as the hydrofluoric acid load-out valve, as if to emphasize its central importance.

'Well, you know,' J.D. started, 'this damn unfortunate Creole kid, LaFlate, was learning how to load the truck. There is no way to learn without doing it, you know,' he continued, 'and, you know, his attention was diverted by Beatrice Sutherland bringing a message out to the area and he messed the connection. Now, normally, without a positive connection, no HF can be loaded, you know,' he said, 'but apparently this kid by-passed the lockout and the high purity gas escaped and got him and Beatrice, you know, and some poor Mexican driving by the fence at that moment.'

J.D. looked at Dan square in the eyes, with that same flat Sour Lake stare he had seen Anne and the waitress use last night, and continued, 'Just one of those goddamn one-in-a-million events, you know, that never happened before and we can't even repeat. Goddamned stupid Creole kid,' he concluded, and spat to the side his disgust.

For the next few moments Dan purposely said nothing. He was wearing neat jeans, a denim shirt with a dark tie and a casual sports jacket. From his shirt pocket he produced a small pad and wrote himself some notes. J.D. was satisfied that Dan was at least taking in his version of the events.

'How did the positive lock valve actuate to let gas escape without a connection?' Dan asked as he fingered the hose and connection.

'Damned if I know,' J.D. answered. 'Except that, you know, one of the men said he'd seen LaFlate dragging it on the ground, so maybe a stone got into it. Damned if we can duplicate that, you know, no matter how hard we try.'

Dan turned to face J.D. 'How do you feel OSHA felt about it when they were in, J.D.?'

'Well, you know,' J.D. started again, 'these state bubbas looked around and I think pretty much agreed with what I told you. We haven't seen their detailed final report yet; sometimes you never see it, you know,' J.D. went on, 'but they understand what happened, you know, and were as baffled as us, when they were here, as to how this happened. We have their preliminary report and they find no willful violation on our part, you know, even though we had fatalities here.'

Dan nodded and asked, 'Did you keep a copy of everything they looked at and took with them?'

'Yes,' J.D. answered, 'but there wasn't much, you know, just some training records and technical stuff about the process here and HF data sheets.'

'The damn kid was trained and we have records to show it, you know, but it takes time to learn it right and treat the equipment right, you know, and he never will have the time now,' J.D. added, spitting again to the side.

Dan made a few more notes and replaced the pad in his pocket while J.D. stood to the side. He smiled and J. D. asked if he would like another of coffee. Dan said he would and they trudged back to the trailer. It was very humid and overcast.

'Gonna be warm today, you know, if the sun breaks through,' J.D. said. Dan took that as an invitation and removed his jacket as they walked. He was ready to peel off the first layer of familiarity with J.D., now that they had J.D.'s much-thought-about version of the events on the table.

'A good environmental investigation peels off layers of perceived reality to sample and arrive at the final truth,' he remembered Dr. Foley saying to him back at Michigan State in his student days, 'like peeling an onion.'

Over coffee, Dan said to J.D., 'Maybe next I should talk to Ray Gapt, and then we can get together again later.'

'Great,' J.D. responded. 'Let's have lunch around eleven and Ray can join us, you know, with Anne, too.'

★

Ray Gapt was short, about five foot six, in his mid-fifties, with graying but still sandy hair and an enormous gut that hung over his belly like a sentence. He was a chain smoker, who couldn't smoke in the plant, so he was constantly going outside the fence for a cigarette. That was where he was now with Dan at about eleven in the morning.

'Well, Ray,' Dan said. 'Your account of the leak pretty much squares with J.D.'s.' Big surprise, they would have consulted for the OSHA inspection, Dan thought. Not one of his more brilliant statements.

Ray grunted and puffed. 'Damn New York City Jew environmental auditor, down here to shoot the wounded,' J.D. had said to him. 'Well, I damn well don't want to be among them,' Ray had responded. A lot J.D. cared about old Ray, Ray thought.

Dan started again, almost casually. 'Ray, when we were walking around, I saw this area covered by tarps. What was that?'

'Just some old equipment,' Ray answered and added in a discouraging voice, 'want to see it?'

'Maybe after lunch,' Dan said. 'I'm hungry, aren't you?'

★

Lunch was at the local International House of Pancakes. J.D. paid. They all had fast food and copious iced tea. Ray nervously smoked from beginning to end.

Anne had given Dan a copy of a note, just before they left for lunch from Paul Atkinson to H. Jeffrey Bush, which troubled Dan. He wanted to talk to Anne about it, but had no opportunity with the others present. The note read:

AMERICAN INDUSTRIAL

TO: Paul Atkinson
FROM: H. Jeffrey Bush

Perhaps you would like to inform Anne Hennessy (and Dan Straus) at Sour Lake that plant chemist B. Sutherland filed with us a sexual harassment complaint against J.D. Hutchinson a week before the accident. We just discovered it as a new entry for action in our access file.

PA 2/ 23/ 95

cc: M.F.
T.O'R.
A.C.

How to handle such a matter? Was there any connection? Probably not. Would Bill Cory want to be involved? Shouldn't he? These thoughts picked through Dan's brain, as they ate their hamburgers and fries, and drank their iced tea.

When J.D. and Ray went to the men's room, Anne winked at Dan, but said nothing. Dan thought, God, she is beautiful and sexy, but only said, 'We need to talk about the note; maybe after some further discussions I'm going to have with Ray.'

During the car ride back to the plant, in a Chevy Blazer just filthy with mud, J.D. received a phone call on the car phone. It was a one-way conversation, but apparently J.D. received a status report on a project that seemed to be completed. 'Good' and 'Okay' were about all the man of many 'you knows' said.

★

They were out there at the huge tarp staked down by wooden pegs. It was maybe thirty feet off from the HF loading station, by the side of a dirt road. Dan was saying to Ray, 'So this is just a lot of idle equipment – could I take a look at it?'

'Why?' Ray asked. 'It's a lot of bother to take up the tarp and hard as hell to put it down again. Here is a list of what's under there,' Ray said, offering several pages of what appeared to be a freshly typed report.

'Well, thanks,' Dan replied and scanned the document with its listing of columns, tanks, piping, etc.

Dan stood his ground. 'This is very useful, thanks, but it is important I be thorough,' he said with more resolve. 'So let's take a quick look, okay?'

Ray said he would check and started off to the office, obviously expecting Dan to go with him. But Dan did not move, smiled pleasantly and said, 'You go ahead, Ray. I'll just enjoy the sun while you're gone.'

Ray trudged off. Indeed the sun had appeared. Dan had his sleeves rolled up, but he still looked quite smart. He walked the perimeter of the tarp in large strides, hands in pockets, counting yards to himself as he strode. His father used to do that, almost as a ritual between them, to measure out the sixty feet, six inches, that approximated the distance between pitcher and catcher, before they threw and caught at the park.

Ray reappeared, sweating into his shirt from his great gut, with J.D. 'I'm getting a few workmen to remove the tarp,' J.D. said. 'No problem, you know.'

'Do you want to come back?' Ray asked.

'Are they coming soon?' Dan responded, again standing his ground.

The reply was an affirmative nod, so they stood there waiting until two workers, one on a fork truck, appeared. They simply and quickly removed the tarp, folding it into a smaller square and taking it to the side on the lift truck. J.D. walked over casually to join them.

Indeed, there was the collection of rusted equipment named on the list, mostly on its side, on a hard-baked dirt pad, slightly smaller than the tarp. Dan walked around touching or kicking various pieces of metal. He noticed bolts in the pad and empty brackets on some of the equipment. There were stains on the ground, which he squatted down to reach and rubbed his finger across. Twice he brought his finger to his nose after touching a stain.

J.D. and Ray watched him, as one would oversee a wild teenager in a royal family – not daring to correct or even remonstrate, but very concerned as to what would be the next outrageous action. Ray was smoking, which was very much against plant rules on the site. His shirt now had a dark, extended sweat patch, where his belt was folded under his gut.

'What was here?' Dan finally asked himself aloud, as much as them both. They could only guess as to his suspicions. It was, at this point in the peeling of the onion, a rhetorical question.

★

They were huddled in J.D.'s little office, which, in fact, was a trailer on the site. Dan was used to this, especially in plants in the South and Southwest, where the people were hardworking and corporate glamour was not a valued commodity. J.D. was talking, while all three drank from paper cups of coffee.

'Well, you know, we have had a few pilot operations down here, trying different stuff,' he began. Dan shifted in his chair, but said nothing. He was pointedly not taking notes. Ray was smoking. 'Well, you know, we have had this corporate order to try and expand our production to make the numbers. We have been looking for new applications and products, you know,' he said nervously.

'About six months ago, a research type from New Jersey, you know, asked us if we could try out one of those new CFC substitutes down here,' he continued, 'and we set up a little unit at their direction – sort of a very little bench research unit – to make this substitute with our HF for refrigeration uses, you know. That's what we had on that pad,' he concluded 'but the work got too complicated, so we took it down, you know. We heard the company is going to take the project on at the San Jose, California, plant or maybe even Mexico, you know,' he concluded.

'When was the operation stopped?' Dan asked.

J.D. looked at Ray, who mumbled, 'I think last month.'

'I think I detected chlorine residue on the pad, is that right?' Dan asked.

'Probably,' Ray answered. Goddamned Jew is smart, J.D. thought.

Dan shifted. 'Shit, yes, I guess so,' J.D. said. 'The products we were working had a chlorine component, you know.'

J.D. knew Dan was good at this now and he wasn't about to get caught in a squeeze saying, 'We just were trying to meet the division mandate for growth and bottom line expansion, you know, by going along with the development boys, under Charlie Moore up at Corporate.'

Just following orders, Dan thought. Where have I heard that before? But his job was to get to the bottom of the accident, not to assess blame, so he plunged on, knowing he was reaching up the organization in doing so. 'Was this pilot unit in operation at the time of the accident, J.D.?'

J.D. sighed a little and answered, 'I think it was.'

'What would the records show about product coming off?' Dan asked.

J.D. replied, 'We didn't keep too complete records, as we were just sort of experimenting – a bench research operation – for Corporate.' He stuck to that explanation.

'Where did the product go?' Dan asked, somewhat bewildered now, but never surprised by the looseness of a small operation lost in the corporate culture.

'Up to Seymour Redfield by FedEx in New Jersey,' J.D. responded and noting Dan's not reacting to the name, added, 'works for Charlie Moore, you know, on special engineering assignment for new CFC alternate products. Hell, it never amounted to much,' J.D. muttered.

Dan was sorry he hadn't been taking notes, but it was too late to start now. He would recapitulate all this that night. There were still a few critical questions he needed to ask, as an environmental compliance auditor, even if the information turned out not to bear on the incident.

Dan turned his attention to Ray, as if responding to his last statement, 'Was any of this activity permitted, Ray?'

'No,' Ray responded, 'because it was strictly research and development, no production. Didn't need to be,' he emphasized.

'But there must have been emissions and waste material, Ray. Where did they go?' Dan pressed on.

'Oh,' Ray answered, taking a drag and exhaling, 'we have general permits for the plant for operation and bench-scale related research, and waste of course, and we just naturally folded this activity into them – nothing was hidden.'

Dan decided not to pursue this further at the moment. He didn't want the session to turn accusatory in the first day, but the thought kept pressing at him – what happened to that famous bubble up process of communication between environmental peers, which Tom O'Rourke and American Industrial are always trumpeting to the world. Did no one in New Jersey know of this operation but Charlie Moore and a few of his direct reports? Did Marv Friedman, who kept track of the smallest details, not know? Would anyone have cared if the accident hadn't occurred?

'J.D., let me ask you this, out of ignorance,' Dan finally said. 'Chlorine chemistry, especially with HF, is very, very corrosive, I think. Were you satisfied with the safety precautions we were taking at the pilot unit?'

'Yes, sir. You know, we were real careful,' J.D. replied and then thinking better of the shortness of his response added, 'We kept a tight handle on everything.'

'Who mostly worked on this pilot?' Dan asked.

J.D. answered, 'Well, you know, it was not a full-time thing, but Ray and I both supervised, and Bonnie

Sutherland was research chemist at the site for us, so she helped out.'

Ray added in a lower voice, 'The LaFlate kid was at the plant, too, in the last few weeks, so he worked a little with it too.'

★

Dan smiled. 'I guess that's enough of that for now. Suppose I just spend the rest of the afternoon wandering about the plant on my own?' He added, 'Okay with you?' He knew they had no choice.

So Dan could be seen from time to time poking around at the HF loading station, chatting with workers, and then at the uncovered pad, with the remnants of the pilot operations.

Dan knew he had to talk to O'Rourke about the pilot and Bill Cory about permitting issues, but that would hold until the morning.

First he would go over the events with Anne, including the sexual harassment bit, and, later tonight, he wanted to talk to Dr. Foley at Michigan State.

★

Dan and Anne sat at dinner at the Holiday Inn. They had had several drinks and were enjoying a California Chardonnay with their Holiday Inn dinners – steak for Dan and a big salad for Anne. They had convinced J.D. that they would prefer to eat alone that night 'in order to compare notes', as Anne put it. J.D. was glad to get away.

Both had dressed very informally. Dan in jeans and a Michigan State sweatshirt. Anne in a running suit, with zipperdown jacket, that was down as far as it could go without causing a Texas Holiday Inn scandal.

'I'm going to go club hopping with Bonnie Sutherland tonight, after we break up,' Anne said.

'About what time?' Dan inquired.

'Bonnie will meet me here about 10.00 PM,' she answered. 'It will be real low-key, in view of her mother, but it gives me a good opportunity to talk to her outside the plant and the home, and see what is really going on in Sour Lake and at the plant. I'd ask you to come, but I think that would interfere with our female bonding,' she smiled, as did Dan, while nodding.

She wondered if he did understand and said, 'I know it seems harsh to you that we would be going to bars so soon after her mother's death, but it's not so unusual down here – in fact, bar hopping is *de rigueur*. A way of letting off steam.'

Again Dan said, 'I understand,' and added, 'What about the harassment action? Will you bring that up?'

'I don't know,' Anne answered, 'but everybody says J.D. and Beatrice had been banging it up in the back room for years. In fact', she continued, 'there are all sorts of stories about Beatrice around, which add up to one sexually needy or maybe just happy woman! Was J.D. banging Bonnie too – sort of like that Smith woman with father and son in South Carolina – I don't know.'

'I don't see how this relates to the accident,' Dan said, 'but I think we need to make sure – tie up all loose ends, so to speak.'

Anne nodded assent. 'No one seems to know about the harassment complaint, and I haven't asked J.D.'

'Maybe you should do that, tomorrow, after you talk to Miss Sutherland,' Dan suggested. 'He won't expect it from you and that will shake the "you know" man a little. We need to shake him.' He added, 'He is too Texas cocksure of himself and his invulnerability – so, even if the harassment has nothing to do with the case, maybe it will loosen him up on other fronts, especially if it comes from the beautiful Anne Hennessy, local girl, who intimates that Dan Straus, that Northeastern Jew, doesn't know about it.'

She laughed and put her hand on his lightly, saying, 'You are a clever and devious man, Dan, but in a good cause.'

Dan let Anne's hand stay on his. He drawled out in a Texas marshall's voice, 'Just doin' my job, Ma'am.' They stayed quite motionless, until she drew back to continue eating. Her touch had been so light!

Then Dan continued, 'Now let's get back to our friends at the Sour Lake plant and their little pilot operation. They know I'm very disturbed,' he added in a disturbed sounding voice. 'First because they were running a bootleg operation, second because they did not appear to have told anyone or applied for specific permits, whatever they say.'

Anne interrupted to say, 'Could that mean fines and public exposure?'

'It could, if we don't fit it under the existing permits as minor R&D work,' he said. 'That's what J.D. and Ray already have worked out as their cover. I'll tell my boss, O'Rourke, and the lawyers tomorrow morning and ask for advice.

'Maybe they will agree with the plant's view that it was only a bench research operation and within already existing permits,' Dan said, thinking out loud. 'But I have an obligation to pass this on, or bubble it up as we say. But more important to us is that I must pin down this renegade operation and its relationship to the loading dock and the emission that killed two employees and a bystander.'

'Do we have to go public with this, Dan?' Anne asked, unconsciously moving her jacket zipper up and down as she thought.

'Not yet,' Dan answered. 'But we may not be able to keep the lid on it. Everyone in the plant saw the tarp being taken off and me walking around it and kicking the tires.' Dan added, 'And I don't know how long we can keep people from putting two and two together. For example, what about Miss Sutherland? I understand she was the plant chemist, among other jobs, and worked with J.D. and the rest on the pilot. She's bright. Won't she raise the question with you – if not tonight, then soon?' Dan asked.

Anne answered, 'I don't know – that's not the kind of thing we would discuss – no gossip factor. Do you want me to raise it?'

'Only if she does, but, if she does, ask her some leading questions. How did she get into the project? Who was involved? Was it successful? When did it end? What was the role of the LaFlate kid?'

'Well, we will have a decision point by Thursday night,' Anne said, 'when we are having dinner with Joe Wiseman and his wife – my friend Sarah. That's set now.'

★

Bonnie Sutherland stood by the table talking to Anne and Dan, while he sought to settle the bill with the waitress and Anne got her stuff on the other chair organized.

'Can I just put the check on the room?' Dan said to the waitress, and to Bonnie, shaking hands, 'It is so nice to meet you. You are clearly one of Anne's best buddies from the past.'

Bonnie was one of those really pretty, long-haired, independent-looking Texas women. Her brown-blond hair hung very straight to her mid-back. She was tall and lean with an open face and friendly smile.

Her body language gave off the message, don't fool with me and don't tell me what to do.

Dan added, 'I'm really sorry about your mom.'

'Yeah,' Bonnie said very directly and unexpectedly philosophical, 'life is so quick to be over after all those years.'

The thought occurred to Dan that this Texas hard, beautiful woman ran deep. 'I'm here to look into it,' he said, 'as you probably know, but that's for tomorrow – go out and try to enjoy yourself tonight.'

Bonnie smiled at Anne and said, 'Yeah, well we have a lot of catching up to do. Since this little girl left Sour Lake for New Jersey we don't see too much of each other.'

Anne turned to Dan and, once again lightly, laid her hand on his, as if to lay claim to him, and said, 'Are we going over to the plant together?'

The question surprised Dan, as did her hand still on his, but Anne may have suddenly realized that she needed to talk to Dan after the visit with Bonnie and before they started at the plant in the morning, so he said, 'How about we meet for breakfast, or won't you be in shape for that?'

'7.00 AM sharp, right here,' she darted back, and she patted his hand to emphasize the location.

Bonnie smiled. 'I'll get her back in good order,' and as they left, 'See you tomorrow probably too, right?'

'Yes,' Dan answered, so taken with his meeting with these two young females that he had almost forgotten that

Bonnie was the plant chemist on the pilot project, and he would need to talk to her.

Dan gathered himself and went upstairs, called Gloria and listened to her complaints and little victories of the day. He felt very homesick for her at the moment, or maybe conflicted would be a better word. Anyway, he loved her no matter how much Anne and now Bonnie made his blood race.

★

Dan woke with a start in the dark of his room. Who was the B. Sutherland? Bonnie or her dead mother, Beatrice? Why hadn't he thought it could be Beatrice? And yet, didn't Anne think it was Bonnie?

Bonnie would be the one most open to harassment! And could that connect to the pilot plant? Why was he so slow to put this together?

He would raise the issue with Anne at breakfast.

★

The first day of the audit on the accident and fatalities had raised more questions than answers. Sometimes audits were like that. And then, if you pursued your contacts, the thread of the story would be uncovered and the ball of yarn would unravel so nice and easy. That is what happened on Tuesday.

They got good and drunk together, Anne and Bonnie, and cried quite a little about Bonnie's mom. Other than Bonnie's anger with J.D., they stayed away from business. Bonnie did tell Anne that the plant was very tight for months. They thought they were going to lose their production to San Jose in the short run, and Matamores, Mexico, under NAFTA, over time. J.D. was so nervous all the time, and aggressive, Bonnie told Anne.

Dan decided to follow with Bonnie in the late morning, but first he talked to Tom O'Rourke from J.D.'s office, while J.D. was out in the plant.

'Well, I don't know how much to say, Tom,' he said. 'But they had a renegade CFC alternate R&D pilot operation here.'

'What?' Tom responded.

'And bad as that sounds, Tom,' Dan went on, 'it's worse because I suspect the leak was from the pilot operation and they are covering it up. There is just so much more possibility of that causing a vapor release that would kill people. And the renegade pilot they operated with no operating procedures, it all adds up.'

'Oh no,' Tom said. 'Well, follow it through and let me know. Did they have any permits?' Tom added.

'None that I can tell,' Dan answered. 'They seem to think it was okay to do things under the cover of their general operations permit as R&D – maybe that's so, too, the more I think about it.'

Silence on the other side of the line. Dan could hear Tom breathing until he said, 'Another thing, Tom. There was a sexual harassment action filed recently by the plant chemist or her mother against the plant manager. Both worked with the pilot operation. It was her mother who was the plant secretary and was one of the three people killed here.'

'My God,' Tom answered. 'Now listen. Do the best you can do with this mess. What do you want me to do up here?' Tom asked.

'Well, could you tell Bill Cory in Law what I've told you,' Dan said. 'I haven't been able to reach him. Ask him to call me with any advice he would offer, including the need to permit the R&D pilot.'

'Sure will,' Tom said. 'I'll get him, but I'll also call Marv Friedman and ask him how the hell he could be running a CFC alternate project down there with none of us knowing and no permits.'

'How about waiting on that one more day?' Dan asked, 'so I don't have every bigwig down here at once until I nail down the facts.'

'Okay,' Tom said. 'One day, but remember we bubble things up.'

'Yes,' Dan said, 'we do, but they didn't down here, did they? But do talk to Cory please,' Dan said to O'Rourke. 'I don't want to do anything unlawful.' They both laughed as they signed off.

Dan then decided to talk again with J.D. and Ray – go over the same ground, so to speak, and then walk the property once again. Peel that onion, he thought. He would have to focus on Bonnie by mid-morning and then have lunch with her and try and draw her out.

★

Bonnie looked really sweet. Her long hair, blonder in the sunlight and combed straight. Long Texas body built on gorgeous legs. Sensuous eyes and mouth. Nice smile. A way of touching you when she talked. She was very direct and Dan could see how harassment would be real easy for a cracker like J.D. with all his preconceptions. All he needed to do to get started was respond to her physical allure, Dan reflected.

Yes, she liked working at the plant.

Yes, she liked Sour Lake.

Yes, she was really troubled by the incident itself.

Yes, she was the plant chemist based on her B.S. in Chemistry from UT She wanted to be a nutritionist, but had ended up in chemistry and at the plant.

Yes, a damn shame, she hadn't gone on, but she was a good employee and good chemist.

Yes, she worked on the pilot project. Damn rednecks thought they would keep it a secret from him but she knew they couldn't.

No, she didn't know anything about the accident. She wasn't at the plant that day, but in Houston on a day off buying dresses.

He asked her to walk the property with him, which she did. She knew the operation very well. She seemed technically competent. She hadn't known Jon LaFlate very well, except that she trained him on the hazards of HF – that was documented. She couldn't believe he made the mistake at the loading platform with the valve.

'But there are three dead to prove it, I guess,' she said, and hesitated, 'including my mom.'

He liked her and her candour.

Yes, she missed her mom.

★

Dan got word that Cory would call him at four PM Texas time, so he suggested he and Bonnie go out and eat lunch. She said okay. They drove to an Economy Inn dining room right in Sour Lake. When Bonnie sat behind the wheel, her little skirt came halfway up her thighs. Dan noticed and noticed he was supposed to notice. She told him two important things at lunch.

B. Sutherland in the harassment action was her, not her mom – who didn't like Bonnie complaining to the company about 'her sexual business' as her mom put it. She told him what her relationship with J.D. was. She said she had slept with him only once, a few years ago, but lately he was patting her ass and even once touched her breasts in public. She told him to stop and he didn't. Their relationship became harder and harder, as she grew more competent at the plant. It was like a war. He bullied her. She filed the action. Her mother was mad as hell at J.D. Beatrice told J.D., 'Your pecker head took over for your head but it has no brain at all.' She was out there all the time in the yard bawling out J.D. It was a carnival, Bonnie said.

Bonnie also told Dan that the pilot plant was put together on a shoestring. 'Many people in the plant said it was set up by Corporate to fail,' she said. 'I only consented to be the plant chemist at the pilot,' she said, 'when they told my mom we had to make a try at progress here or lose the business. We weren't making the numbers or seen as part of the team. Most people blamed J.D.'

'Including you?' Dan asked.

'Yes, including me,' she answered, after a hesitation.

*

After lunch, Bonnie suddenly asked if he would like to visit her mother's grave. Thinking that she wanted to tell him something in total privacy, he said he would.

They drove to the southern end of Sour Lake just past the school, down the main road and then off to the right for a few miles, into wilder and lusher country – sycamores and wild flowers made it quite beautiful. Dan strangely felt himself relaxing in this beautiful, dense and floral East Texas lushness, and in this woman's presence.

She asked him if he had been in this part of Texas before.

'No,' Dan said. 'But it doesn't look much like the Texas I know – more like a rain forest. It sort of makes you want to slow down,' he added, and she smiled her reply.

'I must be tired,' he said rubbing his eyes. They arrived at a turn down a dirt road and then on to the cemetery. He hadn't meant to let his guard down with this lovely, young woman, he thought, but there was something about her which calmed him.

They trod out to the fresh grave in the small, old Texas cemetery. Dan noticed Mexican names on many of the stones, but not on that of Beatrice X. Sutherland until they were before it.

For a few minutes Bonnie was still in thought, as she crouched down by the newly dug and filled grave, to take stones out of the dirt. 'She was a good woman,' Bonnie said, 'who loved having a man.'

'She had lots of men,' Bonnie continued, turning her face to him, with tears streaming down her cheeks. She said, with that full-face, deep Texas look, 'And she gave and got pleasure.'

'I'm sure you miss her,' Dan said, 'and I'm truly sorry if I haven't said that before. What was the X for?'

'The X?' she asked.

'Yes, in her name,' he answered, and she reached forward and touched the X on the marker.

'My maternal grandfather was named X.T. Sutherland,' she said. 'Like lots of Texas people he was known by initials instead of a name. Mother took the X from my grandfather. She rejected my father's name,' she said, 'when he lit out. When I was a little girl, she dropped all connection to him and went back to her family name – that's when she took the X and I became Bonnie Sutherland.'

She sat down on the grass by the grave, and he sat, too, next to her, to encourage her to talk on. She had stopped crying. She clearly had something to say, and he felt comfortable she was going to level with him.

'You know,' she went on, 'my mother Beatrice had an affair with your big personnel guy in New Jersey – what's his name, fuckin' Atkinson – when he was down here. My mom made me swear not to talk about it – although Anne knows – but now she's dead, so I don't feel so bound to silence. I can't help but think that damn guy went up the corporate ladder and just tossed my mom aside like a piece of meat. He is probably glad she is dead with her secret about him, but I know – and the secret won't die with her now, will it?' she concluded.

'No, I guess not,' he said gently, 'but I can't see that the two matters are connected.'

'They're not,' she replied, 'but they are for me.' He looked at her quizzically. 'Well,' she said. 'I had a brief roll in the hay with J.D. I told you about it. Anne knows that, too, but she is like my sister. It meant nothing to me. He just kind of bullied me, like he always does, when I was new and unsure at the plant. Thing is my mom learned about it and was pissed at J.D. He then threatened to fire me unless we kept our mouths shut. He sort of acted like he had this control over me. It was weird. He pushed me into working on that goddamned pilot, too, which I knew was a piece of shit,' she said.

'He harassed me, goddamnit. My mom was out there at the pilot looking for J.D. because he had casually rubbed my bottom, like it didn't mean nothin', the day before the accident, and she had seen him do it. I told him next time he was a dead man, but he just laughed. Hell, the man is such a bully. I wouldn't kill anyone, not even him. But my mom *would* have killed him. She was out there to tell him so, looking for him, although it turned out he was away from the site when the leak and vapor cloud occurred, too.'

She was crying now, the tension released from the nonstop description of what she had told him. Dan touched her arm and, then, as crying turned to sobbing, he put his arm around her. She dug her face in the nap of his neck, sobbing now.

Dan rubbed her back gently. Her crying subsided. He said to her, seizing the naked moment, 'Bonnie, this isn't the right time, but where did that leak come from?'

'What do you mean?' she asked, face still turned inward and lips touching his neck now.

'You know what I mean,' he said. 'Was it the HF loading dock or the pilot operation?'

'You know the answer,' she said. 'They will trash me for sure if they know I told. Everyone is scared shitless you will find out, even the OSHA inspector, who doesn't want this trouble.' After a pause, she said, laughing a little, 'And you already know. I really dig you, you know.' Then they kissed and she laughed again and wrapped her arms and legs around him, as she lay on top of him, and they kissed there on the grass in front of Beatrice's still fresh grave.

★

Eventually the kissing and embracing was spent and the ardor cooled. Bonnie signaled it by rolling off Dan. They lay on their backs unwilling to give up the moment, although their motivations were perhaps different.

Dan spoke first, after getting his breath and gaining his composure. 'Excuse me for such a rush, but you just seemed so sympathetic – and pretty – and I just lost myself for a few moments.'

Bonnie turned and looked him deep in the eyes, with her beautiful, blue eyes wide open. 'No harm done. I rather enjoyed it, didn't you?'

'Yes,' he said.

'And I needed it too,' she continued. 'Sex is my great hedge against pressure, and with you I feel so damn open.' She smiled. 'You are quite a guy.' She paused, then ventured dropping her voice, 'I hope my eagerness doesn't turn you off.'

'Not at all,' Dan admitted, although he couldn't fathom what he was getting into and didn't seem to want to try to think it through.

She said, 'You are terrific, you know.' She paused and added, 'We must keep this separate from our jobs here.'

She smiled and reached her hand forward to touch his face. 'I know you will have to pursue the pilot plant leak being the cause of the deaths, including my mom's, but can you keep it from coming from me.'

'I'll do everything possible,' he said. 'After all, they know I suspect it. I appreciate your frankness – I know it took some guts.'

'It's so easy talking to you,' she said. 'And I don't regret it. In fact, I feel relieved.'

Driving back to the plant, she said to him, 'Will we see each other like this again?'

He thought briefly of the opportunities and said, 'I think I may be going to Houston tomorrow to see EPA people. Depends on my conversation with the home office lawyer this afternoon, but it's what I'm going to suggest. Would you like to join me there?'

'Yes,' she said. 'we could meet in the evening. I'll tell you where, later today, if you confirm the trip. I fall in love fast,' she said real quickly then, 'but don't worry. I don't bust up lives.'

As they neared the plant gate, she kissed the end of his fingers and he touched her knees as she drove.

★

Dan spent the afternoon in confrontation with J.D. and just about everyone else over his 'theory' that the leak came from the pilot. Dan mentioned that the HF process was not corrosive enough or inherently dangerous enough to have caused such a problem. Dan said neither J.D. nor Gapt nor anyone else had offered a reasonable technical explanation for the accident in the H.F. loading. The explanation that LaFlate had somehow triggered the valve was nonsense to him. 'It just doesn't go down,' Dan said.

Eventually, late in the afternoon, J.D. said, 'Look, we told OSHA that the leak was at the HF loading dock, you know, and that was my best information. Do we want to go back on that?' he asked.

'Well,' Dan continued, 'I spoke to Cory in New Jersey, and he says we must tell the state EPA about the pilot operation, and use the argument that we saw it as being strictly R&D, under the general permit.' He continued, 'And you and I are going to have to do that tomorrow in Houston. J.D., how long do you think it will take for someone to put that together with the accident. We are better off bringing it up ourselves if, in fact, it happened there, J.D., than waiting for the agency to ask us,' he concluded.

'Yeah,' J.D. countered. 'But EPA and OSHA don't talk to each other and you know I don't know that the pilot was involved. No one else says it was except you.' J.D. asked, 'Do they?'

Dan paused. 'Well, J.D.,' he said, 'you hear things. Just think about it and, maybe, after we meet for dinner tonight with Anne we can talk about this again.'

'Okay, okay,' J.D. repeated.

★

'Are we all set to talk with EPA tomorrow afternoon then?' Dan asked later.

'I think so. We have an appointment at 3.00 PM So we can go after lunch. I'll have the layout of the pilot, as you suggested, to give the EPA.' And J.D. added, 'But now I've got some plant output problems to solve, you know, so let's get together in an hour, if that's okay with you.'

'Great,' Dan said. 'I need to make some phone calls anyway.'

'Use this office,' J.D. answered. 'I'm going out into the plant.'

★

Dan called Cory back and got his voice mail. He left the message that 'J.D. and I will be at the Texas Department of Environmental Protection office in Houston tomorrow afternoon to make a first local contact with the office about the existence of the pilot under the general permit.'

They had agreed that a low-keyed discussion without lawyers and the rather simple explanation that it was a temporary situation under the general permit and now closed up might suffice, and could later be relied upon with the Feds. J.D. and Ray would do the presentation. He was just there to support and to make sure they did it.

'We will then follow it up with a letter if it goes down,' he said and added, 'if not, I'll be back to you.' It was, in fact, the part of the job Dan liked the best – planning and negotiating with the agencies. Foley often questioned him, based on this personal preference for negotiation, to think about whether he was misplaced as an auditor.

Dan then called O'Rourke to say that he would be going to Houston DEP tomorrow with J.D. He reviewed the strategy, including the message to Cory. He told O'Rourke that he had stumbled on informal confirmation that the pilot was the source of the emissions that led to the fatalities. Dan said that J.D. was thinking over Dan's technical problems with an HF plant emission at the loading dock, and the possibility of the emission emanating from the pilot. 'He is thinking about it,' Dan said, 'and I'm putting a lot of pressure on him to confirm my unconfirmed report. Of, course it might simply remain a suspicion. It doesn't change the facts – I mean the fatalities, I guess.'

O'Rourke said, 'I have an appointment with Charlie Moore tomorrow morning. I will call you immediately after that, but I don't see how he can't know about all this. I don't know what his explanation will be,' he said, 'but you're doing a great job, Dan. I know it's tough. Keep it up.'

'I need to talk to Marv Friedman tomorrow, too,' Dan said.

'I know,' O'Rourke answered. 'Don't worry, he knows all about this, I'm sure.'

'Yeah, that's what worries me,' Dan said.

'I'm behind you one hundred per cent,' O'Rourke added. Dan wasn't sure he appreciated the necessity for an endorsement.

★

Dear Gloria and girls,
How are you all doing? Very hot here in Texas. And then there is the weather (ha, ha)! Hope all is going well. Sorry to miss the family fun,
Love,
Dan/ Dad

Chapter Three

Houston

Dan was lost in thought as he, Ray and J.D. drove into Houston on US 90. J.D. had come clean in a phone call that woke him out of a dead sleep. It was almost midnight. J.D. sounded pressed and a little drunk. 'Yes, he too believed there was a possibility the leak was from the jerry-rigged R&D pilot setup,' as J.D. was now calling it. 'Although,' he was quick to add, 'there is no direct proof because the pilot is dismantled and they were not continuously monitoring the operation, just collecting some last-minute product sample.'

LaFlate was out there fussing with the piping and Beatrice Sutherland had just been in the yard near the pad. J.D. said he didn't know what for. He speculated it could have been an emission from the HF high priority distribution point because they were filling at that time and there had been a question about the valving. LaFlate was sort of moving between the operations, both J.D. and Ray staunchly maintained.

'What's the difference, really?' J.D. said. 'They're dead and so is the Mex, Gonzales. The cause was really the same either way,' he said, 'and we wanted to avoid questions about the pilot, which was going down anyway and with it maybe the business,' he rambled. 'We lost that business, you know, when Mr. Friedman said we were going to take it to Mexico under NAFTA. Son-of-a-bitch government politicians,' J.D. said, as if they were to blame, and it occurred to him J.D. believed Washington was at fault.

'Who else knew that the R&D pad could be the source of the emission?' Dan asked, choosing his words carefully.

But J.D. answered, quite openly, now that he was talking about it, 'Ray Gapt, Charlie Moore must know, Bonnie Sutherland – maybe if the cunt figures it out, and, I guess, LaFlate must have known right at the end what the source was.' Picking up on Dan's phraseology he added, 'But there is no direct evidence, and OSHA was satisfied.'

They had agreed they would tell EPA in a matter of fact way about the existence of the pilot, about that plant's theory that it was a part of the permitted operation for a short time, and being dismantled on the pad. 'No reason to discuss this leak possibility with EPA tomorrow, you know,' J.D. said.

'While the investigation goes on we will stop at that for now,' Dan answered.

They had agreed to take Ray with them because he knew the EPA inspector, whom he had dealt with in the past, a veteran named Tom Horan. J.D. had agreed to tell Ray that morning of the fact that he had told Dan of the 'possibility' that the pilot had been the source of the leak, and to just let Dan's investigation go on. J.D. said he would have to also tell Charlie Moore back at headquarters. Dan said he would tell Anne.

*

As late as it was, Dan called Anne and asked if he could come down and talk to her. Just past midnight, sitting in the little armchairs around the table by the window, Dan and Anne discussed J.D.'s admission to him and its implications. Anne said she would have to tell Bush in the morning, and perhaps they both should be present when they talked to Marv Friedman on the phone. They agreed to call it a possibility as J.D. did, to give Dan some room to maneuver.

Anne then told Dan that, earlier, she had brought the harassment charge up again with J.D. 'He was adamant that Bonnie was a real tease and he had done nothing but be playful after the one incident, which he mentioned was fully consensual. He said he got along fine with Bonnie now and thought she would withdraw the charge, with the tragedy of Beatrice behind them.'

'I think my talking to him about the harassment charge really stirred him up,' Anne said. 'He keeps hinting at unknown conspirators and pressures. He said at one point that the real enemy was a conspiracy between the media, government and the big companies. He scares me with that stuff.'

Anne had obviously thrown on her jeans and a button-down, plaid shirt when he called – she was barefoot. She looked luscious. She asked him playfully, 'Say, you looked a little disorganized when you came back from lunch with Bonnie – everything okay?'

'Yes,' he said, 'but she took me to the cemetery where her mother was buried and told me there it was the pilot, not the HF plant.'

'Between the fresh grave, this really nice, young woman's feelings and the truth, which I had really guessed but she confirmed, it was quite discombobulating.'

'Knowing Bonnie, I can imagine,' Anne injected.

'I didn't tell you because Bonnie swore me to secrecy, said her job was at stake,' he said. 'But now that the cat is out of the bag via J.D., Bonnie's honesty really sets her up as reliable and, maybe, brave too. She gave me the ammunition and certainty with which to confront J.D.,' he added.

'You poor dear,' Anne said. 'You have been through a lot today. Maybe you need a little old-fashioned sympathy.'

She surprised him by leaning forward and kissing him flush on the mouth. They kissed again and this time his hand drifted across her beautiful breast.

Then they parted a little and Anne looked down to the floor.

'Would you go to bed with me for a little while, Dan,' she said. 'I feel so lonely tonight.' They kissed again. 'I have my period now, Dan,' she said, 'and it may be old-fashioned, but I am in my deepest flow and I don't like sex with a man then, but maybe you could just be with me for a while.'

'Yes,' he said, 'let's do that,' and soon they were under the covers in their underwear, bundled together and kissing. When it became apparent that he was ready and deeply aroused, she took him in her mouth and licked and sucked him until he came.

★

The next morning, on the day of the trip to Houston, they met for a quick breakfast. He had returned to his room in the middle of the night for a short sleep. In the morning she was all business, really as if the night was just an interlude. He was very grateful for that because to him Anne had nothing to do with Gloria – or with Bonnie, for that matter, he thought ruefully.

From the plant he called O'Rourke and received permission to talk to Marv Friedman. Anne was going to visit with the Gonzales family so she would miss that conversation after all. He wouldn't see her for the rest of the day. He had told her he was going to visit with friends in Houston that night and he would leave a number at the hotel where she could reach him.

He called Gloria, but got the voice mail, so he told her on tape he had had a rough day yesterday, what with the investigation and going to the cemetery, and today and tonight he would be in Houston at EPA. She was used to his moving around, so he knew it would go down okay with her. He told her he would try and call her that evening from Houston.

★

Sitting in the car, moving from the lush bayou coast of the Beaumont area toward the downtown Houston high-rise skyline, which appeared to rise out of the Buffalo bayou itself, Dan thought about the phone call with Marv Friedman. It had started with Friedman's usual bombast, but Dan could hear Friedman becoming defensive. The situation had put Dan in the cat-bird seat, as the Red Barber of his childhood would have said.

Friedman said O'Rourke had briefed him and rather aggressively asked, 'Is there anything more new?'

'Well,' Dan answered, 'I have a couple of people down here, who say it may have been a pilot plant emission, including J.D. That makes a lot of sense to me, more technical sense than the HF loading station, frankly, but I haven't yet seen the data, on which I can say for sure. Maybe there isn't any.'

Silence at the other end.

'Anyway,' Dan continued, 'we are going to the Texas DEP in Houston this afternoon to low-key discuss the pilot plant. We got Bill Cory's advice we should do it – actually J.D. and his assistant Ray Gapt will do it – I'm just along as backup – that's what Cory agreed was the best alternative at this point, and I know he talked to Mr. Carpenter.'

'Yeah, I know,' Marv Friedman said. 'I've talked to Carpenter, too.'

'Have you talked to J.D.?' Dan asked, falling into his auditor's role.

'No,' Friedman said. 'But I know Charlie Moore has and, before you ask, let me say that I didn't know of any operation in Sour Lake to produce research quantities of test CFC alternate. I knew they were doing that in San Jose,' he said loudly, 'but it's news to me they were doing it in Sour Lake, and they are going to pay for the renegade deception, believe me,' Friedman said.

It all sounded a little practiced to Dan but he let it go by. As long as Friedman didn't interfere, he could not care less. 'And listen,' Friedman added, 'I told the chairman you were doing a good job, so don't make a liar out of me.'

'Well, thank you,' Dan said, figuring they were about finished, 'I'll try not to.' He knew this was Friedman's way of telling Dan he had talked to the chairman.

Friedman went right on, 'Mr. Casey says he wants to see you about this in Austin on Saturday. He said just you and maybe the Hennessy girl,' Friedman practically whispered, 'so see how much you can get done by then, keep the plant working and keep your nose clean.'

Too late for that, Dan thought.

As he left the plant, Bonnie had appeared, looking very fresh and happy, chasing him down the hall saying,

'Mr. Straus, a phone message for you.' She smiled and handed him a note which said simply, 'Hotel Warwick after seven.' He smiled and thanked her saying, 'If they call again, say I'll be there and look forward to it.'

★

Now they were off the freeway and finally into downtown Houston, with its blocks, mixing contemporary glass office buildings, fast-food restaurants, lounges with go-go signs, private homes and gas stations.

Ah Houston, he thought – the metropolis without zoning.

'Well, here we are, you know,' J.D. said, and Ray woke up in the rear seat, or, at least, pretended to awake from a sleep that would separate him from further questions. Let him be for now, Dan had agreed with O'Rourke, just as long as he uses that gut and good old boy manner to support Mr. You Know, here, with the Texas DEP, Dan thought.

★

They entered the Houston local office of the State Department of Environmental Protection, through a spiffy glass arcade, in an ultra, modern building in downtown Houston, only to find themselves on a connecting cat walk to old offices in a warehouse-type structure. Ray Gapt knew the way.

Tom Horan sat in a big swivel chair, by an old window air conditioner, with his back to the door, as they entered. With the knock and the sound of the door opening, Tom started in his chair and turned the page of a book in his lap.

'I had the distinct impression,' Dan was later to tell Bonnie, 'that he was napping and that he followed a regular procedure of page turning when the sound at the door awoke him.'

The office was very hot. A junior man sat at the other end from Horan at a desk near the door. The air conditioner cranked away. Horan wore a well-worn brown suit and a tie, with a pull-over sweater with crumbs from lunch on it. He was about sixty-five years of age and obviously waiting for retirement.

The usual pleasantries ensued while they scurried for chairs. Horan asked Dan where he had worked before Specialty. 'He knew the company only through the division at Sour Lake,' Dan noted later to Anne, 'and I determined to keep him at that more local relationship.'

Ray then, referring to a flow chart, took Tom Horan through the HF facility at Sour Lake to remind him of the physical structure and the permits. Horan listened and made a couple of notes. At one point he said, 'Yes, yes, I understand.' At that point Ray mentioned that they were thinking of some changes at the plant and the permitting implications. Ray emphasized that these changes would expand the plant and bring more employment to Sour Lake, 'a depressed area', he reminded Horan. Again, Horan said, 'Yes, yes, I understand.' Dan thought Ray was quite skillful in his handling of this bureaucrat.

Ray then indicated to Horan that Dan was down doing an audit at the plant. 'Did Tom know that they had had an accident at the plant?'

'Yes,' Horan responded. 'I guess that shook you all up. I saw the report of an emission go past my desk a few weeks ago, including fatalities. Too bad,' he said. 'Had OSHA been in?' Horan asked.

'Yes,' J.D. answered. 'They were quite thorough.'

'You come through it okay?' Horan asked.

'Yes, we think so. Goddamned young kid may have screwed up,' J.D. said.

'Apparently,' Dan added.

Ray then explained that 'While down on the accident, Dan had come across the remnants of our dismantled small, temporary R&D facility, using HF to do a little research on potential uses to maybe land the plant expansion for Texas, and wanted to make sure DEP was aware.'

Horan made few more notes.

'We thought we would carry out this communication technicality with DEP, while Dan was here,' J.D. chimed in, 'and he would meet you, Tom.' He made it sound like they were all just trying to fulfill the rules of this overly technical auditor from up North to satisfy the company and perhaps secure the growth they all – the good old boys – wanted for Texas.

'How long was it up? Where did the waste go?' Tom asked. They supplied the information and referenced the existing permits. Horan asked for a plot of the pilot and they went through the little informal drawing they brought with him. Eventually he looked up and said, 'Yes, yes, I see.'

Ray then said, 'Of course this activity was under our general permit, but we want to confirm that with you. You know the company auditors are very tough on us.'

'We're just trying to keep our plant open, you know,' J.D. added, 'but we want to be technically correct too.'

'Well,' Horan responded, 'that sounds reasonable, but I will check it out. If there is any further review from here, I will let you know,' he added, 'and I'll keep the drawing of this R&D pilot – it's already been dismantled you say – as documentation.' He asked Ray and J.D. to sign and date the drawing, which they did and the interview was complete. It seemed clear they would not hear further from Tom Horan on this matter.

As they left the office, J.D. said, 'Mission accomplished.'

'Yes,' Dan said, 'unless we hear something more I guess that is right.'

'Good job,' J.D. said to Ray, in a voice indicating that he intended to close the matter out.

'Pretty fast,' Ray responded. 'Short and sweet.'

'Let's make a file memo by tomorrow,' Dan said, 'so the record shows the disclosure.'

'Okay,' J.D. said. 'Good idea – you do it, Ray. Give Dan and me a copy and let us know if Horan comes back.'

As they departed from the glass entryway, Dan explained that he was going to visit some friends in Houston that night who would return him to Sour Lake either later that night, or in the morning. He would just take his overnight bag from the trunk of the car. J.D. and Ray were glad to have him off their hands.

★

Dan made his phone calls next to Cory and O'Rourke to tell them of the meeting at DEP, and then to Gloria. He told her about his day and she told him about hers, but the conversation was stiff. He told her he would be in Houston overnight at the Warwick and return to Sour Lake the next morning.

★

He met Bonnie in the bar of the Warwick Hotel, a stately, handsome, older Houston landmark near Rice University. She smiled comfortably at him, when she caught his eye on his entering the darkened room, and she arose and kissed him lightly.

She was a knockout. That's all he could think. She wore a tight, short, red dress, which accented her legs, and a bolero jacket, which parted slightly when she moved, to show her beautiful, white skin and her youthful and shapely bust. Her long hair hung down to her mid-back. A woman of such incomparable beauty and ease he thought... and a chemist to boot, he thought laughing at himself.

'How was your day?' she asked and he briefly described the visit to the agency and the outcome. What he focused on at greater length was a description of Tom Horan, the DEP functionary.

'He was an amazing stereotype of the government bureaucrat,' Dan said and told Bonnie his impression that Horan had been asleep when they entered and then routinely turned the page of the book when the noise of the door awakened him, as if he were reading.

They chuckled and Bonnie said, 'just a Texas good old boy, who Ray and J.D. know how to play since birth.'

'Make his job easy,' he commented, 'and align against the guy from New York, that seemed to work pretty well.'

Again they both had this smooth feeling of ease with each other. They sat talking about life in Sour Lake now, her hand resting lightly on his arm. She described her comfort in growing up in East Texas, as an independent girl without much maternal supervision, who could seek what she wanted without an overbearing preconception of what her goals should be.

'So different from my childhood of expectation,' he said.

'Of course,' she said, 'a Texas girl does not have to be a demure Southern belle, at least not in East Texas – she can be a roughneck, if she wants, and in the context of my life I wanted to be sure I could do whatever pleased me. Anne was a little different because she was ambitious for what I would call worldly success – something I don't give a shit about,' she said honestly, 'although I am ambitious in my own way.'

They ordered two more glasses of wine. She slipped off her jacket and placed it on the third chair at the table. She was stunning, he thought, with her beautiful, bare shoulders, the thin straps of her dress overlying them, and the provocative, just visible rising of her breasts.

'God, you're beautiful,' he said. It seemed the most natural thing to say. She smiled.

'Anne is a really good professional and a nice person, too,' he said. 'You are lucky to have such a friend.'

She told him then about their teenage days. 'Anne and I were the local rebels, but not in the way they expect here, because we both like sex and alcohol, which is okay here, but in a certain mold. We did well in school, too, and expected to make our own way. We were a twosome,' she bragged.

'You are two wonderful individuals, who made up a twosome, perhaps,' he said. 'But your lives are different now. I hate to think I've come in close contact with both of you because of a bad accident and fatalities.' He continued, 'But still I'm glad.' He blushed and stammered, 'Not glad about your mom, of course.' He paused and looked down. 'God, what a shit,' he said. She squeezed his hand and he went on, 'What I meant was I wouldn't have met you.'

'I know,' she answered simply.

They sat there easily talking. Dan was getting better at that Sour Lake direct gaze, as he returned the look from Bonnie's blue eyes. Finally, Bonnie said, 'Are we both staying here? I am.'

'Yes,' Dan answered. 'I am as well,' and added, taking his cue from her, 'would you like to have dinner served by room service?'

'That would be great, just what I had in mind... would you come to my room?'

'Absolutely,' he answered. 'Shall I give you a few minutes?'

'Yes, please do,' she said. 'But just a couple – don't keep me waiting very long.'

★

It was a wondrous night for Dan and for Bonnie. They met sexually with a fervor he had never before experienced. Both suspended the outside world in their closeness and ease with each other.

If Bonnie was attractive with her clothes on, she was dazzling to Dan undressed. She had such a beautiful body and used it in her sex to such advantage. She told Dan she was in the last day of her period, and, if he didn't mind, she didn't.

He didn't, only telling her late into the night, when their sexual sharing was peaking, that 'unhappily there are some things I cannot do for you that you do for me.'

'I'll take a rain check,' she said.

They kissed sucked and licked their way to a commitment that grew past the sex itself and encompassed their growing attitude toward each other. They were devouring each other, sexually but also intellectually and emotionally, and told each other things which they had never shared before. They felt themselves falling in love and said so.

'You know I have such trouble showing myself – I mean my real self – to others,' Dan said. 'I have trouble sharing my doubts with others. I am always worried about my success,' he added. 'By that I mean whether I accomplish what I think I should. That spills over to my personal relationships', he said, 'where I want everything to go positively and that I should look good – above criticism, so to say. With you it's different,' he said. 'I feel I can say and do anything and you will accept me.'

'I know,' she said, 'and I'm happy.'

'I have never met anyone like you,' Dan said.

'Nor I,' she answered. 'We seem perfect together.'

They kissed, then kissed and kissed. She sat atop him, while he kissed and licked her breasts, and then they kissed again. Open and full-mouthed they kissed, she sitting mounted atop him, until they exhausted themselves with climaxes. Then they lay together, arms and legs intertwined.

'I've never understood why sexual activity and analytic thinking are seen as opposites,' Bonnie said, 'not to be found in the same woman. Is that peculiar to Texas?' she asked.

'No,' he answered. 'And not to women either. I've often thought the way we don't admit an athlete can also be intellectual – you know, a dumb jock – is a similar generalization for the athlete, which puts him down. The possibility that a woman can be both sensual and intellectual eludes so many.'

'You know,' she said, 'a dumb jock is sort of the same as a dizzy broad.'

Only one time Bonnie stopped him – when he started to talk about Gloria. 'No,' she said, placing her finger to his lips, 'that's for some other time. Whatever happens, this is our night, Dan.' And she replaced her finger with her tongue, and then her lips and sucking mouth, while he entered her and they rode together to an exuberant climax beyond his previous experience.

★

May 10, 1994

To the Editor
Chemical Technology Newsletter
Michigan State University

Adding to your dialogue on Environmental Technology Assessment, each technology transaction may be recognized as unique; over-regulation of technology cooperation or too strict definition of environmentally sound technology could stifle innovation and limit access to needed technology. In purchasing and requesting access to new technologies, enterprises and governmental authorities in developing countries and countries in transition are trying to balance many needs: economic, social and environmental. Given those parameters, the most appropriate technology can only be determined with reference to those specific needs, as well as the conditions under which the technology will operate. When parties in a technology transaction consider the type of technology to be utilized, they should seek to ensure that existing infrastructure, skills and resources are capable of absorbing and safely utilizing the technologies in question.

Even the best, most environmentally sound hardware can have a negative impact, if misused or mismanaged, or if not supported by the appropriate resources, institutions and infrastructure. Instead, from my own experience, I would say that the partners in the technology transaction need to jointly determine that the technologies, which are chosen, are sound and adaptable to the special needs of the businesses concerned. This is best achieved in the framework of diligence in the company transactions. What is needed is more information about the environmental performance of technologies, which have been identified as being of primary importance, along with the capacity and resources to fully utilize that information.

Flexibility in approach is necessary environmentally or elsewhere, to ensure, within reasonable bounds, that the entrepreneur has the room and incentive to innovate, without harming the public.

Very truly yours,
Dan Straus
American Industrial Inc.
New Brunswick, NJ

Chapter Four
Sour Lake

The dinner at Joe Wiseman's was that night and Dan was drawing together his thoughts, as he sat in the bathtub at the Holiday Inn, early that morning. He loved baths, long leisurely ones, where he soaked, turning on the hot water periodically to replenish the warmth. Since he was a child, he would do what his parents laughingly called 'surfing' in which he would totally immerse himself while lying on his back. When the tub was too short for him by his adolescent years, he would extend his legs out, feet on the wall, and surf with his boyish abandon. His dad, who constantly worried even to Dan that he was too bound up with his responsibilities, sometimes joked that surfing in the tub was his only vice. Not his only vice now, God knows, Dan thought, but still he surfed.

Bonnie was as cheerful and loving in the morning as through the night. She had driven him back to his motel in Liberty, early in the morning. He would be at the plant by 9.00 AM, tired but tremendously happy. He was bemused by the fact that he felt no guilt, and, more than that, he felt a new and real possibility for his troubled personal life. He agreed with Bonnie that he would call her that night after the dinner and evening at Wiseman's. They had established that she would go to Austin with him over the weekend.

'I have a lot of friends from UT in Austin and some things to do,' Bonnie said, when he mentioned he could be quite occupied with the chairman or it might be five minutes on Saturday. 'So, it won't be any problem, just a great slice of fun for me.'

'Me too,' Dan responded.

At the plant, in conferences with J.D. and Ray, and Cory on the phone, as well as Anne listening, they had decided by midday to tell OSHA that they felt they had fully explored the accident, but there was the possibility, unproved, of a connection in LaFlate's activities with a small pilot out there which had been dismantled.

Cory suggested that Ray Gapt do this by himself over the phone, playing it down but answering any questions openly and honestly, to which they all agreed.

By mid-afternoon Ray had had another of his good old boy conversations on the speaker phone with the OSHA inspector, with Dan, J.D. and Anne in the small trailer with him. Ray identified to the inspector that he 'had J.D. and some corporate types with him.' The OSHA inspector indicated that he knew from the records there was another operation LaFlate was working on, which he assumed was the R&D pilot Ray mentioned.

'After a thorough corporate audit, there is some suspicion that the R&D pilot was the source of the emission, but we have no proof,' Ray said.

'So?' the inspector said.

'We're just putting it on the table,' Ray answered.

The OSHA inspector said, 'I assume Texas DEP was informed about the pilot operation.' Ray replied, 'Affirmative, but only recently as we reasoned it was temporary and under our general permit.'

'It's no longer there?' the inspector replied.

'No, we took it down. Never amounted to much,' Ray answered.

'I don't want to open the record for this,' the inspector said, clearly annoyed.

'Make a file memo,' Dan told Ray, with the disgust he felt for the old boy process sounding as a hard edge in his voice, even though the result was favorable, 'and copy Cory.'

Dan also briefed O'Rourke and then talked to Marv Friedman, Paul Atkinson and H. Jeffrey Bush at their invitation about briefing the chairman on Saturday.

'You will be there at 10.00 AM, at the Four Seasons Suites in Austin where Mr. Casey will be staying,' Friedman growled. He was edgy about Dan's meeting with the chairman, although he was very careful now in the conference call to tell Dan he was doing a great job.

'When this is over, heads are going to roll,' Friedman said. 'I don't like being surprised, and I am surprised by the existence of this R&D pilot in Sour Lake, even though we have no proof of its connection to the accident.' This was said for everyone's benefit and perhaps for Dan to repeat to the chairman on Saturday. Atkinson said to Dan, 'The chairman may ask you about J.D.'s competency,' to which Marv interrupted, 'Yeah, well, I think he should retire, so, if you think so, Dan, say so.'

Atkinson then asked if Dan was up-to-date on the harassment issue, relative to Miss Sutherland. Dan said he thought he was. 'Good,' said Atkinson, 'because the chairman may ask you about that, so talk to Anne and maybe J.D., too, each in private, of course.'

'That's another nail in his coffin,' Friedman said roughly.

Bush then brought up the dinner with Joe Wiseman that night.

'You have handled the plant and the Texas government folks well,' H. began, 'but I'm concerned that the press could blow this pilot thing out of proportion. Let Anne handle Wiseman, if you can,' he advised Dan.

'Well, it's a social evening,' Dan answered, 'but, if it comes up, Miss Hennessy will tell Wiseman in some low-key way, and I'll back fill.'

'Well, be careful,' H. said, to which Dan responded, 'We will. We will be discreet and we will stick to the facts.'

'Okay,' Friedman responded and Bush answered with an audible sigh, 'Damn right.'

Dan called Dr. Foley late in the afternoon to roll this meeting with Wiseman over with his mentor, particularly in view of the nervousness in New Jersey, but the professor wasn't there, so he merely left a message that he had called. He then asked his secretary, Caroline, in New Brunswick, to make a reservation for Friday and Saturday night, in Austin, at the Hyatt, across the river from the Four Seasons, and to make the reservation for a room with a king-sized bed, saying, 'I'm tired of sleeping in a cramped bed.'

He also asked Caroline to call Gloria that afternoon and tell her he was going to Austin to meet with the chairman and expected to come home on Sunday. Dan knew Gloria would be impressed by his meeting with the chairman. She would be ambitious and doubting he was prepared for such a contact. He knew also that Caroline's relaying of the message would give an authenticity, which would calm the waters of irritability caused by his absence, although he wasn't quite sure that calming the waters is where his future lay.

*

He met Anne in the lobby to go to the Wiseman dinner.
Dan wore a tie and sports jacket. He felt very dressed up for
Sour Lake, but not compared to Anne. She was dressed up
to the nines in a black cocktail dress and looked great; more
she looked fabulous. She had such sensational legs, Dan
thought, and he had the distinct impression she was out to
impress him, as much as Joe and Sarah Wiseman, with her
physical attractiveness.

*

Joe Wiseman lived in one of those great old East Texas
homes, in the Sour Lake old town, off the west end of
Route 15, among sycamore and pecan trees and a lush
feeling of vegetation and bayou. His wife, Sarah, Anne's
childhood friend, was a sweet, young woman, who
appeared to have no pretense and quite a lot of Smith
College independence in her.

Joe was direct and outspoken. Dan quickly learned that
Joe started most conversations and ended almost all; yet
there was an honest quality about him that seemed to join
Texas and New York City, City College.

Sarah was saying, 'When I first met Joe in New York
City, I wondered if all New Yorkers were so fast-talking
and smart, but now I know it's partly being Jewish and an
intellectual New Yorker, and partly some genetic quality in
Joe that is inbred in his generations of family and strong
men.' She took Joe's hand at the dinner table – they sat next
to each other in the circle like young love birds.

Anne said, 'Sarah was always bowled over, Joe, by guys like you... but she does appear to have made a good choice in your case.'

Joe smiled. 'Flattery from a beautiful public relations person like you, Anne, is likely to get you anywhere. Would you like a job, to start?' he chuckled.

He turned to Dan. 'And what about you, my New Jersey friend. How do you like our East Texas atmosphere?'

'Well, I'm pretty busy, actually, with my plant review,' Dan responded, 'but I am pleasantly surprised by the beauty of this part of Texas. Actually,' he added, 'I had this idea that all of Texas looked the same – hot and dusty – and only now do I realize that Texas has a number of different regions with different climates and vegetation. I really am quite impressed.'

'We are more Louisiana than Texas, in many respects,' Joe countered, 'that's true, but we are Texas here by temperament. Louisiana would never elect George Bush,' he said. 'His family is too patrician, and here we go for the global knockout punch. Lyndon Johnson was perhaps even a better illustration,' he added, 'of the Texas reach for the national stage.

'Speaking of the national stage,' Joe continued, directing his inquiry first to Anne in almost a courtly manner, 'how is the plant situation working out?'

'Well,' Anne said, 'it was a terrible tragedy for the families, but also for the people at the plant.'

'I can imagine,' Joe said.

'But we are coming out of it, doing everything we can for the families.' Anne added, 'Perhaps because I'm from Sour Lake I can help just a little bit more than others.'

Joe nodded. 'And you are investigating the accident, Dan?'

'Yes,' Dan said.

'Anything new?' Joe inquired.

'I have confirmed an emission was the cause, and Mr. LaFlate and Mrs. Sutherland were in the vicinity – Mr. LaFlate probably at the controls,' he added, 'although the whole thing has a freakish quality.'

'A leaking loading valve?' Joe persisted.

'It's difficult to pin down,' Dan answered, 'but the accident was a freak and all procedures and operations are under review so it will not occur again. Inexperience could have been the cause,' he added and Joe's brow knotted at a question forming in his consciousness they knew he would ask.

Dan continued, 'There was some 'R&D' work going on too, trying to keep the plant afloat and LaFlate just simply might have made a mistake, despite his training. It's difficult to pin down the cause with LaFlate – the operator – dead. But we are touching every base.'

'Dan's here to assure it won't happen again,' Anne interjected.

Joe picked up on it going in another direction, saying, 'There have been a lot of cuts recently in industry, Dan, and some cutthroat competition. There have even been rumors in town that the business is moving to Mexico under NAFTA,' Joe continued. 'Could those factors have led to a deterioration or bad attitude, or maybe even poor training leading to the accident?'

As if to take the edge off his question, Joe turned to Sarah and said ruefully, 'Imagine that, Sarah, I sound like one of those damn Texas conservatives who opposed NAFTA – when in reality I favor it,' he added for Anne and Dan's sake.

'No,' Dan answered. 'The OSHA inspector did not find a lack of training, nor did I. Ray Gapt and Bonnie Sutherland were really quite competent. J.D. seems to think it was just a freak occurrence,' he added, 'but I'm trained to find deficiencies if they exist and correct them.' Joe nodded. He looked at Sarah, who was quite white with tension and gripping the table.

'No one could find Bonnie at fault, could they?' she said.

'She's done so much with herself.'

'No,' Dan answered. 'On the contrary, we have great respect for Miss Sutherland.'

Dan continued, seeing a chance to make a point. 'I went to Houston yesterday to see the state environmental people. Quite an old and smart Texas codger in the agency.'

'We call that a good old boy,' Joe laughed.

'Anyway,' Dan continued, 'J.D. was telling this good old boy about the R&D pilot operation Anne mentioned – it's been taken down now. This DEP guy seemed sensitive to the plight of a plant trying to find technology, which would give it a second wind. That is a little different than the Feds.'

'That's great news,' Joe said. 'You'll have to tell me more about it, if it comes about, Anne, and produces some new employment. Of course,' he quipped, still following his own news lead, 'Ross Perot would say you are developing it here to take to Mexico.'

Sarah patted his hand lovingly. 'Enough of that NAFTA talk, Joe – even if you don't mean it – let's have dessert and Anne and Dan will tell us about what they have seen in the theater lately in New York City.'

As they were leaving, Joe asked Dan if he would be willing to talk to the Beaumont Chamber of Commerce at a dinner meeting in the next few months about industrial environmental management and auditing. Dan indicated he would. 'Terrific,' Joe said, 'I'll get some dates and we can fix on one.'

'I'll go to that, too,' Sarah added, 'and perhaps Anne and Bonnie would be my guests.'

'With pleasure,' Anne laughed. 'The three Sour Lake girls back in business.' They all knew Sarah was from a gentler, more dignified background, but Sarah clearly liked the connection.

★

Thursday night, as Dan lay in bed, he thought about Joe Wiseman's question. How right Joe was that cutting staff and cost efficiency measures resulted in poorer maintenance and environmental short cuts for bottom line results.

Was J.D. or poor Ray at the plant an unfair scapegoat? Would the captains of industry take any of the blame? No, Dan decided. Did they deserve it? Increasingly, he thought so.

He thought, when Japan moved ahead on the world market in the Seventies and Eighties, US industry reacted with great purpose. Milton Friedman and the business schools gave the new MBAs the word, 'There is no free lunch.' De-layer and downsize, the advice went out and the public affairs people changed that word – downsize – which meant cut workers and staff – to rightsize, which gave a better spin to it.

Friedman, perhaps, didn't realize the effect of his advice, and clearly didn't give a shit either, Dan thought.

Many companies made large cuts by adopting robotry on the assembly line, by substituting temporary workers for permanent ones, by using contract workers who got no benefits or low pay workers in foreign countries, and by taking out layers of staff and not doing 'the non-essential' tasks. Often maintenance was the first activity to be cut because it could be put off for a year or two without immediate bottom line damage. The same was true of elective environmental expenditures, which were seen by many industry leaders as non productive anyway. The test became, 'Does it add value?' Friedman would love it, but the result was a distortion of good environmental management, in the name of the efficient business process, Dan thought. Environmental expenditures required by law were carried out where there was no way to barter them down, but 'non-essential' environmental activities were passed by as not of value.

So the anomaly was that, while the environmental profession was growing, and scientific knowledge and improved analytical techniques, not to mention public awareness, were spurring the profession on, the companies, under the pressure of de-layering and rightsizing, were devaluing environmental activities. This produced great pressure on the plant folk, who were sweating to meet increased regulatory rules and oversight, created under the public pressure generated by the Love Canals and Bhopal. The chairman of American Industrial was a champion of total quality and simultaneously dynamically urged the organization to de-layer and continuously cut non-value-added activities. The census was going down even as profits rose.

The unmoderated capitalist belief in profits over people seemed to take hold and Marv Friedman enunciated that

belief as his priority. 'Profits, profits, profits,' Dan recalled
Marv Friedman had said. What was J.D. or any other plant
manager whom technology was passing by to do?

Dan had no answer. He knew his job of environmental
auditor was valued because he flagged the danger spots and
zones for correction, so presumably the rightsizing would
not go too far. No one wanted to go back to the old days of
pollution excess and dumping. He was proud of his work,
and knew he did a good job for his profession and the
company, but he also understood the ways in which he was
used.

He knew he had gotten to the bottom of the accident,
and that new leadership would be brought to Sour Lake.
That night, when he talked to Bonnie about their weekend
together in Austin, she said she felt that the end of J.D.'s
tenure, if that happened, would give her a new chance at
the plant to do her job. She even felt that would happen if
he stayed. She said she felt Dan had brought a breath of
fresh air to the plant, and that it could renew itself.

Was she just making him feel good? he asked himself.
She was good at that. Did she really believe the plant could
govern itself better? Was he just a fall guy for the
management to go on 'rightsizing'? Why was he still
worried, when the regulatory agencies, when even the
newspaper only seemed to care about employment? Was he
being too hard on himself and what he could accomplish?
Could he protect Bonnie from any ax that would fall? With
these thoughts Dan put himself to a troubled sleep.

*

The next day Dan wrapped things up and focused on
preparing himself to meet the chairman in Austin. He

arranged to meet with Anne on Monday in New Jersey at headquarters. She was going to visit the LaFlate and Gonzales families once more, before going home to New Jersey, on Saturday night or Sunday morning.

He told J.D. and Ray to 'take it easy,' as he left. They were drinking coffee together in J.D.'s office like two condemned men. They knew he was seeing the chairman and could only imagine the worst, although Dan seriously doubted the chairman would make such decisions.

Dan spoke to Gloria at home from the motel, before he checked out that afternoon, recounting in some detail the dinner the night before, to avoid other subjects.

Gloria concluded with, 'A meeting with the chairman is important, Dan, so do it well.' She was ambitious.

Anne breathlessly arrived at the motel lobby, just as he was getting ready for Bonnie to pick him up, to tell him that Marv Friedman had called after he left and wanted him to call right after he met with the chairman.

'How are you getting to Austin?' she asked.

'I have a ride,' he said. She knew, he was sure, that Bonnie was taking him.

'Good luck,' she did say, as she kissed him lightly but flush on the mouth, saying, 'Be careful, Dan, in Austin, with the chairman there. I really care about you.'

'I will,' he assured her and stepped to the motel entrance and then outside with his bag to await Bonnie.

★

Life's Tale

Death rides the BMT,
headlines *The Daily News.*

The liberal establishment imperils man's advance,
pontificates *The Post.*

Truth enlightens,
informs *The New York Times.*

All fools

The best hope of the West is dying of prejudice
and greed,
While we watch on TV.

To track ascent – delusion;
To search for order – folly;
To seek the freeing truth – inanity.

Life seems an insane progression of events.
Not a tale told by an idiot,
but by an anarchist.

To thine own self be true,
remains the best advice,
that one advice fits all.

Dan Straus

Published in the *Michigan State Journal*, April, 1986,
Graduation Weekend.

Chapter Five

Austin

Dan and Bonnie lay upon the bed of the Hyatt, Friday evening, in Austin, naked. They both knew they were becoming intertwined more than physically. Love-making had spent their passion, temporarily. National Public Radio was playing Mozart. A sheet loosely covered them. A fruit basket was on a side table, with some of the contents partially devoured. A wine bottle stood, almost empty, next to an ice bucket. Clothes were scattered about the floor. Bonnie stroked Dan's arm. Dan was talking:

'I saw this movie on public television about a month ago, made by Roberto Rossellini. You know he was the Italian director, who married Ingrid Bergman years ago. Well, this movie is about Louis the Fourteenth, King of France, back at the time of the Renaissance. He was the first great king of France, and brought the country together under his power.'

'I remember my history books,' Bonnie said. 'Let's see, Louis Fourteen made it, Louis Fifteen enjoyed it, Louis Sixteen paid for it. Right?' She kissed his arm.

'Right,' Dan responded and fell quiet, from the long practice of Gloria squelching his ideas mid-stream.

'Go on,' Bonnie said. 'That can't be the end of the story.' She turned on her side facing him, her lovely breasts pressed against him, eyes wide open – she listened as Dan continued:

'Yes, Louis, the Sun King, had a plan, according to Rossellini. He would assign all his court people jobs responsible to him. Whether in charge of foreign policy, the church, administration, the gardens, entertainment, his wife, the children, the wine, the bed chamber, whatever, they would be rewarded on the basis of performance and devotion to him. Status in the court was made dependent on loyalty and carrying out his wishes.'

'So that's how the Sun King did it,' she said. 'Not just with a big cock but a big brain too.' They kissed ferociously and she rolled on top of him. She looked deeply into his eyes and said, 'Speaking of big cock.' They laughed and she added, 'But the big brain counts too and I think you haven't told me the whole story about this movie yet.'

'Why do you think that?' Dan was honestly interested in her mental processes, she was so different from Gloria or anyone else.

'Well,' Bonnie said, 'so far this is just a story from history, but you are a helluva savvy guy and this story about the Sun King has to be related to why we are in Austin.'

'Why do you think that?' he said.

She responded going back on her side pressed against him, after taking a sip of wine from her glass, 'No, Dan, it's your story and I love it. You tell me.'

He went on: 'As you guessed, my beautiful and tasty companion, Rossellini has more at stake here than just an historical anecdote. For this is a story about government and governance today. The leader establishes a circle of power as a retinue and bestows favors based on whether they do what the leader wants – that's considered good performance. Sort of the way the communists worked in

Eastern Europe, what a Yugoslav writer called the new class.'

'The new class, but as old as the hills, or, at least, back to Louis the Fourteenth,' Bonnie said thoughtfully. 'God, I love you and your ideas.'

'Well,' Dan continued, 'it's Louis the Fourteenth or Roberto Rossellini's idea, but isn't that what we have in American Industrial? All this talk about total quality and industrial democracy. Doesn't the chairman impose de-layering and cutting census, even though we are very profitable? On what they shamefully call rightsizing, his retinue – the VPs of this and that – are continuously tested. He has even gone so far as to say that those don't agree with this process will learn to adopt it or walk the plank! My God, isn't that Louis the Fourteenth in Rossellini's parable?'

'You know,' Dan added, 'the salaries and perks of these high-level executives are really destructive. It's not just that the salaries of the top executives are obscene or set up a new managerial class, but, with that seven figure compensation and stock option, these bigwigs have less care about the long term. The short term pays off for them, it's set up that way.'

'So who looks out for the average Joe, the pensioner?' Bonnie asked, warming to the subject.

'That is the basis of Friedman's wail about money, money, money,' Dan replied. 'He is being paid off on short-term results, so his greed is quite as bad as the capitalists at the turn of the century – for the system of reward encourages a short-term approach.'

'While the average employee gets screwed,' Bonnie added, 'because she or he is going to be dependent on the long-term life and solvency of the company in retirement.

God, I'm glad I'm in Sour Lake, not in New Jersey. Dan... you are going to turn me into a radical yet,' she said, licking her lips.

'A beautiful one at that, honey,' Dan replied. 'But you know better than I what the consequences of these moguls' greed will be on industry. I just hope we don't pay for it.'

'I don't guess you will tell him that tomorrow,' she said, kissing his arm.

'No,' Dan said, 'because I'm ambitious to do my job and get him to help me, despite the fact that his rightsizing is probably the real root cause of J.D.'s disaffection and the problem in Sour Lake.'

'Hey,' Bonnie said. 'I'm for you.' And she sat atop him now. 'I wonder if there was anyone like me in Louis's court,' she said.

Dan responded, 'If there was there must have been one lucky son of a bitch like me, who kissed her beautiful mouth (which he did), sucked her wonderful, luscious breasts (which he did) and fucked her.'

Bonnie placed his extended cock inside her and rode atop him, kissing all the while, until they exploded together in pleasure, and then some.

★

There was a fax from Caroline delivered during the night under their door. The chairman had changed the appointment to 1.00 PM.

Caroline offered the information that the chairman was going to play golf with the Governor in the morning, so he suggested they could meet for lunch at the Four Seasons at one. If the chairman was late because the Governor kept him, Dan should wait at the hotel restaurant until the Chairman arrived or he sent him a message.

Anne called at 7.00 AM. She had met with the families of LaFlate and Gonzales. Both had filed preliminary papers for wrongful death civil actions on Friday accusing the company and J.D., as its representative of negligence. Marv Friedman and the chairman were joined in the suits. The Sutherland family had done nothing yet. She couldn't reach Bonnie. There was talk around New Brunswick of a criminal investigation, but nothing had eventuated yet and she had told them neither Dan nor she thought that would happen, if the company acted openly and resolutely.

'Does the chairman know about this?' he said.

'I don't know,' Anne answered. 'But I would be careful with him. I care about you,' she repeated, 'and I don't want you eaten up by him. I'd rather do that myself,' she ventured with a little laugh.

Dan laughed too, although more nervously and offered, 'This is turning into a lifetime experience for me. I only hope it's a long and happy life.'

Bonnie appeared to sleep quietly at the other end of the room, hair splayed across the pillow, the sheet coming up to her waist, her breasts so perfectly mounted upon her, as her arms reached out and curled up behind her head. Anne's words at best made him more aware of his growing love for Bonnie, this beautiful and intelligent free spirit, he thought. Her kind of freewheeling, sensitive and not judgmental loving was new to him and tremendously welcome.

He said, 'Your concern for me is so sweet, Anne, but I've got to take care of myself.'

'I know,' she said, 'but I like to communicate my lust, as well as take care of business. Is that a folly?' she asked.

'No,' he answered, 'but I don't want you to turn on me, if I disappoint either as an environmental auditor or a friend.' He accented the word 'friend', so she would understand.

She said, 'Okay, but be careful today, please,' and then she added, 'if you talk to Bonnie, tell her I would like to chat with her today or tomorrow. I'll be in my room this morning.'

She knew, Dan told himself. She knew. He remembered that Anne had said 'everyone in Sour Lake knows everything about everyone else.'

He answered part of her statement flatly with, 'Unless you say otherwise now, Anne, I'm going to tell the chairman about the suits. I don't want him to think I would withhold any information from him. After all, it's his company,' thinking again of Louis the Fourteenth.

'Okay,' Anne said again. 'I'll see you Monday morning in New Jersey. If there is anything before that we need to talk about, you can reach me at home by tomorrow night. Have a good day, sweet man,' she said and laughingly continued, 'I won't call you *that* back at headquarters, I promise.'

'You've been a great help to me so far, Anne,' Dan concluded, 'and you can call me "sweet" any time.' They both laughed and said good-bye.

Dan was now released until later in the morning from getting ready for the meeting with the chairman. He climbed back into bed. Bonnie turned to him, smiled and gave him the Sour Lake stare.

'That Anne,' Bonnie said. 'She is falling for you, King Dan. She is going to offer you her sweet body, if she hasn't done so already. And it is sweet,' she said, 'and that makes me envious of her, so kiss me now and then ravish me, sweet king.' She kicked the sheet off and opened her legs, wet in anticipation, but she did not have to wait long for him or the passion which followed as the sun streaked in upon them.

★

Dan had spent about ten minutes going over the situation at Sour Lake as best he understood it. He reviewed the HF process, the allegation of leak and three fatalities inside and outside the fence. He described the plant's conclusion that a leak had occurred in the loading valve or line, with an inexperienced operator at fault.

Tony Casey asked Dan, 'Do you believe that that was how the accident occurred?'

Dan did not know how much the chairman knew about the accident, but they were relaxed in informal clothes, which Caroline had advised Dan to wear. 'Dress down Saturday,' she had said, so he took advantage of the loosening of the protocol to say, 'No, Mr. Casey and, after a week at the plant, I think I established that that is not what happened.'

The Chairman rejoined, scratching, 'Hey, Dan, drop that Mr. Casey stuff, okay. Here, I'm Tony.' He added, 'I appreciate your being straight with me, so tell me what you think you established.'

Dan then reviewed the existence of the R&D pilot, its being taken down, the greater likelihood of a fatality occurring from a leak there because of the corrosive materials and the slapdash pilot construction. 'Do you have corroboration?' the chairman asked.

Dan answered, 'Yes and no. I can't prove it, but I believe it. Our plant chemist first suggested it to me in a very emotional circumstance and then finally J.D. Hutchinson, the plant manager, confirmed that it was a possibility.'

The chairman switched in his chair, examined his pants' leg, took a drink of iced tea and asked, 'What about the agencies and the state. Do they know of this – possibility?'

'Yes,' Dan answered. 'I arranged that we would tell the agencies on a low-key basis about the existence of the R&D pilot, and make record of that. I talked to my boss, Tom O'Rourke, and the Law Group.' He added defensively, 'Whether they put two and two together to a certainty I don't know, or whether they really want to go any further I doubt.' Dan continued, 'After all, it is over and the R&D pilot is, in any case, gone. I don't have the proof to say it definitely was the pilot, but, at least, we have told them about it.'

Casey nodded, 'I'm upset to hear they would have a pilot down here without Environmental knowing.' And he added, 'Did you talk to Marv Friedman about this?'

'Yes,' Dan said. 'He was apparently surprised by the information and upset too.'

'What about that lug Charlie Moore?' Casey asked, surprising Dan with his directness. 'He's been asleep for years, that good old boy. Did he know?'

'I can't answer that for sure,' Dan replied and took a gulp of iced tea.

The chairman asked, 'What would be their motivation down here to pirate a plant, Dan, in your opinion?'

'Well, sir,' Dan answered, 'I think I know that.' Tony Casey waved his hand as if to say go on. 'They were afraid of being closed down and losing out to Mexico, so they took the ball in their own hands.'

'Did you hear that directly from them?' Tony asked.

'Yes, sir,' Dan answered again, very directly now, using the Sour Lake stare. 'Not only from J.D., but also indirectly from the editor of the Beaumont newspaper, although, of course, he talks of their worry over NAFTA as the Perot paranoia.'

Tony Casey laughed out loud, scratching his head persistently, as he said, 'Texas is going to make a lot of money out of NAFTA and the Governor is going to support all of Latin America joining it. San Antonio is going to be in competition with Miami as the gateway city.

'And we are going to profit from that in American Industrial... if these redneck shit-heads down here can keep their powder dry.'

In an offhand manner, he added, 'It is a little discomforting to me, Dan, that you so easily postulated the existence of this renegade CFC alternates plant and so easily got to the bottom of the difficulties at Sour Lake. Why couldn't Friedman's boys have done the same? What the hell are they doing in the chemical operation, if you will pardon me a little heat in this informal conversation between friends.'

'Well, sir,' Dan carefully responded, doubting they were friends, 'in truth most environmental problems that cause bad accidents are easy to spot by a good, professional auditor. Not necessarily by one of those accounting or management firms because they don't know the questions to ask beyond their check sheet.' Dan thought perhaps he had gone too far, but he felt emboldened by a rising self-esteem, professional and sexual.

'An ounce of prevention is worth a pound of cure, eh,' Casey winked.

'Well, yes, yes, sir.' Dan shifted in his chair and then added what he knew his chairman would respond to. 'The best example of that was Bhopal. Any halfway decent professional auditor would have seen the laxness, the lack of emergency training, the missing safety devices. Union Carbide and their Indian affiliate had just decided to economize their audit program away, and they paid the penalty.'

'I like you, Dan,' Casey said. 'You talk straight, but I know you are for me, too. I also like your choice in female colleagues.' He smiled, as he patted the rump of the pretty young thing, who was clearing their table of glasses. She grinned at Casey and said, 'Oh Senator, you are so sweet,' as her breasts sought to fall from her costume.

Dan thought of the validity of this conversation and the absurdity of this aging letch with all that power over lives and fortunes, including his own. 'Thank you, Mr. Chairman,' he said, correcting her designation of Casey as 'Senator' and realizing that he and the waitress perhaps had more in common than he liked to contemplate.

They sat for a minute or two catching a couple of pretty Texas women diving into the pool and then the chairman said, 'Dan, I have an idea I'd like to check out with you. Did you plan to stay overnight? Did you bring any business clothes?'

'Yes,' Dan said.

'Well,' the Chairman said, 'I got invited to a little cocktail reception at the Capitol around 7.00 PM. Why don't you go too and we'll talk a little there. I do have plans for you, young man,' he confided. 'Then I'll let you go as I have to go to a dinner with the Governor – politics you know.'

'Great,' Dan responded.

'I asked the PR gal, Ms. Hennessy, who was here with you, to go too – a real knockout. If you want to bring a female guest you know here, you should... just to balance us out,' he said.

'Well, actually,' Dan answered, taking the plunge, 'the plant chemist is in town at the university on an alumni weekend – she gave me a ride into Austin. If I could reach her, I'd ask her.'

'Great idea,' the chairman said, rising to leave. 'We'll meet at the Capitol Rotunda at seven. Be a real American Industrial delegation. See you there. Thanks,' Tony added, 'you're doing a great job, son, and I appreciate it.'

Dan knew the chairman was pleased. The scoop was that when he called you 'son' you had become one of his retinue, Louis the Fourteenth style, Dan thought.

★

Bonnie and Dan met back at the room at three thirty in the afternoon, as they said they would. Dan explained to her that she was going with him to the reception, and how that came about to be okay. Bonnie was surprised but found the chance to be together at the Capitol in a fun event just great.

'I like the fact that Anne will be there, too,' she said.

'He must have caught her right before she left, since at 7.00 AM she was talking of going back to New Jersey,' Dan answered.

Bonnie observed, 'She will be dressed, to the nines, if I know her, so I will wear the little cocktail dress I bought to seduce you. It shows off my figure, if you don't mind.'

'Mind?' Dan retorted. 'I get a hard-on just thinking about it and I think the chairman hinted enough to lead this auditor to say he likes tits and ass, as they say in *Chorus Line*.'

She laughed. 'Just don't get a hard-on at the cocktail party or I'll be forced to take you into some closet and suck you off right there, sweetie.'

'Is that a threat or a promise?' he said. They stood gazing at each other.

'Let's go for a little walk just by the hotel along the river,' he said. 'I want to try some ideas out on you, which might come up this evening. The chairman hinted at some further proposal for me, which I would like to prepare for, if that's possible,' he said. 'And I value your reaction.'

'I'm glad you don't like me just for my cunt,' she replied and they kissed so sweetly, 'but please like that too.'

'I do, I do, my darling Bonnie.' And he knew he meant that commitment.

'Come on, let's go,' she laughed, 'before you get in more trouble.'

The path along the river, flowing down from Lake Travis, is closely vegetated, as it passes in light and shadow through the city. They walked holding hands. Mostly Dan talked and Bonnie listened.

'I have this feeling that Tony Casey is going to use this incident to clean house in the chemical division. I don't know what he will propose, but I think I am going to be asked to do some wider investigation. He sure doesn't like Charlie Moore,' Dan said.

'I don't much either,' Bonnie interrupted. 'He is a professional Southerner.'

'His good old boy relationship with J.D. will hurt him,' Dan added and then continued, 'I'm not sure how much the chairman trusts Marv Friedman, either, but I sure don't want to get caught between those forces. Friedman is sort of a professional New York City Jew, which I don't much like either – kind of the same reaction you have to Charlie and J.D.,' he said.

'Well,' Bonnie interrupted, 'I like that big circumcised head of this Jew I'm holding hands with.' And they swung their linked arms in merriment.

'Seriously,' he continued, 'I'm just the garden variety, liberated type, but Friedman, with his pose of unreconstructed tough capitalist and New York Jew, happening on a pugnacious, almost prize-fighter's frame is a stereotype, that I not only don't like but which worries me, because he will stop at nothing to get his way.'

'I'm with you, lover,' Bonnie said.

They walked in silence under a bridge which bats were flying away from in the thousands, it seemed. He stopped to watch, fascinated. 'When I went to UT,' she said, 'they told us Austin was the second largest bat haven in the US, second only to Carlsbad Caverns in New Mexico. The bat is a bird that follows its genetic code of sleeping in clusters in the same place each day and feeding in enormous groups at night. As long as you don't fool with their code they are harmless, even beneficial, eating mosquitoes and flying critters.' They walked on in silence. 'Go on, Dan, about the chairman,' she prompted.

He stopped and kissed her on her open mouth. 'Casey is like those bats,' Dan said, taking, her suggestion. 'He seems hyped up, even manic up close, but he is a leader with ideas. Actually, he was quite supportive and a good listener this morning, but I feel that that is because I am going the way he wants to go. If I went another way and he couldn't steer me in the direction he has willed, he would drum me out without hesitation, I think.

'Casey is a little like the king with no clothes in the fable. His nakedness, when you really look at him up close, is that there is nothing special about him, and yet he wields such power.'

'Sort of a naked Louis the Fourteenth,' she teased.

'Talking about movies, there is a scene in Federico Fellini's *8½*. Did you see that?' to which she shook her head no. 'Well, there is a dream scene in which the movie director in the film – Marcello Mastroianni – goes to a Roman steam bath to meet the producer. Everyone is wrapped in towels. There is no way to determine status from the way they look. Steam everywhere. It's very disorienting. Well, in some way, the fact that I can see the chairman's manic side and even persistent physical manifestations, like that crazy scratching, makes me wonder why I don't realize his limitations and treat him accordingly. Why? I know why – he has tremendous power, and I have a chance to tap it or be trampled by it.'

They stopped to look at the Four Seasons Hotel now just across the river. 'I don't want to be flattened in some contest between the chairman and Friedman, but I am ambitious to do a bigger and better environmental job and advance myself,' he admitted.

'My old prof., Dr. Foley, at Michigan State, says you must accept the opportunities adversity present in business or someone else will. I think what I will hear from the chairman this evening will be one of those opportunities, Bonnie.'

'Go for it,' she said flatly. 'You've got everything it will take.

'Let's go back now, Danny boy,' she said, 'for a quick fuck before we go. I've got the hots for you. I guess all this talk of power turns me on,' she laughed.

★

They stood upon the great seal of Texas in the Capitol Rotunda. Around that seal were the various flags that had served the state, including as an independent county, as part of Mexico and France, and in the Confederacy. They were being pointed out by a vivacious dark-haired guide, who was saying to her group, 'We should hurry up to the legislative chamber before this obviously very fancy party with the Governor begins.'

She had reference to Bonnie standing with Dan by the seal. It was 6.45 PM. 'The chairman likes punctuality,' Caroline had said and so he and Bonnie arrived early. 'We don't want to keep Mr. Casey waiting for us,' Bonnie urged excitedly.

They had talked about whether the chairman would be uncomfortable or even resent her being there with them, when her mother was a victim. 'I'll make him comfortable with me – and you – right away, or as soon as possible,' Bonnie said. She looked down. 'I think I can make him see that I want to go forward from Mom's death. She loved her work and her life, and she wanted me to feel the same, even in the face of that stupid J.D.'s pressuring me.'

As they stood half-dressed in their hotel room preparing for the evening, her mouth still warm from her contact with him, tears were streaming down her face in what Dan could see was real grief. A remarkable woman, he thought, and then said it. 'Bonnie, you are one wonderful, complex, remarkable woman.'

'I love you too, baby,' she said, 'and don't worry about tonight. I'll be fine.'

Now, upon the great seal of Texas, she was an absolute knockout, Dan observed with pride, in a short-black dress, with a flared skirt, showing off her beautiful legs and low-cut in front and back, exposing much of the shape of her beautiful bosom and, not incidentally, shoulder blades under her flowing, long, blonde hair.

'Old Tony Casey will not forget me tonight,' Dan said to Bonnie, 'because he will not forget that I came with you.'

'Oh, I don't know,' Bonnie practiced. 'I'm just glad you found me at the university alumni party I was attending, and I had a nice dress to wear, meant for my fellow grads.' They both smiled and she added, 'And besides, Danny boy of mine, I know how Anne will dress for this event, and the chairman will be hiding his hard-on all night.'

They both laughed and he touched her back, as they saw Tony Casey and Anne walking toward them through the entrance.

'Look at that beautiful woman. Maybe you will have that hard-on for Anne too,' she whispered.

'Only for you darling, only you,' Dan countered.

They made their introductions and Bonnie said to the chairman so sweetly, extending her hand in handshake, 'I am so happy to meet you Mr. Casey.' She held Casey's hand in hers assuring his attention, saying, 'My mother, who you may know, died in that terrible accident at the Sour Lake facility, and I have worked at the plant practically all our working life. I'm so proud of the fact that the company asked Dan and Anne to do a thorough investigation. I have felt comforted by their dedication, which I'm sure your leadership inspired. And my mother always said go on, go on to the next good thing in life, so I decided to attend a dress-up alumni reception at the university this evening, sort of to get myself recharged back at my UT roots.'

'Yes,' the chairman responded. 'I'm happy, too, but how did Dan find you?'

'Well,' Bonnie said, 'I drove him to Austin last night and I guess, in the chitchat in the car, I told him the reception was for a well-known chemist from the University of Texas and Michigan State – Dan's Alma Mater. I'm a chemist, you know,' she added.

'We do have all sorts of talent at Sour Lake, don't we?' The chairman chuckled and then his face straightened. 'But I am sorry about your mother, my dear.'

Bonnie leaned forward toward the hand joined with hers and kissed Tony Casey so lightly on the cheek, and said, 'Well, thank you, Mr. Casey. It is so dear and caring for you to say so, but please, your sincerity is already demonstrated by Anne's good care of us and this very earnest and competent young man you sent us to set the plant right.'

With that Bonnie took Anne's arm, Anne, whose eyes were widened in amazement at her friend, and said, 'Anne, I thought, maybe I would see you at the UT reception tonight, but not here. What a great surprise.' And she led Anne, with Dan and the chairman following, to the elevators to the legislative chamber.

Tony Casey said chuckling and scratching his head, 'Dan, I am very impressed with you. I think the Governor will not forget our little company delegation.'

★

The Governor was largely what Dan had imagined. He was a younger George Bush with Presidential ambition written all over him. He smiled a lot but was suitably serious and thoughtful in conversation.

It was obvious he was used to having his way, like most people who are treated as important.

The Governor was clearly taken with Anne and Bonnie as two Texas women, who were making good, with a company that intended to forge a commercial relationship with his state. 'Remember Anton,' he said, laughing, to Tony Casey, 'we not only want your PAC money in our campaign chest, but we want you employing the best of our Texas folk – like these two intelligent and beautiful Texas women.'

'We are doing our best, Governor,' the chairman replied, equally formally. 'But you know we need the incentive of those border-free zones to really give the Texas economy the goose it needs under NAFTA.'

'You know, Anton,' the Governor would have the last word, 'Texas comes from the Indian word "*Tejas*", which means friendly, and that's what we mean to be, especially if it benefits us.'

'So that's the tit for tat with the Governor,' Dan said to Bonnie and Anne, as the chairman and the Governor moved a few steps aside to continue their conversation in private.

'Maybe,' Anne said, 'I know Mr. Casey's secretary caught me just before I was ready to leave and asked me to escort the chairman. He has been talking both the PR issues in Sour Lake and NAFTA with me,' she added. 'So I guess I can think of myself as the Dallas cheerleader of our company. By the way, Bonnie,' Anne said, 'you probably recognize this revealing dress – it's yours. I took it from your closet, as soon as I knew I was coming. Thank God I still know how to get into your house and your clothes,' she continued, 'even if this is a little snug for me.'

'I'm glad you found it, Anne,' Bonnie answered, 'and we like it snug, don't we, Dan?'

'Yes, I must admit I do,' Dan replied. 'At least on both of you, how did Anton put it, Texas women.'

Bonnie gave him a playful tap on the chest and Anne knocked his head twice, saying, 'hello, hello,' and they all laughed. The chairman turned to them for an instant to see what was funny. He smiled and then went on listening to the Governor.

Bonnie excused herself to the ladies' room. 'Did the chairman ask you about the R&D-plant?' Dan questioned Anne.

'No,' she replied. 'He only said you were doing a great job, and talked NAFTA to me. Luckily I got a hold of our Jeff Bush this afternoon – he had been apparently rather frantic – and talked Mexico and NAFTA, so I've been able to hold up my end. You know, don't you Dan, from your meeting with him,' she continued, 'that the chairman likes you and is going to ask you to stay on this job and expand your role.'

'Yeah,' he said, 'but what does he specifically want?'

'I don't know,' she answered. 'He's kept that to himself.'

'By the way,' she said, taking his arm, as they walked over to get new glasses of wine for themselves and Bonnie, 'Bonnie looks wonderful.'

'Yes,' Dan replied. 'She is a beauty and quite nice, too.'

'Yes, she is that,' she answered. 'But I meant that she is glowing like she is in love. Anyone I know?' she asked, and then continued, 'Never mind answering. Any secret you might just have on that score is safe with me.

'You are my bosom pal in the company, Dan, and Bonnie is my greatest lifelong friend,' she said, laughing a bit. 'After all, if we hadn't gotten to UT and made our way out of the Sour Lake girl bait trap, we would have ended up local call girls together, servicing the visiting oil men, or maybe fat housewives. And that's what I hope I'm not going to end up doing tonight with old Anton, although knowledge of that possibility should help assure you that I'm not about to spread any rumors about you.' And she leaned close to Dan and concluded, 'I mean it, Dan, I so love you and Bonnie. I'll only behave in your interest.'

Bonnie approached. Dan gave her the extra glass of wine and Anne said, 'Here is that wily beauty we were talking about. I've just told Dan, Bonnie, that it seems we are all in love with you, starting with the chairman over there.' Anne continued, 'But he intimated it was our bodies, encased in your Victoria Secret dresses, that has got Anton's blood running.'

'Maybe the Governor too,' Bonnie kidded. 'You may have to sleep with them both tonight, to prevent too much competition between them for you, leading to a bad deal for the company.' Again the three laughed, attracting the attention of those around them.

'Hey,' Dan said. 'I'm startled at the position of grace and opportunity you two have placed me in down here, and the way you attract and deal with attention. I have very little experience – no, I have no experience – in fending off admiring glances. It is my good fortune in being with you two. But I am learning from both of you.' He continued, taking their hands, 'You two are the treasures I found in Texas.'

To his surprise they both blushed a little and tears brimmed up to the lower lids of Bonnie's beautiful eyes before she willed them away.

Anne changed the subject. 'Say,' she said. 'More seriously, I don't know what you two are doing when this reception is over, but I have to go to dinner with the chairman at the Governor's mansion.'

'Well,' Dan ventured, 'if Bonnie will stay around, I'll take her to dinner, as payment for her having to hobnob with the élite here.'

'Great. I'm in no hurry,' she said to Anne, as if to insist on the fiction they three were now creating for protection from Tony Casey and the others. 'But I'd like that real finger-licking good barbecue you get at the County Line restaurant.'

'My thought is that, if we could make a date to meet at midnight at Sante Fe Rose, for country-western music, I will have an excuse to leave,' Anne said. 'If I don't show up, then you will just have to imagine the worst, I guess.'

They laughed. 'I'm staying at the Four Seasons. They got me a room – and I'm going home tomorrow morning,' she volunteered.

'I'm at the Hyatt,' Dan said, 'and I plan to go back to New Jersey in the late afternoon – I thought maybe the chairman might want me again tomorrow, at least that's what his office said to be prepared for.'

'I'm staying up at the university with a cousin,' Bonnie lied, 'but I'm not on a leash. We would be glad to give you that out from the chairman, if you like. I'll show Dan some line dancing to work off that barbecue.'

The female tour guide, from earlier in the evening, approached saying, 'Say, I'm a party-crasher and I thought you three could provide me a little protection from security by talking to me – I know you two know I'm okay, from seeing me before with a tourist group here.'

'My name is Sally Jane Espena,' she said hopefully, flashing those black eyes against her creamy white skin and Hispanic features.

'Hey,' Bonnie said, 'we welcome your addition to our little group, although, if our friend Dan, here from New

Jersey, is surrounded by many more Texas women, he may undergo a personality change and imitate Dan Juan DeMarco.' They all laughed.

'My name's Anne Hennessy and this is Bonnie Sutherland from Sour Lake. We are UT grads too, Sally, and we too used to lead tours of the capital.'

'Like this is great,' Sally said. 'But how were you so sure about UT?'

'I'd like to be clairvoyant and logical like my friend Anne here,' Bonnie answered, 'but I heard you talking in Spanish to your group when we were waiting down there, and I knew a bilingual girl leading a tour of the capital was for sure a longhorn.'

Sally made the Texas sign with her fist and fingers. The three women laughed again, Bonnie saying to Dan, 'We're just fraternizing, Dan. This is Texas talk. You Easterners wouldn't know much about this,' and she made the sign of the longhorn steer again, at which they all laughed.

'I do too,' Dan said. 'I mean I know the sign, as I once watched the Michigan State football team demolish Texas in Lansing. The Texas band bravely made the sign at the game's end, while they played the *Eyes of Texas Are Upon You*.'

'Well, they are upon you now, my friend,' Sally said. 'Here in the capital with your two stunning Texas women in hand, you are the talk of the Governor's party, let me tell you.'

'You know,' Anne said to Sally, 'I recognize your last name, Espena, your voice and your way of talking – do you have a much older brother, who was an opera singer – I think he is now a big producer in Chicago?'

'Yes, that's us,' Sally said brightly. 'You are talking about my brother Primo – my oldest brother.'

'I remember him,' Bonnie joined in happily. 'He was a really nice guy – from Brownsville.'

'No, Corpus Christi, but we did go to Padre Island a lot,' Sally Espena answered.

The chairman joined them and was introduced as Tony Casey to Sally. 'I'm not going to ask what you do,' Sally said to him, 'except that I know you were talking quite a long time with the Governor, but you are connected to my two friends from the University of Texas here and their wonderful and smart escort, Dan, so I'll just say welcome to our capital, sir.'

'Well, thank you, young lady,' Tony replied. 'You are all so friendly here.'

'Texas means friendliness in dialect, sir,' Sally answered.

'So I've been told,' Casey said laughing. 'If you three lovely women will pardon us,' the chairman said, 'I would like to take Mr. Straus away to that little table there for a short conversation.'

'Oh that is perfect for us,' Anne responded, in her best PR voice. 'It gives us some time to relive some old times at UT and really get the buzz on what's happening now.'

Bonnie looked at Dan, with her Sour Lake stare, and said, 'Just don't keep him too long, sir,' and then smiled at the chairman.

'I won't spoil the party, and anyway, we must go to the Governor's dinner soon, mustn't we Anne,' he said, looking at his watch, scratching his head and walking away with Dan.

★

They sat at the County Line Restaurant devouring their barbecued ribs, chicken, pot roast, potatoes, salad, along with drinking the mugs of beer that had made them quite drunk. They were quite aware of the fact that Bonnie, with her striking beauty, in a dress too fancy for the surroundings, made every head turn. To that challenge she acted kittenish and they repeatedly kissed and gently fondled, while they ate and talked.

Dan told her of the proposal from the chairman. 'A proposal that can not be refused,' Dan kidded, 'although no one said I wanted to refuse it.'

The chairman had asked Dan to continue with his attention to Sour Lake by 'making sure everything is really buttoned up tight and on the up and up. I can't afford any more slip-ups in Texas,' he said, 'and I want you to assure the Governor's people that everything is fine bringing them to Sour Lake. We will arrange for that level of contact for you in a few weeks or months, when you are ready there. We are going to put a new CFC alternatives plant in Sour Lake and in Mexico and you will oversee that,' he said, 'to make the Governor happy and end this confusion.'

Dan asked if that wouldn't be J.D.'s job and Casey said, 'J.D. will retire or be fired, as will his environmental staff. You will train Miss Sutherland for the job of environmental specialist and she may be the acting plant manager eventually, too,' he said.

'I'm going to get some goddamn good women into key jobs. We know she can do it, don't we? The fact that you and she get along is a big plus,' he added, 'but not the determining factor. This will also get us past this goddamned sexual harassment business,' he said.

'Of course, this all depends on your getting the plant straightened out and up and working at Sour Lake,' he added, 'with Miss Sutherland assisting and maybe eventually taking over when you move on.

'And by the way,' the chairman concluded, looking about, 'we will expect you to do an audit of the pilot plant at San Jose and investigate the suitability of Matamoras for a permanent installation while you're at Sour Lake. We are looking for young blood in Environmental with impeccable standards. I won't stand for less,' he said.

'In short, Dan,' he said, 'you get these sensitive locations buttoned up and you will be VP of the Specialty Chemicals Division environmental unit within the year. Your days as an auditor are numbered now, Dan,' Casey added. 'I hope you are going to take that old fart, Charlie Moore's job. In any case, he is a goner, Dan,' he said, 'so don't feel bad – we are going to move you into the leadership in Environmental.' He added, 'And Miss Sutherland will move up with you, if she performs.'

Dan was stunned. As he said to Bonnie, he could see the manic planner taking advantage of opportunities in this: fixing several wrongs, making headway on a number of what he had called 'leadership issues,' and protecting himself and the company. 'He even told me to sound you out on this before we parted tonight,' Dan said. 'That's the way he put it – "before we parted," – so we could talk about it again next week, when I return to New Jersey.'

'When?' she asked.

'He thought Wednesday,' he replied.

She knew he wouldn't leave it like that. 'What did you say then, darling, for yourself and for me?'

Dan laughed. 'I said I'd do it and do my damndest. I also said,' Dan added, 'I couldn't speak for you, but I thought you wanted your future to develop in Texas.'

'Ah, but you are allowed always to speak for me, Dan,' Bonnie said, 'and the whole package makes me happy and a little dizzy. Not that I can't do any job in that plant now,' she added.

'I want these young, intelligent beauties you have surrounded me with to think of me as a leader,' Dan reported the chairman had said.

Casey laughed then, Dan said, and imitating the Chairman by scratching his hands and arms wildly, said in Casey's voice, "'Of course, I want my wife and children to think that way too, but I'll get a good start tonight with this sweet pussy, Anne." Just kidding,' Dan said, 'he didn't really say that about Anne.'

Bonnie laughed and looked apprehensive too. She licked her fingers and dug into a rib. 'We won't see Anne tonight, poor girl – I hope she isn't going to have to grin and bear it,' she said. 'Or take it, I might say, for her own good and some might say yours and mine, too.'

'No,' Dan contradicted. 'Casey was real clear that all of this was in mind before he saw us tonight, and I believe him.'

'I get the better deal,' she said and kissed his fingers, exaggeratedly licking them clean.

He kissed her mouth hard and said, 'These battlefield promotions – that's what they are, isn't it – with promise of so much more, worry me. Suppose he changes his mind, somehow thinks he is paying us off,' he asked.

'For what?' Bonnie said, a little drunkenly. 'You are the best,' kissing him again, 'and I'm almost as good.'

'Well, I would say for managing this Sour Lake deal without causing a scandal and to work out with NAFTA,' he responded.

'But I'm part of that too,' she said, 'and I'm satisfied that you have found the truth and exposed J.D. My mother and I will be avenged – I'm proud of you, Dan... and you have kept things going at the same time too. God, the plant is going to grow – that will make Joe Wiseman happy,' she added. They kissed again.

'What about J.D. and his harassment of you,' Dan asked. It was the first time he had raised the issue directly.

'I guess I'll just keep my two little actions going,' Bonnie said. 'One against J.D.... till the bastard settles or at least apologizes, and the other against the company and J.D. for my mom, until I see some real cash in that one. Is that okay, baby?' she said, kissing him again and squeezing his leg between hers below the table. 'Because, if it is not with you, I'll give it up now.'

'No,' Dan said, 'I think it is right to make that worm J.D. squirm, you know, and the company should pay big.'

'I mostly just want something,' Bonnie said, 'to build a little park or something in Sour Lake for Beatrice.' And again her eyes filled with tears followed by an expression of radiant happiness.

'Okay,' he said, 'okay, as long as you will take the job of helping me run the plant.'

'Help you!' answered. 'I'll positively motivate you, baby, but only you and I will know that. We will have to protect ourselves,' she said, 'so maybe you should stay outside Houston to give you access to the agencies and the airports as well as to us.'

'Sounds okay,' he said. 'Just not too celibate, please.'

'Don't worry,' she replied. 'We will keep it strictly business at work, but I'll make plenty of visits and keep your pipes clean.'

'Thank you, Madame Acting Plant Manager,' he chided.

'Let's listen to some country music and dance the two step,' Bonnie said. 'Anne won't come,' she added, 'but we owe it to her to be there.'

The music was fun for them. His arm round her waist; the dancing was athletic and sensual.

Anne did not come.

★

Early Sunday morning and Bonnie and Dan lay upon the bed entangled. They had woken early in love-making, a continuation from the night before. They had opened the curtains to enjoy the illumination and caress of the sun rising to the East over the river and downtown.

Physically they were united now through every pore, and they felt a oneness with each other that satiated them, but made them continuously eager to explore their sexuality together. Now they lay, he against her back, silently drinking each other in.

Bonnie said, reading Dan's thoughts, 'Dan, we will always be together now, but I'm not a home buster – you need not be concerned that I will feel abandonment when you leave.'

'I know that baby,' he replied. 'But being with you has confirmed the reality for me that what you call "my home" is a thing of the past.'

'I don't want to take on the responsibility for that,' she replied.

'You don't have it,' he said. 'Acrimony and bickering are what did that in for me, not you – you are perfect. I will miss you every second I am away. In fact, I already miss you,' he quipped.

She turned toward him and they kissed. She placed him inside her and he responded immediately. He rolled over on top of her and kissed again and again, while he rode atop her on his elbows.

'Ah, darling, yes,' she said in passion. 'I love you so much,' as he came inside her. They lay there then, he still inside her. 'And I love your cock too,' she finally whispered.

★

They ate breakfast in the room – a big, sumptuous breakfast – fresh juice, fruit, eggs, pancakes, ham, bacon, toast, rolls – the whole works, to which Bonnie pointedly added her birth control pill. Dan paid for the breakfast in cash with a huge tip. They laughed and fell into each other's arms – wrapped in their Hyatt robes.

Bonnie opened Dan's robe and said, 'Now, sweetie, now for dessert,' and took him in her mouth. Then, against the glass wall of windows of the bedroom, he opened her robe and they joined, standing up, her legs wrapped about him.

The phone insistently rang, but they just let it go, she licking his ears, his eyes, his lips and his mouth, while he told her he was going to reach up into her until she told him how much she really loved him. To which she said, kissing and biting at his mouth, that she loved him beyond all else. 'I will do anything for you, Dan,' she said, 'anything. Darling, there are no limits for me with you,' as he thrust into her with a passion and climax for both, as she kissed him with wild abandonment of purpose.

She said, 'Baby, I'd die for your love.'

Later, lying stretched out naked upon the bed and quieter, Bonnie said, 'I am yours forever, Dan, whatever happens. But once you get home there may be complications or second thoughts, I know.'

He interrupted, 'No, Bonnie...' She stopped him with the tips of her fingers on his mouth, saying, 'No, Dan. I understand how much we are committed to each other. How much we love each other. How much we adore each other's bodies. But it is because I adore you so that I would not engage in a pulling match to pull you apart.

'You will do what you need to do and want to do,' she said, 'and soon you will be back here on your assignment and I will be waiting with my arms, and less you doubt, my legs, wide open.'

She laughed in a low voice. He kissed her fingers which were still on his lips. 'Let's take a shower together,' she said and then laughing, 'I'm going to wear that cock right off you, Danny boy.' He picked her up in his arms and carried her into the shower room and they embraced.

★

The message from the phone call was from Gloria. She told him she would stay at her mother's on Shelter Island on Long Island until Monday morning, since he didn't expect to return until that evening. She asked him to call when he got home, if he could, unless it was after 10.00 PM, as she had had a headache all weekend and would go to sleep early.

She said in the message rather curtly, 'I hope you did well with the chairman, Dan.' When he hung up he felt burned by her coldness and distrustful ambition.

Bonnie sensed the cold wave that crossed his horizon and said, 'We have time before your flight for a Tex-Mex lunch at the university, Dan.' She made the sign of the UT steer.

He said, 'Great, just what I want, as long as we can go under the table together before I leave.'

playing hard to get. I'm no tease, Dan. I'm just flat out yours whenever you want me.'

★

Bonnie drove back to Sour Lake, listening to a retrospective of Patsy Cline singing sad, introspective country-and-western songs on the Beaumont country station. She felt melancholy but happy too; bittersweet is the word I think, she thought.

She was so sure of herself in her exploding love for Dan. They had ducked into one of those dollar photo booths in a drugstore by the UT campus and taken a still of each of them for the other. She had her copy of him on her dashboard. She would move it to her wallet, when she reached Sour Lake, as they agreed their relationship would stay secret, while he pursued the chairman's mandate and his uncertain future back home.

Dan said he would call her each day whenever he could – either to her home or at the plant. Bonnie seemed, by dint of the strength of her desire, already to hear his voice, no less feel his touch. She determined to use time alone – without Dan or her mother – to ready herself for her new plant duties – study the processes, the jobs, the output, the customers, the problems.

'I'm going to push hard, when I get back, for J.D. to be immediately cashed out,' Dan told Bonnie over the Tex-Mex lunch. 'There is no reason to wait,' he reassured. 'Whoever else is culpable, he is, and there were three fatalities. I will take over, if they wish,' he added, 'but only for the purposes Casey proposed and only to make a transition to you, so make yourself ready any way you can.'

'That's a good idea,' she answered and thought now of her preparations, but her readiness for Dan too. Anytime, anytime, she thought and said aloud with Patsy Cline, 'I love him, I really do.'

★

Dan stared out at the clouds as his airplane sped toward Chicago *en route* to Newark. Piled about Dan, on the open seat next to him, were plant maps, workbooks of data, and his daily notes. He was preparing his audit report on his laptop on what he found at Sour Lake and the outcomes and recommendations, directing it to his bosses, O'Rourke and Friedman, but knowing it was destined for the chairman and carefully constructing it, to support Casey's recommendations where he could. Casey had said to him, in Austin, at the capital, 'Say what you want to say in the report, Dan, but remember what it is I want to do, too.'

Dan had started the final draft of the report in the airport when Bonnie left him off. She did not go to the gate with him. She said,

'That would be too sad, Danny boy, and besides I would want to eat you up just before you go, which would make a scene.'

'Sounds nice,' Dan said, a little disappointed.

'Maybe I should just drive off into the woods here,' Bonnie pointed to a park, 'and take that wonderful lollipop of a prick of yours into my mouth so you won't forget me.' She laughed.

'Sounds nice,' Dan repeated, 'but I won't forget you, baby – I love you.' And he rubbed the back of her neck in affection as they drove into the Austin airport.

They said a quiet if intense good-bye and he repeated his pledge that he would call her each day. That was important to them both.

'In the meantime, I will study,' she laughed, 'so that you are real proud of me.'

'You mean this is the serious face of the woman I love,' he joked, flashing to Bonnie the unsmiling photo of her they had just taken that lunch time.

They smiled at each other, kissed ever so gently and sweetly.

She said, 'See you soon, my love.'

He was glad Gloria would not be home that evening. He needed time to digest what had happened and what his next steps should be. Bonnie had reasoned again at lunch for caution on his part in going too fast, breaking up his life. 'I'm ready for anything and everything with you, Dan, but you need to be ready, too,' she said. She suggested again then that 'the period you are next in Sour Lake on the chairman's assignment would give us time to find the way for us to go forward with each other. Don't you think that's right, darling?' she questioned. He told her he wasn't sure, but he would think on it.

'I would do anything for you, Dan,' she said. 'I would give up everything for you, sell myself for you, die for you. I love you and I'm sure, darling,' she added, 'but you must be, too, before you break things apart. We have that time offered to us, so let's take it,' she had reasoned, and, kissing the fingers with which hers were interlocked she added, 'and I will enjoy every moment with you – I won't be on edge or waiting for some decision you might make, but just luxuriating in our love.'

Dan answered, 'It will work out, I feel it in my bones.' He blushed then. 'Quite a statement for a scientific auditor!'

With the plane late in leaving, Dan had sat at the gate working on his report and finishing it in the plane. He wanted to arrive at work Monday morning ready to go. Dan dozed between Chicago and Newark, while the plane circled over Pennsylvania above a thunderstorm. He was then working on a speech he was going to give that Tuesday night to a local New Jersey bar association about the environmental process in industry. He intended to use that to refine the talk he would later give in Beaumont.

He had called Dr. Foley from Chicago, to summarize the week and vet his ideas for the talk. Foley was supposed to be the speaker (Dan had invited him months ago with the pleasure of hosting his mentor in what he hoped would be a happy evening with Gloria – she would not argue with him in front of Foley), but Foley had canceled out a few weeks prior, pleading tiredness from the flu, and Dan was the substitute. Dan was worrying about what to say.

He put his writing tablet aside and daydreamed and then dreamt a scenario to be delivered at the meeting which would shake them up. Into and out of daydreaming and then to dozing, he passed – almost in a semi-conscious state, brought on by his exhaustion and elation. Dan consciously and then subconsciously planned his speech and met some demons.

★

Perhaps the bumpy turbulence of the ride helped explain the frenetic nature of his thoughts and dreams, in which he was a master of ceremonies at an environmental awards dinner, but dressed in a clown's costume with a big red nose.

'*It's time for the annual* Have a Nice Day Environmental Awards,' *he said to the assembled guests, in formal tuxedos. They were a raucous audience hardly paying attention. 'In the spirit of Alfred E. Newman of "What Me Worry" fame,' he shouted like a circus barker over the din, 'who never let the facts or the human condition influence that daffy smile, with the sunniest of intentions and an eternal prescription of "have a nice day", here are the American Industrial environmental awards.' Dan was still barking it out:*

'*The Jay Alfred Prufrock Should I Eat a Peach Award goes to that little known French environmental bureaucrat in Europe, who, this year, at a university conference, opined in a learned way that the Germans should stop eating oranges because of the cost in energy and environmental degradation to get the oranges there from sunny Spain, Israel or, heaven forbid, Florida. No matter that, at least since the Renaissance, people and products move about more freely, that open borders are a measure of such freedom, and that oranges just may make life a little more palatable as compared to staying on the feudal lord's manor for life. No matter, too, that life in those good old days was much shorter, partially because of nutritional diseases (no oranges). No matter, too, that oranges are tasty and useful to those addicted Huns. No matter that when the east block of Europe fell, the central and eastern Europeans were starved for western fruit, including not only oranges, but bananas. And forget the agricultural revolution of the eighteenth and nineteenth century in Europe.*

'*Please, that's only history. Our fanatic environmental bureaucrat in Europe deserves this award as the symbol of those who follow the Club of Rome dictum that the sky is falling and they know what is good for all of us. Better our European take note of the conclusion at the Cairo population conference that, rather than condemning women for their free expressions and choices, we should be providing resources and education for the poor among them and widening their choices – need I exemplify by saying and the availability of oranges.'*

Now Dan was back to consciousness, but happy to while away the time in absurd reverie:

'The Ross Perot Great Sucking Award *goes to all those who collaborated unsuccessfully to defeat NAFTA and GATT but particularly to Ralph Nader, whose anti-humanism goes from restricting the pay of federal judges to less than the lawyers who litigate before them, to denying the poor of Mexico their best chance of this ebbing century to make their lives better.'*

Now Dan fell asleep and a Fred Astaire smoothie of his imagination sang, *'While the movie censors tried the facts to hide, the movie goers up and multiplied. Lordy, lordy how they multiplied,'* and then danced about the stage with someone, who looked like Bonnie in her short, sexy, black dress, while the people in tuxes threw oranges at them.

The thoughts continued in the dream: *'The fact that the large majority of the people to our south support these trade agreements from Rio to Miami matters not, we suppose.' Ralph Nader appeared as Fred Astaire in tux and smoothly sang 'We purists know what is best for them.' Dan said to Bonnie, as they sat crammed into the audience, 'When the idle poor of these countries become the working middle class, with the improved environmental protection they will demand under their own national laws, then we will hardly know or care about who is who or which is which.' Dan tunefully sang some bars, while Bonnie stood and showed her breasts to the audience. Gloria appeared on stage brandishing a large butcher knife. Now Ralph-Fred argued his case directly to Gloria, and Bonnie took her seat topless next to Dan in the audience.*

Dan jolted awake, sweating, but then forced the daydream to go on:

'The Mr. Bumble Irrelevance Award *goes to the countless theorists telling us all the correct path to follow in solving highly technical scientific environmental controversies. Would they dare to tell the architect how to build a bridge, or the surgeon the fine points of organ transplant, or the pianist proper technique in transferring Chopin from the sheet to the keyboard? And yet we are constantly warned of mind-boggling dangers from straying from the straight and narrow.'*

The motion of the plane circling lulled Dan back to full sleep:

Dr. Foley now appeared in dungarees, sport coat and tie, but not shirt, to save his serious name. He said in the style of Polonius, 'The real shame of the situation is that we have really pressing health and environmental needs and we have the technology and the trained and experienced people in the government, in the public sector, in industry and at the universities, to solve many of our most pressing concerns, if we apply our resources and our smarts, instead of throwing up our hands and our wallets because the sky is falling or worrying too much about the perfect solution.'

Back in clown costume, with Gloria wildly slashing at his groin with a knife, Dan continued barking at a large herd of Texas longhorn steers, 'The Lysenko Economic Planning Award *goes to the central planners who still think they have the right answers to all environmental problems, if those business and government knuckleheads out there will only listen to them.*

'Greenpeace has all the answers because its mission is to stop the adoption of the western industrial economy. When will these environmental extremists learn? Ideologues since Lysenko ('No, since the Pope, in the case of Galileo,' Sally Jane Espena yells from the audience) have hurt people's lives by dictating conditions and outcomes from afar. They inevitably do harm.' 'How careerist,' Foley barks.

'*Finally*,' Dan announced to himself absurdly, as he rouses himself from his dream, 'The Rip Van Winkle is Asleep or Merely Oblivious Through the Years Award *goes to those businessfolks who are egging on Congressional know-nothings – Newt Gingrich is prominent – to abandon rather than reform the environmental regulatory process. How quickly some hardline industry advocates forget how we need regulations in our balancing act to compel good conduct in the face of other priorities.*' As he extracted himself from his dreams and daydreams, Dan felt first somewhat pleased that he had defined a liberal agenda at the dream's end, and then he felt crushed by the implications of his own moral doubts.

★

e-mail from Dan Straus on the Internet

Dear Bonnie,
I increasingly feel I can turn to you not only as a lover, but as a friend, companion and confidante.

I am disturbed by the juxtaposition of what I say and what I do. Maybe I am just in an anxiety state! I know I am a damned good environmental auditor, but I'm not sure how it all adds up.

I have been working under a deadline on the final draft of an article which will describe in an entertaining way some of the theories of my thesis. I am sure of my theory and the backup, but I'm feeling that I'm too cocksure (no jokes please).

Anyway, maybe next time we are together (very soon) we can talk about this and my crazy dream on the airplane last night. Am I in early mid-life crisis?

Anyway, thinking of you.

Love,

Dan

P.S. – I'm sending this to you via the Internet. Please read it and then delete it, for obvious reasons.

Chapter Six
New Jersey

1. The Chairman

The chairman sat at the end of the examination table in the company clinic at headquarters in New Brunswick. 'Well, Doc,' he said, 'I thought I was doing pretty good, so I laid off the Prozac for a couple of days.'

'You can't do that, Tony,' Dr. MacDonald replied. 'You've got to take your medicine every day to keep your mood up. There are these little chemicals in your brain that stimulate your mood,' he said, 'and the Prozac releases them.'

'Okay, okay,' Tony responded. 'I'll do it, Doc. I got so much to do, I need to feel good.' He scratched his head furiously.

'I want to try something else, Tony,' MacDonald added. 'There is very good experience in combining these mood elevators with something more permanent that will keep you from such violent shifts – lithium. I'm going to suggest to you that you take lithium each morning,' Dr. MacDonald said, sitting down on a little stool opposite Tony Casey. 'And we will monitor your blood levels and your glandular activity.'

'Okay, Doc, you're the doc,' Tony answered. 'I just gotta feel well,' he said, looking at his watch and scratching again.

'Tony,' Dr. MacDonald ventured, 'it might help, too, if you had some support therapy. I could arrange it. I know a good therapist in Princeton who would be very discreet,' he added.

'I can't do that, no time and, if it got around, it would kill me,' Tony responded. 'Just give me the pills, Doc, and I'll come in and talk to you.'

'Okay for now,' MacDonald answered. 'But maybe I'll bring it up again when the medications are more established. You are what is called bipolar Tony, and therapy would be good for you.'

'Okay,' Tony said dubiously. 'Bring it up again.'

'You said you had another question,' MacDonald said to Tony.

'Yeah,' the chairman stirred. 'I spent last Saturday night in Texas and I slept with this young woman. Real good fuck, although she cleared out fast enough. She told me she had no interest in blowing me once a day in my office,' he laughed. 'Just kidding, Doc.' He laughed again. 'But I ought to get checked out for, you know, urinary infection or whatever.'

'Do you have any symptoms, Tony?' the doc asked. Tony shook his head, no. 'Well then, I guess there is no infection, but we'll do a urinalysis, to check, anyway. Did you use protection?' Doc asked. Again Tony shook his head, no. 'You should, Tony, if you are going to do this sort of thing.' He reached over to a counter display and gave Tony a pamphlet. 'You can't be too careful about AIDS, Tony.'

'She is a nice, clean, executive type,' Tony answered.

'You can't see those microbes, Tony,' the Doc concluded.

Tony felt good now. He liked Doc MacDonald, and had made him the company's medical director, besides being the site physician. He needed now to talk to that obnoxious New York Jew, Friedman, about Sour Lake. He would do what he wanted or he would be out, too, along with that J.D. homeboy schmuck. Then he would meet with Dan Straus.

Undoubtedly, he would accept the assignment – he would move that Jewish kid up. There would be a big gain out of this in control and shaking up the troops.

At the end of the meeting with Dan he could ask Public Affairs to join in discussion around the conference table – with Anne there too. Let's see what guts she has to face me. He liked her, he thought scratching. Maybe she would give him an occasional blow job at his desk, he fantasized and scratched again. Shit, he thought, I'm starting to scare myself. The holy mother at home has got to loosen up or I'm going to do something stupid.

2. The President

'So that is the way I see it,' Tony Casey told Marv Friedman. They sat across the chairman's large desk from each other. No cups of coffee, no informality. 'There has been a lot of lying or at least deception, not only at that redneck plant of yours but also in your staff, Marv,' he said, 'and we are going to control it and take no hostages.'

Friedman had expected the worst from the chairman, but not quite what was being proposed. 'I had not known about the Sour Lake R&D operation,' he said.

'Maybe you didn't know,' the chairman answered. He was really into it now. 'I got a real ear load from the Governor in Texas, Friedman. Real nicey-nice, you understand,' he said, 'but we need to act fast and clearly.

I'm not fooling around,' Tony said. 'Either you are with the plan or you walk the plank too. I'm looking for a big new and profitable Mexican plant under NAFTA, with Texas support, but not until we demonstrate we are a modern company and,' he raised his voice, 'know what the fuck we are doing. So decide, Friedman, you little shit, and decide now,' he said. 'Straus goes in to clean up in Sour Lake and San Jose and establish us for Mexico and then we put that woman Sutherland in. Shit, you chauvinistic prick, Friedman, you have her for advancement on your charts.' He raised his voice. 'So do it! That will be your first woman plant manager, you little shit. And I want that redneck liar, J.D., out today and that goes for your VP of Operations, Charlie Moore, come to think of it, too. Yeah, let's get old slow-motion, slow-talking Charlie out, too. He's dead now, isn't he? He had to know, right, Marv?' Casey added. There was a moment of silence. Then, 'do you get it – are you with me?' Casey asked in a big voice. 'Because, if you aren't, I'll assume you are not on the team.'

'No need for that, Mr. Chairman,' Marv responded, shifting his legs as he did. 'I'm with you – J.D. and Charlie Moore will retire – no Tony, they *have* retired. No delay, and Dan Straus will put the package together,' he added. 'He has done a great job.'

'Atta boy,' the chairman responded.

'And you're right, Tony. Miss Sutherland has been ticketed for a bigger job for a while now,' Marv was warming up. 'She will assist Dan and then be our first female plant manager – and a goddamn good one,' Friedman got up some steam. 'I'm proud of her advancement. We have been grooming her. We will lead the way.'

'Good,' the chairman said. 'Now you are with us. We'll continue to be a great team, Marv.' And Casey asked his secretary, Miss Lazzori, to enter the room. He asked the pert, young woman, carrying a notepad, to record a file memo, with copies to them both and Paul Atkinson, VP of Human Relations, of their conversation, which he transcribed to her, and then added, 'Put a note, Miss Lazzori, that a new staff VP for Operations or Environment in Specialty is not be filled without my approval.'

'Well, Mr. Chairman,' Marv piped in, 'I really like your idea that, if Dan Straus does the job, he's got the VP job for Environment, within my organization.'

'Damn right,' the chairman said. 'Thank you, Miss Lazzori. Now, Marv, I suggest we meet with Dan Straus to see if he wants to work with us. Then I'd like all of us to meet with the Public Affairs people, including that gal you sent down there, Miss Hennessy, who joined us with the Governor, to see where we are in terms of the community and the state, including what announcements should be made.'

3. The Vice President

Late that afternoon, Marv met with Charlie Moore and said, 'Charlie, we are going to give you a twelve-month severance and then full retirement. Don't say anything, Charlie,' he added. 'Just smile and take it because it's more than you would get from anyone but me, and, goddamnit, you are a lucky guy the way you endangered this organization by putting that bootleg plant in Sour Lake.'

'You knew about it, Marv,' Charlie answered. 'I told you about it six months ago and you acquiesced.' He drawled it out. 'You liked it – you said no one knows where Sour Lake is.'

'No, I didn't, goddamnit,' Marv said. 'And don't you forget it or your golden package will disappear as fast as your dick, when that Hennessy gal gives you the come-on.'

'Okay, okay,' Charlie said. 'I'll take the fall, don't worry about it. Just keep the bargain.'

'You'll do more than that,' Marv answered, 'or I'll make you a poor retiree with no golf money. Charlie boy – you are going to call J.D. and give him the minimum package and make that red ass understand he could get nothing or even worse, just like you, you son of a bitch. You got it, Charlie,' Marv yelled. 'Your future depends on carrying this off at the plant with J.D. smoothly, and he doesn't have to know that you are out, too, or what you're getting, when you talk to him,' Marv brought his red, flushed face up close to Charlie and talked very softly. 'You on board Charlie boy?'

'I am,' Charlie said. Marv relaxed and returned to his seat. 'Sure, goddamn right,' he said calming down. 'And we'll have a grand retirement for you, Charlie boy, too, with all your old golf buddies present.'

4. Public Affairs

The Executive Council, or all who could be assembled at short notice, sat around a large, elliptical-shaped table in the chairman's boardroom. Coffee in china cups was on the table and a great stack of chocolate chip cookies was being attacked.

The chairman had asked Dan to briefly describe what he had found at Sour Lake and his conclusions. As Dan did, he kept his attention focused on his boss, Tom O'Rourke. Casey and Friedman would take care of themselves. He knew that Anne Hennessy's chance to talk would come. She had given him the Sour Lake stare on his entering. When he gave her the thumbs up sign, she had smiled. Later, he told her how absolutely terrific she looked. 'Who could resist you,' Anne he said.

'You,' she responded.

'No, particularly not me.'

At the conclusion of Dan's report, the chairman looked at Marv Friedman – Louis the Fourteenth, Dan thought, as Marv, on cue, announced that J.D. and Charlie Moore had accepted retirement. 'We will not countenance the kind of deception that took place at Sour Lake,' Marv said and he went on smoothly, 'This gives us the opportunity to invest in Dan – who has done such a good job – the confidence that he will lead our environmental efforts at Sour Lake and related facilities, while we move our Senior Chemist, Bonnie Sutherland, into management at that Texas plant.'

Anne looked over at Dan and smiled again. 'Fabulous,' the chairman said. 'Now we are cooking with gas. Miss Sutherland will become our first female plant manager within the year, I hope.' Then he asked for a review of the public affairs aspects at Sour Lake in Texas. Paul Atkinson started out, saying, 'Ms. Hennessy has done a real good job of damage control.' The chairman cut him off, 'Excellent. Ms. Hennessy, tell us about the Sour Lake community reaction, including the press.'

Following Anne's discussion, the chairman said, 'This young lady did a fabulous job with the Governor too. We are poised to open up new product manufacture, at a low cost manufacturing base, in Mexico and, through a Texas free trade zone distribution network, to the US and Canada.' Tony added, 'And I want Dan and Anne, and

Ms. Sutherland to be the local A team through the development period to work with the Governor's office.'

'Excellent,' Marv said. 'We have identified these three as on a fast track for our company and Specialty Chemicals is delighted to lead the company on this product and people development.'

Paul Atkinson said, 'I'd like to have a little press conference on Friday as a soft management and diversity story for the Saturday papers.'

'Good thinking, Paul,' Tony said. 'Okay with you all?' Dan and Anne nodded.

Marv said, 'Great, I'm looking forward to publicizing our new development work in terms of these great young people, but shouldn't we get Ms. Sutherland up here, too?'

'You better,' Tony said. 'But bring her up on Thursday so she can be briefed. I met her briefly. She's a bright young woman and will make a terrific impression.'

'Are they any problems?' Tony concluded.

'We still have Ms. Sutherland involved in a harassment action against J.D.,' Cory piped up in a cracked voice from the rear.

'That will go away for us, I think,' Casey answered, 'and, anyway, that redneck bastard deserves what he gets. Anything else?' Tony asked.

'We also still have some suits at the plant over the fatalities – including Ms. Sutherland's mother,' Anne said.

'Good point, but I think this will be seen as a positive reaction by us,' the chairman smiled at Anne, 'when the local press makes the connection.'

The chairman then surprised them by suggesting that they could stage a little reception, Friday night, at the company, at the time of the press meeting, to put some emphasis and light on their dedication to diversity. 'Set it up will you, Paul, or maybe you'd like to do it, Marv.'

'Yeah,' Marv said, 'I'd like to take charge of this because it's my operation and I'm really proud of the progress the team is making.'

'Good,' the chairman said and he looked around and in a stentorian voice said, 'this meeting is adjourned.'

5. The A Team

The chairman asked Anne and Dan to stay around for a few minutes to chat with him after he made a phone call. While he was gone, Anne asked, 'Have you talked to Bonnie this week?' knowing he had. Dan said, 'Yes,' and played it straight. 'She knows about the possibilities for her and is all excited.'

'What did you tell her?' Anne said, crossing those beautiful legs.

'I told her to get prepared,' Dan said, not replying to the question he thought she meant to ask.

'I'll call her,' Anne said. 'You are discreet, Dan, and I love you both.' Anne gave up the questions on that line and stated, 'I'm sorry I did not join up with you for that country-and-western music, Saturday night. Actually, I enjoyed knowing the chairman better, but nothing dire happened – it was just a late night.'

'I'm sure not,' Dan said, 'but I tried to avoid being too interested and asking.' He smiled easily and comfortably and Anne did too.

She looked to the closed door and then covered his hand with hers, leaning forward to say, 'I think that little bash at the capital will propel us all up, Dan.'

'Well, you do a really great job, Anne, and Bonnie is a gem, so how can I go wrong?'

She answered, 'That's right; we need to stick together and do really good work. Friedman is dangerous, Dan,' she added in a low whisper. 'Don't trust him.'

'I don't,' he admitted, 'although the chairman seems to handle him.'

'It's those big bonuses,' she concluded, as the chairman re-entered the room.

'What big bonuses, Miss Hennessy?' the chairman asked, scratching his shoulder.

'Why, the ones that Marv Friedman gets that keeps him in line and the ones I would like to get,' she replied. She had balls all right, Dan thought.

'Well, the doc just told me I'm in real good health,' Casey said, leaving his gaze on Anne and then turning to Dan, 'and I feel really great getting this turned around and off the ground.

'Dan,' Casey said, 'I asked you to stay behind with Anne because I wanted to tell you both that you have my full support. I think you know that. I've suggested to Marv Friedman that you be down there, at Sour Lake, Monday morning, to open the plant,' he said, 'with Miss Sutherland doing all the day-to-day managing for ultimate transition to her, okay?'

'Okay Boss,' Dan replied.

'Anne, I want to suggest to you that we settle the cases with the three families generously,' Casey said, turning to her. 'We owe them that and besides I don't want any nasty controversies in Texas now. There is big, big money to be made. I asked the lawyers to arrange for us to use the Governor's law firm in Austin and give them a local fee based on the settlements,' he said. 'So the Governor will know we are trying to settle on good terms. You use them as your local reference and contact. Don't be afraid to make a big show of it.'

'I'd like you to start these negotiations on Tuesday down there,' he added, 'but you can talk to Miss Sutherland when she is here this week. Let her tell you what she expects,' Casey said. 'I want these cases settled amicably – this is worth hundreds of millions, maybe billions of new business to us, if we get the Governor's cooperation, okay?'

'Fine, chief,' Anne said.

'And by the way, Anne,' the chairman suggested, 'I'm expecting really good publicity in the Houston and Dallas papers about our new woman manager.' Before she could respond, he added, 'But let her go in and sue that creep J.D. We'll make that son of a bitch the villain of this piece.' She nodded.

Casey was really flying now, the Prozac was back in charge. 'Dan, everything is going to be best in class, state of the art, at Sour Lake and at San Jose. I'm relying on that – and when we go to Mexico, I want the exact same. Any problem with that, Dan?' he asked but he knew Dan's passion for environmental excellence.

'No,' Dan said. 'Actually, I'm rather committed to that.' They both smiled. 'And I think Mexico should develop with equal environmental processes, so I like that too.'

'I know, I know,' the chairman concluded, and, as he left the room, he turned and added, 'Work hard on this and keep Friedman in the loop, but remember, I'm the boss.'

6. The Environmental Manager

As they walked the three floors down the interior staircase, Anne squeezed Dan's hand and said, 'I meant it, Dan, when I said I love you both.'

'Don't worry,' he answered, squeezing back. 'If we do the good work we are charged to do, we'll all do all right. Casey's rough and he has his own motives, but he's doing the right things.'

Anne paused and then plunged forward with a new direction in the conversation. 'Has it occurred to you how easily you unraveled the systems and intrigues of Sour Lake?' she asked, repeating a conversation he had had with the chairman in Austin.

'Yes, it does often,' Dan answered, 'but then that is what an environmental auditor is all about, if he or she has the technical smarts, the experience and the independence to follow his own course.'

'Too bad you weren't there before the accident,' she added.

'But the plant wasn't open to me,' he countered. 'Friedman or his boys kept it closed. Besides,' he continued, 'we are talking about some very widely held beliefs among environmental professionals about access and diligence.'

They both contemplated the impact of what they were saying.

★

Back in his office, he sat with a cup of coffee and stared out the window at the suburban corporate campus, lost in his doubts. There were a lot of complications.

While Dan knew he could do the job, it would be challenging and there were variables at the plant, in Texas, in Mexico and maybe at San Jose. He had never even been there. And was Matamoros the right location, despite the fact that the chairman seemed set on it.

Anne had warned him quite explicitly about Marv Friedman. He seemed more power-happy than the chairman. He must have known about the pilot, Dan reasoned. Maybe that was not his concern. They would try and make Friedman an ally by having a family day (Bonnie's idea), when the plant was in good shape, and inviting not only Friedman, but the EPA guy – Horan – and the Governor. He would suggest to Friedman that Marv invite the chairman, so that it would not look like a set-up.

Dan's thoughts went personal. He and Gloria seemed to be at war. He had, of course, told her of the chairman's plan – she liked the possibility of advancement but harped that he couldn't carry it off. 'What do you know about running a plant?' she asked. When he said a gal, who was a chemist and familiar with the operation, would help, she scoffed, 'One of your protégés, I suppose.' He said maybe he shouldn't do it then if she doubted him. 'No, Dan,' she said, 'make the most of this chance. Don't lose your nerve.' They finally agreed that they would rent out the New Jersey summer house at the shore and she would spend the summer, at her mother's, on the beach on Long Island, with the kids. 'When you come home, Dan,' she said matter-of-factly, 'I'll come, if you are here for more than a day.'

'If I come on weekends,' he said, 'I'll come out to the Island, as I'll miss the girls.

'You son of a bitch,' she said, her temper flashing. 'You won't miss me, just the kids.'

'No, Gloria, don't say that. You're not in competition with them.' And he reached forward to hug her, but she moved away. He felt they had tacitly agreed to a trial separation, without saying so, and he felt relieved, but disquieted by the easy planning of a break-up. He would take her to her mother's on Saturday.

★

Dan called Bonnie at 6.00 PM at her home, as they had arranged. He had spoken to her every day – they were frank, thrilled by and jealous of every moment they had on the phone.

She had established the pattern. First they would talk about work. Then they would talk about their longing for each other. This night Dan would have a lot to talk about with Bonnie, starting with her trip north the next day and the meeting with the chairman.

★

Talking to Bonnie made Dan feel good. He realized that even over the phone she was accessible to him. He told her it was all moving forward nicely. 'I know it will go well, if we do our jobs,' Dan said, 'because doing a quality job in this case exactly fits within the business goals.'

'I'm so excited by this, Dan,' Bonnie replied. 'I'm going to make this work.'

Bonnie would come up Thursday afternoon. They would have dinner together with Anne and be together on Friday at the Public Relations event and then Marv Friedman's little party. They agreed their relationship over the two days would stay professional and she would seek to stay with Anne, which would make a point for the staff in New Jersey, if it needed to be made. Bonnie said, 'I don't know if I can keep my hands off you, but I know we will be together the next week, won't we?'

'You won't be able to keep me away,' Dan answered. 'My biggest problem will be mastering myself, so I don't follow you around with an erection. I have one right now just talking to you,' he added.

'I wish I were there to suck it, Danny boy,' she said and they both laughed.

★

At home that night with Gloria, they fell off the track of civility and common interests, particularly the children. He found himself in a corrosive, gut-ripping argument, before he knew what happened. He had the feeling that it began with Gloria's drinking, which had started that day with wine, before he came home.

The hysteria focused on a common theme for them – Dan's competence in Gloria's eyes. She questioned Dan when he explained what was going to happen over the next several days. Dan asked Gloria if she would like to go to the Friedman party. She asked if other wives or husbands would be there. He said no. She said, 'But you should care about that, Dan. You don't want to look like a novice.'

He said, 'I don't give a damn about that.'

'Your such an idealistic baby, Dan,' she said crossly. He tried to stay even. Obviously, he thought, I don't want Gloria there with Bonnie. She pressed on. 'You have got to be a businessman now, Dan, not just a greenie.'

'Well, Gloria,' Dan replied, recalling the reasonableness of the conversation with Bonnie on the corporate strategy, 'the chairman has told me exactly what he intends, and the job I have been asked to do in a quality way as a "greenie" (he gave it a special accent) reinforces what he wants. If I do a good job,' Dan said, 'I'm sure I will be rewarded.'

'You are so naive, Dan, she said bitterly. 'Goddamn it,' she said, 'my future depends on you, and you – you hardly take any strategy into account – must you talk and talk about doing a good job, when you should know, if you had half a business brain, that they may just dump you when they have used you up?'

Then she rather wildly returned to one of her favorite themes, 'I guess you probably talked to that pansy guru, the great Professor Foley,' she underlined the professor with great satire, 'who tells you from that ivory tower of his to just be a good greenie.'

Dan took the bait and answered angrily, 'You always attack Foley, when he is helpful to me, as if he's a threat to you. I did talk to Dr. Foley,' he said. 'He cautioned me to keep track of the chairman's objectives by finding reasons to stay in contact with him.'

'What did you say, Mr. Genius? Isn't that what I've been telling you? You must be listening if Foley said it,' she taunted.

'Well,' he answered not as evenly as he intended, 'I've already raised the issue with the team I'll be working with about meeting the chairman's goals – and I do have experience which should get the chairman's biggest project going in Mexico, so I'm confident I can do it, even if you don't think so.'

She shouted back, interrupting him, 'You don't know dittlysquat about Mexico, Mr. Big Man.'

'Thanks for your usual vote of confidence,' he replied icily. 'I'll do pretty well with little support from you.'

'I'll be so glad to get away from you this summer,' she spat out at him, crossing a bridge she had never before crossed.

Dan sat down and tried to take in what was happening, but he was too angry, so he said simply, 'Let's stop now, before we say anything we will regret.'

'I don't regret anything and you won't shut me up, you son of a bitch,' she said and hit him on the shoulder with a flailing fist.

He backed up. 'I'm not going to respond, Gloria. I'm going upstairs to take a shower and get in bed and read. Please calm down, too,' he continued. 'We have time to talk this over, but calmly. There is too much emotion here.'

'Yeah, Mr. Big Time Corporate Auditor,' she said. 'Always with the steel-trap mind, so cool and collected. So reasonable. Fuck you, Mr. Jesus Christ,' she yelled after him as he went upstairs. He heard the TV go on and the laugh track merriment of a sitcom filled the downstairs. He also heard the refrigerator open, as she took another bottle of white wine and began working the cork out.

The next morning he tried to leave early to avoid a confrontation. The girls were downstairs watching television and he shared with them a cold cereal breakfast.

She came to the staircase, as he was leaving, and called, 'Dan.'

'Yes,' he said, coming to the bottom of the stairwell.

'I'm sorry,' she said, 'it's just that I don't see how you have enough experience to pull this off.'

'I understand. Everything will be all right,' but in truth he didn't understand and he knew it would not be all right.

'I'll be home late tonight, as the team is going to have dinner together,' he said.

'That's okay,' she said. 'I'm going to substitute teach today and then have a massage to relax me, so I'll probably be asleep when you get home.'

'Bye,' he sort of waved.

'Love you,' she replied.

In his car he thought, We are going nowhere but down. Am I to blame? I'm the unfaithful one, but I can't deal with this anger anymore. It will destroy me.

7. The Press Conference

The next three days went by quickly and in a blur. Bonnie's presence made him happy and it was clear she continued to be thrilled by him. The fact that their contact was all intellectual and platonic if anything drew them closer together. Bonnie stayed with Anne, a fact she made known to the New Brunswick corporate folk. They agreed to meet in Houston, at the Warwick, on Sunday afternoon. He would fly down midday. 'Be ready for me,' she said.

The publicity events went well, especially because Joe Wiseman was flown up and focused particularly on the potential rise in the employment base at the plant. The chairman was pleased. He was quite polite to Bonnie, saying, 'Hello, Miss Sutherland. I'm so glad to see you again.' They shook hands.

Bonnie wore a conservative dark suit with skirt just above her knees. Her long, blond hair was a contrast to the business attire. Dan told Bonnie she looked stunning, saying, 'You always will outshine me, Bonnie. You are so bright and beautiful.' She gave him a playful look that said don't flatter me, but she knew he meant it.

The chairman asked Dan and Bonnie to join him at the rostrum and opened it up with the statement: 'American Industrial is dedicated to the values of excellence in servicing its customers, fair profits for its stockholders, the welfare of its diverse employees and the good of the community. Recently,' he continued, 'we had an accident in our Sour Lake, Texas, plant, which resulted in three fatalities. We were shocked,' he said, 'and have been examining that operation and others similar, to make sure we live up to our values. We talked to the regulatory community in Texas,' he continued, 'to assure ourselves that we were operating with their approval.

'While we are confident,' he said, 'that we continue to be a leader in our operations, including in safety, we have decided to use this terrible event as a catalyst to reshape ourselves. So,' he announced, 'we are accelerating our planned promotion program by appointing Dan Straus as plant manager at Sour Lake and operations environmental leader for the CFC replacement business we are developing. We know Dan will do a great job in organizing our activities in Sour Lake and that the Texas region will grow.'

He added, 'And, to ensure that he has the right team with him, we are also announcing the appointment of Ms. Bonnie Sutherland, the plant chemist and one of our high potential managers, as operations manager there, and plant manager designate to succeed Mr. Straus, when he accomplishes his tasks of rejuvenating Sour Lake with Ms. Sutherland's assistance.

'A special note,' the chairman said, putting his hand up, as if to ward off questions. 'Ms. Sutherland's mother, Beatrice – a longtime and trusted – and I should say treasured – employee, at Sour Lake, was one of the fatalities, which greatly saddened us.'

The chairman paused. He turned his gaze on Bonnie, and said, 'We know she would be proud of her daughter today, as she moves toward being our first female plant manager. I only regret – and I deeply regret – that we did not make this promotion sooner, as we had planned, but unfortunately, sometimes it takes adversity to spur you on.

I am personally committed to continuing to build American Industrial into a leading company in North America.' Casey concluded, 'And that includes taking every advantage of our diverse workforce, and giving every one of our employees every advantage they earn.

'Miss Anne Hennessy,' Casey pointed her out and asked her to stand at her seat near the rostrum, 'has helped us so much in developing our interests in Texas. She will continue to support Miss Sutherland and Mr. Straus.' He smiled at Anne and asked the news contacts there to be sure to talk with her when 'this little ceremony is over.' Then the chairman asked Marv Friedman, President of the Specialty Chemicals operation, 'to make a few comments before we enjoy the wine and punch, and the tasty little morsels our kitchen has cooked up.'

Marv took the rostrum and said, 'I am proud to be a part of American Industrial today and for the Specialty Chemicals Sector to lead the company in this announcement of a new expansion initiative of a product which our pilot tests show us will meet the needs of the air conditioning and refrigeration industries without depleting the ozone. We are expecting plant growth in the Texas region and expediting a bold initiative to elevate three of our most promising young managers. We are proud,' he said, 'of the work Mr. Straus has done and we are expecting much more of him in our effort to continue to produce products and profits with continuously improved environmental integrity and safety.'

Friedman focused on Joe Wiseman and continued, 'We have every intention of increasing our business in Texas and the southwest with those wonderful new products, as the chairman indicated, but first we will be settling the cases with the families of the three fatalities, in a way that will be very fair to them. Our heart goes out to Ms. Sutherland and the other families.' He continued, 'And while we have very little experience in terms of industrial fatalities – thank goodness – we do not intend to stand on ceremony or on our innocence of any wrongdoing in this case. We are going to demonstrate to the people of Sour Lake, and Texas, and to all our employees and their families, our dedication to them, by demonstrating our intention to reach a fair – no, a more than fair – agreement with the families in this tragic matter.'

'Miss Sutherland and I,' Marv concluded, 'are co-employees of the Specialty Chemicals Sector. I offer her my condolences. We – Mr. Straus and I – offer her fairness and assistance in her new job. American Industrial has given its generous vision of integrity and support in making these promotions. What Ms. Sutherland and Mr. Straus and Ms. Hennessy will deliver to us,' he laughed, 'is their dedication and one hundred and ten per cent effort.'

★

The press party at Marv Friedman's was mercifully short. Friedman's wife appeared to be very angry and took it out on Marv with harrowing looks. She glared and glowered, and obviously was waiting for them all to leave, jealous of her privacy.

Anne was terrific with Joe Wiseman and the local press, as Bonnie and Dan agreed. She would be a tremendous ally to them both. In private, she didn't hide her feelings for Dan from Bonnie, but they seemed to deal with that in a way which underlined their mutual support. The process between Bonnie and Anne was a mystery to Dan. His focus was entirely on Bonnie now.

The trip to Long Island was a quiet one after the hysterics of the Wednesday night. Gloria was generally contrite, although she continued to insist that Dan was too inexperienced and non-political to pull it off. He enjoyed the Saturday, playing with the kids on the beach. The truce he and Gloria agreed to, on Sunday morning, before he left, sitting on the porch together in the sun, was that he would come there the first weekend available to him and he would call to talk to the girls as often as possible – at least a couple times a week. 'They will miss you, Dan,' she said.

★

Draft letter to Dr. Foley on Dan Straus's computer in New Brunswick.

Dear Tom,
How are you? I have been concerned with how you are pushing yourself and the strain on you the last several phone calls. This flu has been with you too long, Tom. Even the giants among us like you, need relaxation and recreation!

As you requested, enclosed is my final draft of our joint article for Business Economics. *I am proud to be working with you. Let me know your thoughts.*
DS

Dr. Tom Foley, Professor, Michigan State University; Dan Straus, American Industrial, Inc.

In developing countries, the key element to sustainable development is prosperity and how that acts as a positive stimulus to environmental protection. As a matter of fact, without economic well-being or progress, you don't get sustained environmental protection. What we are presenting, therefore, is the opposite tack from those who argue cutting back is the only course to follow.

In the developing world, among many concerns, there are companion problems with which they have to deal: poverty and unacceptable environmental degradation. Those twin problems are on the minds of the people in those countries. At the Rio conference on environment and development in 1992, people from the largely northern developed world, the OECD countries, generally came with environment on their minds. That was the agenda that was brought to Rio by the more prosperous. Even those leaders from the North, who didn't seem to put the same emphasis on environmental issues, focused on Rio through the lens of environmental concerns. In comparison, the people at the conference from the southern, developing part of the world, came with poverty and increasing prosperity on their minds. The reality of the Rio conference was that it was about environment and development. Whether you thought of development or environment first, depended largely on where you came from.

The crisis that we are facing in the developing or lesser developed world is the crisis of poverty first and then the environment. Professor Paul Kennedy of Yale in his book, *Preparing for the Twenty-first Century* (p. 22), focuses on this issue: 'In 1825, as Malthus was making his final amendment to his original Essay on Population, about one billion human beings occupied the planet, the race had taken thousands of years to reach that total... In the following hundred years, the world's population doubled to two billion and in the following half century (from 1925 to 1976) it doubled again to four billion. By 1990, the number had advanced to 5.3 billion. By 2025 – a year in which perhaps about half the readers of this book may still be alive – the earth will contain, at a conservative estimate, 8.5 billion.

'How the crowded populations will be fed, especially in times of famine, and what will happen to the always sensitive relationship between city and country, are not at all clear... even if food is available, will it be possible to give these billions of young people decent health and education, and afterward to provide new jobs at the rate needed to prevent mass unemployment and social unrest. The phenomenon is roughly similar to the crowd of one hundred thousand vagrants who roamed the streets of Paris in the 1780s but today's numbers are fantastically larger. At present, the labor force in developing countries totals around 1.76 billion, but it will rise to more than 3.1 billion by 2025, implying a need for thirty-eight to forty million new jobs every year.'

We think perhaps those kinds of statistics give some frame of reference for the way in which this problem should be viewed. Within that perspective of population growth, poverty and the need for jobs is the environmental concern.

Two seemingly irreconcilable points of view were evidenced at Rio. One point of view basically is to pull back. The 'beyond the limits' argument makes a clarion call for this action. We in the prosperous nations have to pull our industrial development back, the argument says, because we are beyond our environmental carrying capacity and because we have to give room for the development in the south. The other point of view says grow and develop new technology. That point of view argues, as Dr. Kennedy does in *Preparing for the Twenty-first Century*, that the calamity Malthus predicted (for Malthus clearly felt Europe had gone beyond its limits) did not occur because of the development of new technology and the industrial revolution: society was able to provide for itself through the development of technology at a point when there was real concern about the future.

So what happened at Rio? Forget the circus, the expectations, and the fact that the US didn't take positions it apparently could have taken as the environmental leader. What really happened in Rio in the face of these two apparently conflicting approaches to crisis?

We think the direction is shown in the Rio Declaration, the set of principles on which the Conference agreed. Those principles, unanimously adopted in Rio, reflect every other matter that was considered there. The Rio Declaration is an expression of policy. And what it said was, 'The right to development must be fulfilled so as to equitably meet developmental and environmental needs of present and future generations... In order to achieve sustainable development, environmental protection shall constitute an integral part of the development process but cannot be considered in isolation from it... All states and all people shall cooperate in the task of eradicating poverty as an indispensable requirement for sustainable development, in order to decrease the disparities and the standards of living...' (Principles 3, 4 and 5).

What the countries at Rio decided was that they would straddle the two points of view. They would not come down on the extreme of either side. That is a pivotal policy decision. It's a movement away from the pure capitalists' or developers' dream, and it's a movement away from the club of Rome's doom and gloom dictum that the sky is falling and we all better pull back. It is pivotal to decide that we need both economic prosperity and environmental protection to have either.

Agreement by governments that economic and environmental well-being are not in conflict, but are mutually supportive, is the evolutionary political advance at Rio. We would like to mention one study reported at Johns Hopkins in the 1980s. Briefly, in that study, the relationship of a misery index made up of measures of personal and societal grief to the movement of the unemployment index in the inner city of Baltimore was charted, as reported on April 6, 1982, in *The New York Times*.

What they concluded shouldn't surprise us. They concluded that when the unemployment index went up, the misery index went up. When the unemployment index went down, the misery index went down.

In other words, what they concluded is that there is a clear link between jobs and economic well-being, on the one hand, and the personal well-being of the individual and the community, on the other. Much of the background for the agreement between nations which developed in Rio was built upon the United Nations report, *Our Common Future*. The UN Report, on page 1 in the overview, said, 'This Commission believes that people can build a future that is more prosperous (with) more jobs... Our report, *Our Common Future*, is not a prediction of ever increasing environmental decay, poverty and hardship in an ever more polluted world among ever decreasing resources. We see instead the possibility for a new era of economic growth, one that must be based on policies that sustain and expand the environmental resource base. And we believe such growth to be absolutely essential to relieve the great poverty that is deepening in much of the developing world.'

That UN report seems to call for a new technology revolution to meet the Malthus-type challenge, which formed the basis for what happened at Rio. These theories in the UN report and principles agreed upon at Rio are a basis of Vice President Gore's book, *Earth in the Balance*. Al Gore's ideas did not develop out of a vacuum; they developed out of the work that had been done in the UN and elsewhere, before Rio, to bring the confounding extremes together.

There are things you need for environmental improvement in a society. You need public awareness before anything else can happen. You must have leadership, and without awareness you can't have leadership. You need commitment and that comes with leadership. You need unfailing attention to problems, which requires even-handed legal enforcement, given the way we humans are. And you need environmental programs to comply and go beyond compliance. You need a dedication to total quality, including good, environmental management, voluntary programs, above and beyond legal requirements, as already carried out in many companies, including:

- Safety excellence
- Wellness programs for employees
- Waste reduction/ management
- Pollution prevention
- Product/ process design for the future
- Hazard assessment
- Transportation care
- Energy conservation
- Global standards/ practices
- Environmental auditing
- Community action/ emergency response
- Technology cooperation
- Public disclosure

Good environmental management processes and programs, like Responsible Care or the global environmental management initiatives Environmental Self-Assessment Program (ESAP), based on the ICC business charter for sustainable development, were discussed at Rio. They were reported on by industry in *The Greening of Industry* and in the World Resources Institute's *Beyond Compliance*, detailing those voluntary sustainable development initiatives.

Environmental problems cannot be solved without money. And it often takes a lot of money. You build one water treatment plant in Juarez, Mexico, or on the New Jersey shore, and that costs maybe sixty million dollars or more. That money has to come from somewhere; it has to be generated by somebody. Good intentions do not solve environmental problems.

You need money and you need physical resources, plumbing infrastructure. You need knowledge. Most environmental problems require the application of knowledge by skilled people. You need technology and receptivity to the technology. And finally, most importantly, in order to get these things, you need prosperity. It's true in the United States. It's true in Mexico. It's true in China. Without prosperity, there is little chance for sustained environmental improvement. Mexico is a big country, with lots of people, resources, hopes and problems. The border area (Maquiladora) is an example of a developing region – one of the most rapidly developing on earth – that has environmental concerns in common with the US. What we are looking for now in this region are jobs and prosperity, on the one hand, and protection of the environment on the other.

The increase in protectionism in industrial countries stifles export growth and prevents diversification from traditional exports... Countries – especially from low income Asian and Latin American nations – seeking to follow the same route have found themselves severely handicapped by growing trade barriers...

About Mexico – could that potential be written about any case more clearly than

Mexico and the United States, now that they are bound by NAFTA? The Maquila area of Mexico is one of tremendous development, compared to fifty years ago or even thirty years ago. Whether we can take the next steps to marshal the resources to further develop and protect the environment now is clearly before us.

The environmental awareness in Mexico clearly exists. There is a commitment and NAFTA, we would say, underlines that commitment. Although there is much to do, a tremendous amount to do, there is an increasing knowledge basis. And where technology does not exist there, now, it can be developed or transferred.

If Mexico can continue to develop its economy, the money and the resources can be found to make the kind of progress that is being talked about in the UN report. Increasingly, even environmental advocates grasp this reality: 'Even with the peso crisis, the environment is better with the (NAFTA) treaty than without it'.

There is a powerful argument for sustainable development through trade and operation of the free market, both as to relieving poverty and want and to promote good environmental practice. Furthermore, during the course of the negotiation for ratification of NAFTA in the US, there was a separate, side environmental agreement negotiated among the countries. The three parties, the United States, Canada and Mexico, basically agreed to set up a tripartite commission to focus on environmental concerns not receiving adequate attention. A mechanism has been set up, paralleling the trade agreement, which allows meaningful attention to the environmental area. Many trade and environmental experts call NAFTA and its environmental side agreement the 'greenest' trade agreement.

Will this juxtaposition of development and environmental protection, with the reality of total environmental quality approach by industry, get lost and not transpose itself over to the GATT? The success or failure of this multilateral approach between Mexico, the US and Canada will be of significance.

Turning to China, let us set the base for a moment. We're not talking about Singapore here. It's easier to talk about Singapore. A little island, with a strong central government, which is very, very prosperous. The poverty is over on the Asian mainland, on the other side of the strait.

China is a country of nine hundred million people, going on 1.2 billion. That's because they held their birth rate down! And right now it is the third largest economy in the world, and soon will be the second largest. Not on a per capita basis, of course, but on a total basis. The annual growth rate in GNP per capita is up around six per cent. In grain production, as compared to the Soviet Union, for example, they're doing quite well. They have adequate food. They feed themselves. They are a country of nine hundred million people who feed themselves. It's a country which has accomplished a lot – and still has a lot of problems.

Nine hundred million people going on 1.2 billion. A five thousand-year-old society – not many countries can say that. Entrepreneurial and business crazy. Everybody has a sideline. China is looking forward to absorbing Hong Kong, which has a tremendous capacity to generate prosperity for the mainland. And the Taiwanese are investing heavily in China. In China, growth is the number one priority.

There is a national environmental protection agency and it is getting increasing support. Potable and agricultural water is a significant problem. In the newspapers in Beijing and in Shanghai there are environmental articles almost every day. The populace ask: Why are our rivers getting so dirty? Why is our air so terrible? And so forth and so on. Same things you read everywhere else in the world. The awareness is growing.

China's strengths are its workforce, its decentralization, its agricultural base, its resources, including coal in more than ample supply. They have a very good educational base. Education is prized. The reliance on bicycles (in Shanghai alone, twelve million bikes) is also inspiring.

They have serious weaknesses. Population is still their biggest problem and their unchecked development causes environmental problems. Air pollution is a concern, from coal dust and S02 in the air. It's a particularly high-sulfur coal in China, so it's particularly bad. There is a plan, framed by the World Bank and industry, to get natural gas in replacement for coal usage for Shanghai, and coal gasification technology is a possibility, too. Technology should provide a tremendous environmental plus. Rivers are terribly polluted. There is another big project going on in Shanghai to clean up the local river. What they plan to do is to close off the inner city industrial outfalls and move industry out of central city. They have a tremendous water problem generally and, as elsewhere, people care about the quality of their water, China needs sweet water to meet its mighty agricultural thirst. How are they going to overcome these problems? Assuredly, not by being less prosperous. Let's go back to the Rio Declaration. Here is a rapidly developing country, one of the biggest countries in the world, with some of the biggest environmental problems. Surely, they are not going to overcome their problems by having a less prosperous country and less capacity for new technology or applications of existing technology.

A good industrial hygienist knows that the most important thing to follow is her nose. A good industrial ecologist knows that, when she gets inside a facility, the first thing to pay attention to is housekeeping and her own senses. Later on, you take a lot of measurements and gather data, but what really counts first is your impressions. Is the facility dirty, the housekeeping sloppy, does it smell, are there spills, are the workers disinterested? Our noses tell us that, in China, whether we look at the newspapers, personal energy, the environmental agencies or the growth of the laws or their environmental awareness, technology in their factories, multinational standards in their joint ventures, or the projects they are working on, they are going in the right environmental direction. But that they can only go in that direction, if they continue to be prosperous.

Let's go back to the example on the New Jersey shore about ten years ago, when the ocean and beaches were full of refuse. One of us lives near the Jersey shore, and the idea of swimming there was repulsive: the water had a smelly, brown foam. Your nose and eyes told you there was really something wrong there. And so the public awareness arose, the enforcement of the laws arose and the voluntary programs beyond compliance, to meet the environmental challenge and restore confidence, rose. They built sewage treatment infrastructure in a number of towns on the shore that had none. They cleaned up the beaches. They punished transgressors. They pursued waste minimization. Last summer the ocean and beaches were much cleaner. It was like the Caribbean: clean, clear and light blue. You couldn't believe you were in the same place. With awareness, commitment, knowledge and money, much was done. As Dr. Kennedy pointed out, 'Ideally the best thing to happen would be for all China and India entrepreneurs, peasants, technicians, and laundry girls – to enjoy a steady rise in real standard of living. This would not bring per capita income up to western levels for the gap is simply too great, but it would surely be an immense improvement... Already there is mounting evidence of the damage caused by population growth and modernization. China's headlong rush into industrialization, after 1950, was undertaken without regard for the atmosphere, water supplies, or the country size in general... thousands of miles of river are contaminated by industrial toxins, one-third of the coastal fishing grounds are ruined by pollution, and the air in Beijing is sixteen times dirtier than it is in New York and an astonishing thirty-five times more contaminated than in London... As *The Economist* has noted '[China will] build more power stations and factories. These will depend mainly on China's own coal, with its average ash content of twenty-seven per cent, and sulfur content of up to five per cent. Millions more Chinese will suffer from respiratory disorders and a few more cities will disappear from satellite photographs... If they fail to escape from their Malthusian trap, a large proportion of the earth's inhabitants in the early twenty-first century will witness continued poverty and malnutrition... It would be inconceivable and ridiculous for the West to press China (and India) to abandon their plans for economic growth... The only logical solution remaining, therefore, is for the developed world to try to apply its capital, technology and brainpower to help these two giant populations escape from poverty without harm to themselves and the planet... It is already clear that unless rich and poor nations recognize that they inhabit the same biospace, the dilemmas facing China and India will intensify – and the results will not be merely local.'

That is a very reasoned extension of sustainable development and the Rio Conference commitment between nations on the interrelationship between meeting the needs of development and environment. If we are not going to stop the world and get off, then we have to sensibly and rationally – but urgently – make these principles of economic prosperity and ecological protection a reality.

Chapter Seven
The Border

1. Matamoros, Mexico

Bonnie lay on her stomach in the hot sun on the beach at South Padre Island. It was 10.00 AM on Saturday morning. She was lying on a large beach towel, flattened against the towel, arm and legs outstretched. Her bikini top was off. Her blonde hair was wet and carefully pulled to the side so that her shoulders were bare to the sun. She seemed asleep, but she was listening.

The Gulf was calm and flat. They were encamped just over a small dune that gave them privacy, although they were the only people on the hot beach. Anne and Dan were sitting on their towels, talking. Both were wet. Anne was applying suntan cream to her long legs, arms and chest above her wet suit. Dan was leaning back on one arm, sipping an ice tea from a bottle with a straw.

The temperature was ninety degrees Fahrenheit, on the large digital thermometer spinning at the pool above them, at the Radisson Hotel, where they were staying, ostensibly with Bonnie and Anne in one room and Dan in another, but Bonnie and Dan were coupled openly now in front of Anne.

They had gone swimming in the Gulf while the beach was still not too hot to touch. Monday morning Dan and

Anne would go to look at the proposed plant sites in Matamoros and meet with a local lawyer.

This weekend had been set aside by the three of them as their first opportunity to relax, since they had come back to Sour Lake over three months before.

'I agree with you that we have made a lot of progress,' Dan said. 'It's been cleaned, painted, graded and planted. The operation is much better, thanks to Bonnie really taking hold.' He reached over and touched her shoulder blade with his finger.

She drowsily smiled and said, 'The best thing is that the pilot is also now going in properly built, even if it is a stalking-horse for Matamoros, and we are beginning to increase the workforce.'

'No doubt about it, there is a real feeling of doing the right thing,' he continued. 'I'm going to tell the chairman that, when I see him on Friday.'

'Don't forget to invite him to the Family Day at the plant and check the date at the end of the summer,' Bonnie added. She reached out and covered Dan's hand with her own. 'I think the plant council picked August twenty-fifth, didn't they?' She kissed Dan's knuckles, lying back. 'God, is it hot? I forgot how hot Padre Island gets.'

They lay there quiet for a few minutes. Then Bonnie said, 'Turn your head toward Anne, Dan, while I sit up and put my top back on, so I can lie on my back.'

'You mean he's never seen your breasts?' Anne retorted. 'My, oh my, has this Texas plant manager-to-be gone conservative?' Bonnie sat up, her beautiful, perfectly shaped breasts exposed and kissed the back of Dan's neck, as she put her top on.

They were in perfect harmony, she thought. Then she reached over to the sunbathing Anne and kissed her coolly and sweetly on the lips. 'Now I've kissed you both,' she said. 'So I'm going to get us three more iced teas.' She moved off toward the Radisson pool, saying, 'No lovemaking while I'm gone, kids. I'll be keeping an eye on you.'

Dan said, 'Want me to go instead?'

'No,' Bonnie answered. 'I have to go to the toilet and I thought one of us ought to call the plant and see if everything is okay. I'll just check.'

When she was out of hearing, Dan said, 'I'm going to propose to Friedman and the chairman next week that she be made the plant manager now.'

'I'll support that through my chain,' Anne answered. 'As a matter of fact, I have already said to H. Jeffrey that we should not wait.' They were both on their elbows. 'I think the Family Day is the day to announce her appointment,' she added. 'And that gives me a good reason to get Joe and Sarah Wiseman to come.'

'Maybe it's a good reason to get the chairman and that louse, I mean our leader, Friedman, too,' Dan said.

'Now Dan, he is your boss,' Anne rejoined, 'so be nice, nice.'

'I always am.' He turned toward her and smiled.

'I know,' she said. 'It's one of your best qualities.' And she added privately, 'But, then again, I haven't experienced all your attributes, have I?'

'Seriously,' Dan said. 'I get so tired of Friedman's bullshit. Let's face it,' he continued, 'all he cares about is, as he says, profits, profits, profits, but he is so goddamned transparently greedy. My father would have hated him,' Dan added.

'Why?' Anne asked.

'Because my father hated Jews who acted out the Jewish stereotype and fed into the prejudice of anti-Semites. He didn't like Jews who gave other Jews a bad rap,' Dan said, 'and he was always pointing out in disgust to me, as a kid, people who did bad things and were Jewish too.'

'Well,' Anne answered, 'the worst things in our little case were done by J.D. to Bonnie.'

'Let's not forget the three dead innocents,' he reminded her.

'But he is going to pay through the nose to Bonnie, I think,' she continued.

'Goddamned right and he should, damn his ass, for messing with her,' Dan replied.

'Say, you are really getting in the swing of East Texas talk,' she laughed. He looked at her sheepishly.

'I guess so. I love her, you know.' She smiled. 'You too?' she responded and she patted his hand.

Anne turned on her stomach and asked him to put suntan lotion on her back. 'I burn so easily I should have grown up in Montreal, not Texas,' she said. While he applied the lotion, Anne said, 'Has Bonnie told you that we have offered settlements to all three of the families?'

'Yes,' he said, 'although we have tried not to deliberate on it between us. Maybe it's a conflict for me if I get involved. Very generous though,' he said.

'Yes,' she said. 'A million dollars to the Mexican family since he was a bystander, and five hundred thousand each to Bonnie and the poor Creole kid's parents to settle all claims. Bonnie has already said she will take it,' Anne said. 'Did you know?'

'Yes,' Dan answered. 'She wants to build a little park with part of it in Beatrice's name in Sour Lake.'

Bonnie approached them with the iced teas in a paper holder.

'Any messages?' Dan asked.

'All's well,' she replied. When she gave Dan his iced tea, she bent down and kissed him. 'Hey, I missed you on that little walk across the hot sands with the bottoms of my feet burning up right through my sandals. And, besides, we are so careful not to touch in Sour Lake that I thought I would let go here and touch on the whim of the moment.'

'Sounds right to me,' Anne said, 'as long as I don't get too horny.' She and Bonnie smiled at each other, as the three of them sipped their iced teas and baked. 'Soon we'll have to get off this frying pan,' Anne said. 'I'd like a delicious lunch in the shade by the pool, wouldn't you two?'

Bonnie said, 'And then a nice nap.'

'Sounds terrific,' Anne started gathering up her things, then stopped. 'Let's just bake a few more minutes.' They all three stretched out on their towels, sipping their iced teas.

2. Lunch

At lunch, they sat in the shade of the pool, nibbling at fajitas and drinking Margaritas. Indeed, as they ate and talked and laughed, they and their cares seemed to drowse in the dappled sun.

Dan had changed into a Michigan State tee shirt, a pair of blue gym shorts, tennis sneakers and a Michigan State cap. Anne laughed that two UT longhorn gals were being shepherded to their table by the pool by the Big Ten. Indeed, Bonnie wore a longhorn tank top shirt and short flared skirt. Bonnie sent Anne back to put on a UT shirt much like hers, to their laughter and increasing merriment.

There were few people around the pool in the heat of the day, but, at one point, a big, thick-necked rather drunk salesman approached and said to Dan, 'Hi, fella, hey you got two beautiful women there and either of them looks like more than a real handful.' He winked and continued to Dan in a confident tone, 'Maybe I can make it worthwhile for one of these lovely girls – either one – while you focus on the other.' He slid down in the open chair and looked at one woman and then the other, and said, 'Lovely, lovely, shit, what a pair on each of this pair.'

Dan was stunned, but, before he could answer, Bonnie put her hand on Dan's arm and said, smiling, 'Hey, hotshot, you sound like you're from down here somewhere. I would say McCallum, am I right?'

'Well, yes, my beauty,' he said. 'How about I buy you all a drink?'

'Well, I think you have had more than enough, but I ask you because I think I know your wife in McCallum,' she said, pointing to his wedding ring. 'So, maybe, I'm going to have to tell her that you propositioned two nice and proper Texas girls, if you don't get the hell out of our line of sight right now.'

His face turned red and confused, and he turned to Anne, 'What about you, beautiful? You want to make a few hundred this afternoon?' Anne turned full face toward him and gave him the stare. 'Get lost, buddy, or I'm going to call the hotel security.'

He didn't move, but said, 'Oh, come on, girls. I'm sure this gent doesn't mind sharing you all.' Dan stood up and said very firmly, 'Look, guy, you have made a big mistake and now it's time for you to remove yourself, before you get in a lot of trouble, believe me, you don't want to have.' With his one arm Dan took the fellow's elbow and raised him from his chair and walked him away from the two women, whispering in a low voice to him. When they had gone a few steps, the intruder turned and said contritely,

'Sorry ladies, have a good day.' He gathered up his things and quickly left the pool area.

As they laughed about the incident and the women toasted Dan, Anne said, admiringly, 'No one kicks dirt in your face, eh, Dan?'

'No,' Bonnie responded. 'This is one helluva man.'

'What did you say to him,' Anne asked, 'that so turned him around?'

'Well,' Dan said, laughing. 'I told him I was from the Mafia in New York and I didn't appreciate his barging in. I told him,' Dan added, 'that since the blonde-haired young lady thought she knew his family, it would be best if he returned home quickly or he might find his house had had a sudden fire.'

'My God,' Anne said. 'No wonder he took off.'

'I told him that, if he were still here in five minutes,' Dan answered, 'he was going to blow me, while you ladies watched, or I would break his kneecaps.'

'You make my heat rise with your audacity,' Bonnie said, as she wrapped her arms about his arm and kissed his upper arm.

'You are really something, Dan,' Anne echoed, and she leaned forward and kissed his cheek. 'On the lips, his lips,' Bonnie said to Anne. 'What's this European cheek stuff? This is a Mafia don. Kiss him on the lips like this.' And she kissed him lightly on the mouth. They each took a sip of drink and Bonnie said, 'Hey, I'm not kidding, Anne. We are friends here and in love with each other.'

Anne hesitated and then leaned to her left and said, 'I kiss the don, Dan,' and kissed Dan ever so lightly and delicately on the mouth and laughed.

Dan turned to Bonnie and asked rhetorically, 'Say, how do you break kneecaps? I know they always say that about the Mafia, but I had this silly thought, while I was whispering to him, that I have no idea how to break the kneecap, besides bash on it.'

They sat quietly. Then Bonnie stretched back her arms and yawned. 'I'm ready for a nap with my don.'

'Fabulous idea,' Dan answered. 'I'm ready.'

'I feel like I've been given a sleeping potion,' Anne said, discreetly. 'So the idea sounds good to me today – I feel so relaxed.'

'Can Anne nap with us, Dan? – would you like to, Anne? – we could nap in your room. Dan and I could share one bed, Anne. You can have the other.' She knew she was in new territory but she was determined. 'I just don't want you to be alone, Anne.'

'By all means,' Anne said. 'Let's all zonk out together.'

'No kinky stuff,' Bonnie said and she laughed.

'God no,' Anne piped in. 'Okay, Dan?'

'Sure,' Dan said. 'The don will nap with his friends.'

★

They had closed the shades and turned the air conditioner up to high. It hummed away. Classical music, Mozart's *Clarinet Concerto*, played on National Public Radio from Brownsville. Dan and Bonnie were sprawled over one of the twin beds, the covers still in place. They had joined hands between them. Her head rested on his shoulder, his on the pillow. Her eyes were closed, his open.

Anne had gotten under the bedspread of her bed. She was reading a report by a little halogen night-light. She said, 'My experience is, Dan, that the Mexican appreciates and maybe even requires to get things done with politeness and a personal touch. We are offering a very generous settlement to the family, maybe more than they expected in their wildest dreams.' She spoke softly. 'But still it should be done in person and not by lawyers. I suggest that I make the offer with the lawyer. You would be my backup, leaving Bonnie out, only because she is the subject of another settlement offer.'

'Okay,' Dan said. 'But Bonnie is the plant manager elect and the person who stays in the town. Maybe, if they accept, as I assume they will, we would figure some way to include her in the tender of the money.'

'Okay,' Anne said. 'Let's try that. Bonnie, are you listening to this?'

No response. Anne went back to reading. Dan closed his eyes. In time, Anne switched off the light and dozed, her arms cradled behind her head. Bonnie stirred and kissed Dan's ear. Then she kissed Dan full on the mouth, first very sweetly and then with great aggression. Anne turned toward the opposite wall, her breathing very regular. Bonnie pulled her shorts off and covered them both with the bedspread. Then, under the spread, she put her hand down his shorts and shifted on top of him.

While they kissed and exchanged tongues in simulation of the action going on down below, Bonnie moved almost silently upon Dan, in this mode of maximum stimulation for her, until they climaxed. She collapsed on top of him and whispered into his ear, 'I love you, Dan, I'll always be yours.' Then, beneath the bedspreads of the twin beds separated by a night table, they three slept, while classical music, now Vivaldi's *The Four Seasons* on NPR, soothed.

★

That night they got very drunk in a Tex-Mex canteena-club in Brownsville. Bonnie and Dan were later to remark at Anne's aggressiveness, reflecting her depth of attachment to them they thought.

Anne had dressed in a little, short, white, cotton dress, with thin straps holding up her loosely collected breasts in its clinging midriff. When they had met for a drink in the Radisson lounge before driving the twenty-five miles to Brownsville, Bonnie had given a low whistle when Anne walked to their table, saying, 'Hey, no fair, we went for a run and you made yourself the sexiest good old girl in Texas.'

'You look pretty good yourself,' Anne said to Bonnie, who was glowing from her closeness with Dan, in short shorts and a long polo shirt with a V-neck that plunged. 'You have a man,' Anne said, laughingly, 'so this songbird has to dress to attract the glances of the male of my species.'

Now they were sitting in the Brownsville Canteena. Anne sat next to Dan on the little curved bench seat they shared and put her arm through his. Bonnie had her one arm around him on the other side. 'Do you feel trapped by the females of the species?' Anne laughed.

'On the contrary,' Dan replied. 'I feel wanted and loved, and I hope I give off those signals to you both in return.'

'Oh, Dan,' Bonnie said. 'We are both head over heels in love with you.' She continued, 'You have made this little Texas plant manager-to-be and her faithful public affairs manager both feel special, Dan.'

Anne laughed, 'And we will continue to dress up for you. We know you like it.' She added, 'And if your Sour Lake plant manager-to-be doesn't give you enough lovin, you just tell me and I'll straighten her out discreetly but fast.' And they all three laughed.

A mariachi band stopped at their table and over strong coffee and drinks they listened to Mexican music. *Bonita, bonita*, the lead band guitarist sang, and they played a song, kneeling close for each of the women, while Bonnie and Anne hung on to Dan, drank and smiled.

Anne said she had heard about Mexican dancing at the Best Western, why didn't they see what it was. It turned out to be a local party which, given the attractiveness of the women, Dan said, they had no trouble joining. They danced, they drank, they talked, they let their hair down.

Late after midnight they piled into the car, Dan still sober. He laughed, 'One of the curses of the Straus family is that we can't get drunk. I mean flat out, unable,' he said. 'Some sort of genetic deficiency which resulted in my always being the designated driver in college.' He drove the road and causeway back to Padre Island and the Radisson.

Back in their room, Bonnie said to Dan, 'Would you like Anne to sleep with us tonight, Dan? It's something I've never done and maybe won't ever do again, but tonight it seems right.'

Dan smiled and kissed Bonnie. 'I don't think I could resist her in the same bed, Bonnie. It's you I love, Bonnie,' Dan continued, 'but I couldn't resist either of you in bed.'

'Hey, I know that, Dan,' Bonnie replied. 'But I feel every step we take together adds to our love. I want to do it tonight, Dan. I know you are attracted to Anne, too, so let that be acceptable tonight. Then I'll never doubt,' she said.

And so Bonnie went to Anne's room and invited her to come and sleep with them, recounting Dan's conversation with her and her response. They both returned, dressed still in their clothes of the evening flushed with excitement. When they entered the room, Bonnie kissed Dan, who was in his shorts, while she lightly held Anne's arm. She put her hand down on the bulge in his pants and said, 'I think this don is ready for both of us, Anne.'

*

'I'm just here as dessert; she's the main course,' Anne said to Dan.

Dan was clearly ready. He turned the lights off and opened the curtains to the ocean and the Texas night. Bonnie and he kissed and licked each other's tongues, bodies pressed together, standing by the bed. 'I've got a fever for you, Dan,' Bonnie whispered to him. Dan rubbed her flanks and then between her legs, as they stood pressed together kissing mouth, eyes, ears, necks, breasts.

'I love you, only you,' he whispered to Bonnie.

'I know it,' she answered softly. 'This is my present to you. Just enjoy it.'

Anne came up behind Dan and pressed herself against him. She kissed the back of his neck touching both his sides. She was excited and suddenly wet. 'Fuck her,' Anne said, and then, kissing him on the neck and the back and the shoulders, she repeated over and over, 'Fuck her, Dan,' while she rubbed herself against him and raised her own response.

Bonnie lay down on the side of the bed, legs extended to the floor, open wide. 'Put it in Dan,' she said. 'I'm crazy for it.' Dan thrust in but so easily and, as he pumped, they kissed and licked, and he fondled her breasts. Anne kissed and rubbed and licked his back, pressing her moist pussy against his gyrating backside. 'Oh, Dan,' Bonnie said over and over.

The presence of Anne stimulated Dan and, at the same time, held him off, so Bonnie reached multiple climaxes and Dan achieved a height of emotion, which resulted in a crescendo of stimulated climax for Anne, too, that left them gasping.

They crawled into bed, arms and legs locked about each other. They lay there panting and quiet for a while, folk music on the FM dial this time. Judy Collins was singing about clouds and life's illusions. Bonnie broke the silence. 'Hey, this is going to sound funny right now, gang, but I've decided to accept the company offer for settlement – five hundred thou – but I'm not going to relent on my suit against J.D. I'm going to sue the bastard till he apologizes, pays up or his prick drivels up and falls off,' she added.

'I'm not surprised,' Dan answered.

'Hey, friend of mine for life,' Anne added. 'We are with you. What are you going to do with all that money, gal?' Anne asked in her best Texas twang.

Bonnie answered seriously, 'Why, I'm financing a little corner park near my mom's house, where she used to walk the dog and me when I was little.' Then she leaned over Dan and kissed his chest, muzzling around each nipple. 'I'm going to spend the rest on Dan.' She kissed Dan and then playfully licked his ear. 'He deserves it,' she added. 'He has such a great cock.' She slid her hand down inside the sheet and then said, 'Oooh la la, Dan, so soon, you really are a don.'

Bonnie pulled the sheet back and lowered her head licking about his groin and sucking the again extending and throbbing member.

'Ah, Bonnie,' Dan exclaimed.

With a loose arm, Bonnie pushed Anne toward Dan. That was all she needed. She kissed Dan with full lips and then they kissed open mouthed. Dan felt the passion that had been building over the months for Anne. 'Such sweetness,' she said.

Bonnie kissed Dan's hips and then his navel. Dan rubbed Anne's pendulous breasts, moving his thumb over the darkened tips which became greatly extended. Bonnie kissed Dan on the mouth and then licking Dan's lips said, 'Fuck her, baby, fuck her.'

Anne sat on top of Dan, while Bonnie continued kissing him, saying, 'Fuck her, sweet one, fuck her with your sweet cock, fuck her.'

Anne was open and ready and received him. She then rode him while her juices covered them both. Bonnie kissed Anne on the lips and then licked her ears in excitement. Anne reached down with her mouth to Dan's and kissed him. Anne exclaimed, 'My God, my God, my God,' as she moved her face down and kissed Dan, while accelerating the motion pressed against him. Then Dan was stroking Anne's nipples while Bonnie resumed kissing him.

Anne reached repeated climaxes and moved off Dan saying, 'No more, No more. Oh God, I need some water,' and taking a drink from a glass by the table. 'Oh, God,' she said, 'I love you both.'

Dan was still extended and ready. 'Put it in her,' Anne said. 'Finish with her, love her to death,' Anne said, turning toward Dan and kissing his ear and his neck. Bonnie was wet and excited by all the foreplay, and, with Anne lying beside them there, arms up and extended about her head, as she had been when sleeping that afternoon, Dan re-immersed himself inside Bonnie, this time lying on top of her and, with serious protestations of love, they reached yet another even greater climax together.

Eventually the three fell asleep, Bonnie in Dan's arms and Anne smiling alongside, arms up.

3. Border Crossing

On Monday morning at 10.00 AM, Anne and Dan walked across the Peace Bridge from Brownsville to Matamoros. Dan had driven Bonnie to Harlingin Airport for the 6.00 AM flight to Houston and on to Beaumont.

Bonnie had said to him, as they drove, sipping orange juice from a Tropicana carton, 'This has been the best weekend of my life, Dan.' She had stroked his arm and said, 'Saturday night was wild and wonderful, Dan. I have no regrets about that, don't worry. What works for you works for me, Dan,' she had added.

'You work for me, Bonnie,' he had answered. 'You know that, don't you?'

'Yes,' she had said. 'I just don't want you to worry.'

'Hey,' Dan had answered. 'All I know is how much I love you.'

'Last night together, just the two of us, was beautiful, Dan,' Bonnie had continued. 'Don't think I need any kinky stimulation with you.'

Dan had smiled. 'I'm going to get another hard-on, if you keep this up.' He thought back to the beautiful motion of her mouth sucking on him, in the early morning, while he stroked her billowing hair, and indeed he did get a hard-on thinking about her. She leaned toward him, and touched him through his suit pants, between his legs and said, 'Oh, I do love you, baby.' He would fly to Houston that night, where she would meet him at the airport. After a day at the plant, they would have a last night together, before his trip back to New Jersey.

'I can't wait to put this inside me tonight,' she said.

'Neither can I,' he answered. 'Maybe I should just leave it with you, while I'm back at the head shop.' They both smiled.

Walking over the Rio Grande and thinking these thoughts, Dan stopped to look at that impossibly small ribbon of water that was no trouble at all to Mexicans looking for something better.

'No barrier at all,' Anne said, as if reading his thoughts.

'True,' Dan answered. 'But at least it looks fairly clean – no oil slick, foam or garbage. Those water treatment plants in El Paso-Juarez, del Rio and Acuna must be making some progress,' he added, 'because the last time I saw the river it was much worse, kind of green in color and full of foam.'

'Can you tell from such simple visual characteristics?' she asked. 'Not definitely,' he answered, 'but visual indicators are usually pretty good markers of a problem and are the best rough gauge I know.' She looked at him, so he continued, 'The environmental business is really quite simple and the basic indicators work well.

'You know,' he said, as they walked on toward the immigration point and the Mexican lawyer who would be awaiting them at the other side of the bridge, 'the Sour Lake plant was a mess when I first saw it. Unpainted, rusting, piping and vessels from the pilot lying on the ground. That was my first indication that J.D. didn't have a handle on the local situation,' he added, 'but it also told me that a little housekeeping and maintenance, and a lot of care, would quickly improve the situation and productivity. Bonnie knew that too and bought into it,' he concluded.

'She is going to make an outstanding plant manager, isn't she?' Anne added. 'And the chairman will go with her into a new era for the company, pulling Friedman along.'

'Yes,' Dan said. 'I'm going to help her all I can as a professional, and you too, Anne, because you are a part of this team.'

Dr. Jose Carlos Orantes was there at the foot of the Peace Bridge in Matamoros. He was a small, thin, nattily dressed, young Mexican professional, with a pencil mustache and deferential manner.

Dr. Orantes had mainly been involved with American Industrial as the lawyer representing the company's local interests in the law suit filed by a public interest group on behalf of Mexican peasants, living in poverty on the border, who had had babies born with brain injuries, presumably from the drinking water. Not knowing who else to sue of substance in that ramshackle industrial border town, they had focused in on all the American companies, including American Industrial, with its small repackaging operation.

Orantes was happy to have a more positive reason to deal with American Industrial for he understood that the reason why this environmental expert, Mr. Straus, and his public affairs staff person, who was with him that day, were there was to view alternative properties for a plant he had been discussing with the Corporate real estate people.

Personally, he was more anxious to deal with a positive issue, like industrial growth in Matamoros, than the wearying politics of a law suit, which probably was unfounded but also indefensible, in light of the imbalance in the equities.

Orantes was surprised to see how young they were – and how '*muy bonita*' the woman was, but he had long ago become used to American aggressiveness and impatience. As a member of the Matamoros town council, he knew how important it was to land a blue chip company like American Industrial under the NAFTA agreement. He also knew this project was important to the Texas governor.

Orantes spoke good English – learned in his years in San Antonio, in school, but he started in Spanish, '*Buenas Dias,*

Señor and *Señorita*,' and other niceties. They shook hands and smiled. The Americans seemed so open. He admired that. Orantes suggested they first go back to his office and view the plot plans and have a little coffee. The Mexicans always insist on ceremony and are so polite, Dan thought in confirmation of Anne's point over the weekend.

The day was a montage of looking at plans and visiting the two main property possibilities. One was on the Rio Grande, a little upstream. It had an old plant on it, which would be demolished. Dan showed a lot of interest in inspecting the infrastructure, including sewage. The other facility was a few miles inland, in a middle-class residential area, but bordered by a railroad on one side and a highway on the other. The land had been part of a railroad switching area and then had been cleared for development. Dan liked the cleared lot better because of the transportation options and it was not near the river, although waste treatment and disposal might be more of a problem.

They had a Mexican-style lunch at a restaurant called, The Parking Lot. It was obvious to Anne that Dan wanted to think, so, during lunch, she and Dr. Orantes talked about the availability of trainable labor and the problems of corruption and organized crime in the region. Anne said there had been a lot of press about drug murders, but Orantes countered that 'the press exaggerates these things,' and he continued smiling gently. 'Being from the New York City area, you must know that.'

Dr. Orantes was quite taken with this beautiful Texas woman, who was on her way up in the corporate world. He told her she was like a breath of fresh air for him in Matamoros. 'All I usually get are Yankee engineers, with bushy mustaches, and desperado businessmen,' he kidded.

They switched over to Spanish, discussing the growing changes in Mexico.

Finally, Dr. Orantes turned to Dan and said, 'Well, Mr. Dan Straus, what are you thinking?'

Dan answered, 'I like the inland site because it steps aside of the long-term water problems here, but only if we can get it free and clear of past concerns.'

'I will look into that in detail,' Orantes countered, 'although I think that will be so as I took the liberty of making preliminary investigations before you came.'

'Also,' Dan added, 'this would be a high technology, complex chemical plant – the transportation and distribution chain, look good, but the plant would need, reliable, uninterrupted energy source and a state-of-the-art environmental air protection system that would depend on top-flight, dedicated personnel.

'And,' Dan added, 'I would like to know the tenor of the community as to handling sophisticated, hazardous chemicals, to produce a product in Mexico, which would be highly welcome by industry and the government but would get a lot of attention in the press and presumably by the environmental community.'

'*Bueno*,' Orantes responded. 'Perhaps *Señorita* Hennessy would like to work with me to establish the right level of community receptivity.'

'We would like that,' Dan pre-empted the response, 'since this latter request is not strictly a legal request. I will be talking with the real estate people in the Corporate office later this week,' Dan continued. 'So perhaps Miss Hennessy could be ready to work with you by next week. We assume we will get the approvals as we want to move this program along.'

'*Bueno*,' Orantes repeated, and he spoke directly to Anne. 'If you will let me know by week's end, I will arrange for us to talk to a good public relations firm and the city officials, to get a better handle on community receptivity to a high-tech chemical operation.' Orantes was positively beaming now.

Dan had another subject to raise with *Señor* Orantes, one which he and Anne had discussed on the beach the previous day on Padre Island. So Dan added, 'We're also concerned about the housing for our employees. We wonder whether, at the basic wage rates we will pay our lowest-level workers, let's say three to four times the Mexican minimum rate in our experience,' he estimated, 'whether they will have decent housing.'

'Well,' Orantes answered, 'that is not exactly my expertise, but my experience is that the poorest housing – the *colonias* – is generally utilized by recent peasant immigrants to this area from interior Mexico, or even from the South of Mexico. As soon as they get an economic foothold,' Orantes added, 'those who come to the *colonias* move out. I believe your employees would have already moved out,' he said.

'Could we drive past a *colonia* on the way to look at the site again,' Anne inquired. 'I would like to see one – so as to have some personal recognition.'

'An excellent idea,' Orantes responded.

'One other matter you might look into, *Señor* Orantes,' Anne added. 'At our larger facilities in other parts of Mexico, for example in Juarez and Mexicali, we have the advantage of a childcare facility in association with the industrial park. I know this plant with its one hundred employees approximately, at start up – it may grow much larger – cannot afford such a facility on its own,' she nodded to Dan and Orantes, 'but we would like childcare available to our employees.'

'I'll look into it and we can talk about the options when you are next here, *Señorita* Hennessy,' Orantes responded.

'So,' Dan concluded. 'Could we go and walk the property once again and then we will take leave of you, Dr. Orantes, until quite probably next week, when, besides Miss Hennessy, our plant manager, in training in Sour Lake, Miss Sutherland, might also come down to take a look.'

'Outstanding,' Dr. Orantes said finishing his demitasse, coffee and signaling for the check in the large, cavernous restaurant.

'But please to call me Carlos.'

'Our pleasure,' Anne answered, 'as long as we are Anne and Dan to you.'

As they left The Parking Lot restaurant, two little street children came up to Anne. The older, perhaps six years, was a pretty Indian girl, in a little dress and sandals. She carried a box of Lifesaver packets, which she offered to them – 'twenty-five cents,' she said. What they took to be her brother – perhaps aged four and quite disheveled and dirty in tee shirt and shorts, with bare feet – had a pack of Wrigley's Spearmint Gum in his hand. He didn't establish a price; just offered the pack, saying '*pesetas, por favor.*'

By the side of the curb sat their mother in peasant smock with a baby at her breast.

Anne stopped and tried to communicate with the girl, but the price she had uttered – twenty-five cents – turned out to be her only English. Anne said something in Spanish to her and the girl frowned and pulled back the candy. Anne turned to Dr. Orantes and said, 'I would like to give her a dollar, but not for the Lifesavers, but for her and her brother to have hot food. I told her it was for hot food only,' Anne said to Dan.

'The money will simply go to her mother, *Señorita*,' he responded. 'You will pardon me, but you should not encourage her begging.'

'Nevertheless, she doesn't seem to understand my Texas Spanish. Please tell her, Dr. Orantes that she should not be selling on the street. She and her brother should have hot food, and please add she is old enough for school,' she said, as she handed the uncertainly smiling girl a dollar bill.

'*Señorita*, you are very kind-hearted,' and he directly communicated with the young girl in Spanish, while he kept his hand on her shoulder to insist she listen to the suggestion.

As they stood in the warm sunshine, Anne said, 'I'm torn apart by these little children on the street.'

'Yes,' Dr. Orantes said. 'I am very sure that the economic activity of this Maquila region continues to draw these poor rural Indian peasants of Southern Mexico here.'

'It seems to me,' Dan said, 'that only increased economic activity under NAFTA and enlightened responsibility by the companies and the community can solve the problem.'

'I think you are right,' Dr. Orantes responded. He focused on outside help by saying, 'This town is too poor to cope by itself – there are too many needs.'

When they were walking across the bridge to their parked car, Dan said to Anne, 'Thursday, when I see the chairman and Friedman, I'll show them these drawings and get a preliminary go-ahead. You will play an important role here, Anne,' he added. They smiled at each other.

'You seem more and more the strong corporate type, Dan,' Anne responded. 'The assignment and Bonnie must be good for you.'

'You, too,' he answered, and they smiled again.

They drove to Harlingin Airport where Anne went to Chicago and Newark, while Dan returned to Bonnie's arms and Sour Lake.

Chapter Eight
Long Island/ New Jersey

1. Long Island

Dan sat alone on the beach. It was 6.00 AM on a warm, early summer, Long Island Sunday. He had so much to think about, but, for the moment, his thoughts had wandered back to the time of his childhood on the Coney Island beach near his parents' Sheepshead Bay home, where he and his father, on early summer mornings, had a ritual of a baseball throw and catch. Dan thought about the pressure his childhood stammer had placed on him. His father always said it would go away as he got older, (it did disappear in adolescence), but although it was no comfort then, he would be a better person for undergoing the isolation and very real pain because he would be sensitive to the difficulties of others. Dan missed his father since his death a few years before.

This had been a hard weekend – the hardest, Dan thought. They had had a bitter argument about Dan's absence. Gloria had struck him and bloodied his nose in anger, and Dan had then shook her to stop her tantrum. He and Gloria had agreed to separate. He told her he could no longer accept the screaming, the recriminations and the doubts. 'You have worn me out,' he said.

Gloria said she was tired of him and his philosophizing. 'You never let me be myself,' she said sharply. They agreed to go their own ways.

Dan suggested that Gloria approach a lawyer for the right steps for separation and divorce. 'You bet I will,' Gloria answered. 'And you better not try to cheat me or the children out of what we are entitled to, Mr. Corporate Executive.'

Dan tried to say calmly, 'That's unfair, Gloria. I know my financial responsibilities to you and the kids. You can't say I have ever skimped on that.'

That calmed her and she answered, 'Well, I'll see a lawyer, Dan.' She started to cry. 'Don't worry about seeing the girls. We won't shut you out. They love you so much.'

He put his hand on her shoulder. 'I guess I still love you,' she said, 'but I can't live with your expectations and such anger toward you.'

'Nor can I,' he said. She buried herself in his arms crying. 'It's time for the break, Gloria. We both need to get on with our lives.'

Dan sat looking at the ocean lapping at the shore. Was he guilty as he himself charged? Had he tried to change her once too often? He was the unfaithful one, he repeated to himself. Had he fallen out of love and then in love with Bonnie, or was the timing reversed? He knew how much he ached for Bonnie and how supportive she was of him, without question or reservation. But was that Gloria's fault? Wasn't he the culprit? These questions he asked himself in the absence of the father he had so long trusted, to whom he stammered out his unvarnished truths as a boy, playing catch.

When he called Bonnie to tell her of the decisive conversation with Gloria, she had sensed his exhilaration for their freedom and the simultaneous feeling of misery and failure. 'Poor darling,' she said. 'Carrying this all alone – I miss you so much.'

He told Bonnie of his statement to Gloria that he would not nickel and dime her. 'I do think she feels vulnerable and exposed without me.'

'Tell me about it, my wonderful Danny boy,' Bonnie replied and then softening, 'I got five hundred thousand dollars in settlement, Dan, and minus the twenty-five thousand for the park, it's all yours. Give her what she wants, Dan,' she continued. 'I just want you to be happy and come down here and to be close to me whenever you have the chance – I love you, Dan.'

'And I you, baby,' he said. 'Don't worry, I'm okay – just talking to you makes me feel better, less lonely and, besides, if this phone is not bugged, I will add that I am getting a hard-on just listening to your voice and thinking about being close and making love.'

'Oh, Dan,' Bonnie replied. 'I couldn't imagine saying this six months ago, and it's trite, I know, but we were meant to be, physically and in every other way.'

'What you say sounds trite, Bonnie, but it's true,' Dan responded. 'I guess my relationship with Gloria had so flattened out that I couldn't imagine before we met being in sync with anyone personally ever again.'

'Oh, Dan,' she said again, 'you are sympathetic with everyone. But as long as you think it's only me, keep thinking that,' she laughed.

Dan thought again about his dad. He had asked Dan when he brought Gloria home that first time from Michigan State, 'What qualities she brings to you, son?' He had thought his dad just wanted to know more about Gloria, but, maybe, he was really hinting that, when the first blush of romance wore off, there would be trouble. He said aloud, 'I should have listened better.' But then, he felt ashamed, as the two girls came dashing helter-skelter from the house door on to the beach to greet him. Without her, they wouldn't be here either, he thought.

2. New Jersey

Early that afternoon, Dan drove back on the Southern State Parkway to New Jersey from Long Island. The beach traffic was moving the other way. Dan had the chilling thought that it was at the tollbooth in Nassau the brother was callously murdered in *The Godfather*. Why he would have such a thought about fictitious lives he did not know, except that he felt they were all vulnerable.

The chairman and Friedman, of course, had approved of the interior site in Matamoros, at a full-scale meeting of the executive committee that included the real estate fellow, Solomon, who was an ex-marine, with his crew cut, continuous optimism and 'yes sir, no sir' mentality. Dan had tried to introduce the subject of conditions in Matamoros, but Solomon rolled over him with the optimistic, bravura approach that the company could work with others to make things better. Dan could not really object to that statement, so he let it go, although he did note that the chairman picked up on his concern by saying that 'we supported NAFTA not only to make money, but contribute to improving conditions there, and we will do that. We are in this for the long haul and the big bucks.'

At a meeting, on Friday, in New Brunswick, Friedman and the chairman both agreed to hold a family day a little over two months from then, just before Labor Day, at the plant. Bonnie would officially be named Plant Manager at that function. In the meantime she would be Deputy Plant Manager.

They told Dan that morning that they planned to name him VP of Environment for Friedman's operations, expressively delivering on the chairman's word to him in Austin. Friedman added for him to hear, as part of an aside to Casey, 'Miss Hennessy will become Director of Public Affairs for the Environmental Quality team across our operations, as an important part of her responsibility, to make sure the careers of these people progress.'

They were happy for each other, but Dan felt Bonnie should not have to wait through the summer to be the full-time plant manager. 'The chairman wants an event,' Anne replied. 'It will hold, but you can tell her.'

He said he would be in New Brunswick the first couple of days the next week and 'I intend to pursue Friedman then about Bonnie being made Assistant Regional Manager to spell me at all the locations.'

Anne indicated she would meet with Orantes with Bill Cory the following Friday. 'I hope to meet with community people,' she said, 'and I'll set it up for you the next week to go over all the details.'

'Good,' he replied. 'You are a prize, Anne. You should bring Bonnie with you to look at the property – she knows more plant-related questions and details than I do.'

'Will I see you on Monday?' Anne had asked.

'You will,' Dan replied. 'Let's each make a list of those things which have to get done and compare notes then.'

'I'm going to call Bonnie at the plant,' Anne said. 'Any message?'

'Yes,' Dan answered. 'Tell her she is Deputy Plant Manager. It doesn't need to wait for me. And tell her to study up on her Spanish.' He winked. 'She is going to be the Assistant Regional Manager – not just the Sour Lake Plant Manager,' he added. 'But don't tell her that until I get that sold and she makes it happen.'

'Lucky, lucky lady,' Anne said.

★

Dan spent an uneasy night at his home in New Jersey, haunted by the ghosts of his past. He alternated between squirming under memories of Gloria's bitter, debilitating arguments with him and her sobbing in his arms at their break-up on Long Island. Recall of the noisy squealing and laughter of his daughters found him wandering into their room and staring at their bunk beds.

He thought, too, again, about his father, who so patiently stayed in contact with his private pain and humiliation as a stammerer. He pictured his dad in a short remission from the brain cancer he died from, sitting in the kitchen of this house with Gloria and him, after a particularly withering, angry outburst of hers, over a triviality, enveloped the three of them (his mother had retreated to reading in the living room), counseling by model the good humor and steadiness he always advised.

Sitting in that kitchen now alone, Dan thought that the decisive step away from Gloria and toward Bonnie would be good for him. He knew he was on the verge of real accomplishment at work and that he could have an effect on the selfish industrial process he basically distrusted, to his own advantage, while making the company better. He laughed at himself for such idealism, but he knew that was what he basically believed. Gloria always mocked me for my idealism, he thought. Maybe she is right and I'm heading for a fall and taking Bonnie with me, he thought.

She called his seeing of both sides of problems 'his noble neutrality'. 'My Jesus,' she would say, with acid deprecation and satirically referred to him as 'Prince Dan'. Gloria's furious insensitivity was so hard on him – was that what attracted him to Bonnie?

She was not only so goddamn sexual, but she really believed in him, and threw her lot in with him without reservations.

To get himself out of this introspective state, Dan made some phone calls. First to Bonnie. He started with Bonnie in a manner to which she had become accustomed saying, 'Hey, what's going on?' She knew she shouldn't probe him for what was on his mind until she had responded. No need to search for simple mutuality and trust. It was there. Sometimes she would simply zero in on her feelings of loving and missing him, but this night she had an apprehension and fear to share.

'Dan,' she said. 'I'm getting a little scared of J.D.'

'How so above and beyond his usual bombast and machismo?' he asked.

'Well,' she said, 'today I saw him on the street and he was really aggressive – told me he was going to beat my ass, if I didn't back off on the harassment suit.'

'What did you say?' Dan asked.

'I told him – full of piss and vinegar you know – that he should have thought about that when he was the big shot – except I said big shit – at the plant. He said, "Now you are really the hot shit at the plant, aren't you? Well, I'm gonna get your ass, honey!" He got real red when he talked,' Bonnie concluded. 'I thought he might take a swing at me right there.'

'You should tell your lawyer and maybe the police,' Dan advised.

'I will tell my lawyer, but telling the police might invite him,' she said.

'I don't know about that, baby,' he answered. 'I worry about you – you are everything to me.'

'I know, darling,' she said. 'Well, soon you will be back down here. How are you doing now?' she asked.

They talked about work, about his introspection, about his dad, and about the two of them. He told her again in detail about his decision and break with Gloria.

She sensed his need to step out from his mood. Later that night he was to think about the wild abandon of the conversation that then followed, because what they talked about was so frankly and blatantly sexual. Dan was amused by the similarity with some of the explicit sexual phone talk in the movie *Short Cuts*, although their talk, in distinction to the market approach of the movie, was loving and full of commitment and follow-through. Dan marveled at Bonnie's ability to adapt to his needs out of her love and desire for him, whether it be in running the plant at Sour Lake or releasing the power of the great sexuality between them.

As they signed off, Dan repeated, 'And, Bonnie, tell your lawyer about the conversation with J.D., tomorrow.'

'I will, baby. I promise,' she said. 'But I feel better having talked to you. He can't touch us.'

Next he talked to his mother in Florida. He reached her while she was on her other line, so he decided to fan the illusion of bliss for now by asking her to call him back at his home, as if all was as it was. She was an old and frail lady now, living in the past. They talked about the grandchildren, her medical problems (daily there was a problem with Medicare), and his assignment in Texas. He told her Gloria was out on Long Island with her parents enjoying the beach. He told her he found himself thinking a lot about his dad. They shared some fond memories, which brought her to tears, he knew, but also would reinforce the validity of her past with her husband.

Dan's mother, suddenly, in a distracted voice, raised an issue from the past. 'Dan, do you remember much about when your dad left us for about six months? It was such a long time ago, Dan, and you were a little boy. Your sister was a little older, but I remember our little family just became too much for him for a while. He went to the Catskills originally – in September – for his asthma and just sort of kept extending his stay – commuting into New York City.'

'Mom,' Dan said. 'Why do you torture yourself with this old memory? Dad loved you,' he went on, 'and it was just a short phase in his life.'

She continued over the phone, taking no heed of his reassurance, 'He seemed to need to be away from me. At first I joined him for weekends, and he was always nice and polite. I thought there was another woman but there wasn't and it became clear that I was a disruptive force to his solitude.'

'Mom, this doesn't do you any good,' Dan said, but she continued, 'My inability to reach him over that period was devastating to me. My friends said I should retaliate by cutting your dad off, sort of teaching him a lesson, but the lesson I learned was how dear he was to me and how much I needed him.'

He could hear her choke back a sob, and knew that he should not admonish her again for reliving her past and intense love for his father. He also knew that the incident had never been explained satisfactorily to his sister or himself. He knew he should go to see her soon. She was a woman who took great solace from her lifelong interest in books and painting. Now, in the isolation of her old age, he was sure she needed him too.

Finally, he called Tom Foley, at Michigan State. They had a leisurely conversation about work, Sour Lake, CFC alternatives, NAFTA and Matamoros. Foley was particularly interested in Dan's contacts over these weeks with Governor Bush. 'Imagine that,' Dr. Foley said. 'To be a part of and help launch the Texas initiative toward the border under NAFTA. And our article is done with the changes, Dan, so let's get it published.'

Dan could see Foley in his armchair by his desk in his study, puffing on his pipe, keying on Dan's policy issue over the next month – support of the chairman's commercial focus on Mexico through demonstrating environmental responsibility, working with the Governor's office. Dan realized, again, in talking to Foley, that his goals of good environmental management in Texas or Mexico, or China, or whatever, were critically intertwined with the chairman's, and, in this case, the Governor's ambition in Mexico. He suddenly also realized that that should be the subject of his presentation to the Beaumont press group the following week. The fact that he would have to work on it gave him an optimistic feeling of a project not completed.

Dr. Foley then turned suddenly, precipitously, inward to his own concerns as the conversation about Dan's new options wound down. Increasingly, Dan felt that his mentor was trying to spell out a problem, which was hard for him to talk about, faulting himself with unwarranted introspection. Sometimes, lately, Dan felt a disquieting concern that Dr. Foley was somehow losing what had always been his powerful grip.

Foley went on, 'I'm not sure how much longer I'm going to exercise my tenure or teach undergraduates. I'm not really sure I have anything left to tell young people. Maybe I can still help a graduate student here or there in a specific focus, but I think I'm out of touch with these kids now. Sometimes I feel confused by my contacts with them. I'm not sure what's wrong.'

'I don't know about that,' Dan said hopefully. 'You give me awfully good advice.'

Foley continued, disregarding Dan, 'And then I'm not much interested in publishing anymore. I have this book in draft I've done on industrial environmental management with that fellow at A.D. Little, and, while I know it's good stuff, I don't really even care if it's published. Maybe they should take my name off it. I've made so many enemies in my life maybe it would be better if I wasn't credited as an author.'

Dan was uncomfortable with his mentor's new pessimism and self-doubt. They talked more about their long relationship and then Dan told Foley about the field day at the plant at summer's end. 'Would you come if we invited you as my guest?' Dan asked.

'I will,' Foley answered, in a happier voice.

Dan sat at the kitchen table, following these phone calls, making lists. It was a habit of organized thought he had learned from his dad. Write down things to do, mentally list the barriers for each task and think about how to overcome them. Try to understand who were the others with a stake in what was to be accomplished and see where their needs could be satisfied, so he could reach his goals.

★

Dear Mother,
I felt badly that I was not able to adequately respond
to your memories of Dad. You know how much I
loved and respected him, as you do. I think so often of
my father and his great respect for truth and patience. I
remember him saying to me – perhaps more than once
– that the necessity to care about other people's feelings
should not allow you to recoil from honesty, just deal
with the truth without malice.

I remember him telling me at the rostrum of my
Bar Mitzvah that the most profound advice of the
bible is Hillel's 'treat thy neighbor as thyself.' I
remember him saying it is not only a golden rule, but
a code for a kindly life. In other words, it isn't just
that you deal honestly, but in a caring manner.

I feel guilty at not seeing you more often – and I
will be to see you over a weekend very soon. My being
busy in Texas and Mexico is not really an excuse,
although you are very understanding and solicitous of
me.

But it is deceitful of me to withhold from you the
news that Gloria and I have split. I know that you
know our marriage was in trouble. We were probably
both at fault, and the arguments were getting worse
and worse, and more corrosive to the girls' well-being,
as well as, quite frankly, mine. So Gloria and I have
separated, but, of course, the girls will not suffer from
either of us, and I know Gloria will be supportive of
me as their father. She has already expressed her desire
to bring them down to see you in the Fall, if you are
well enough. She is at her mother's for the long school
summer recess, on Long Island. She took off early, I
think to get a hold of herself (one of the advantages of

teaching at an upper-class private school, rather than the NY city public schools). I am here in New Jersey and in Texas at work.

I have lovely memories of you, Mom, with Dad, when I was a child with you supporting Dad's idealistic view with your own set of compassionate realism. You two were quite a pair and role models for me. Anyway, I can hear you saying with that wonderful musical voice and wit, 'Remember, Dan, because many of your friends' parents are divorced does not make them lesser people than you, just children in different circumstances.' I remember, too you saying, when I asked you rather haughtily about your divorced sister, Aunt Eunice, (you may not remember this, but a child's memory on such a thing is to be trusted, I think), 'Dan, get off your high horse – many is the time your father and I have come close to divorce; we are just such good friends we wouldn't want to lose each other.'

Well, Gloria and I are somewhat the opposite, I think. While I believe we still do love each other in some baffling way, we argue so much and so corrosively and have so little compatibility that life is too much of a strain together. So, we will join the majority statistics of those in the over fifty per cent divorced category. Dad always told me not to become a member of the majority just to get along with them, but I don't think he had this in mind.

Anyway, I first decided I would not tell you of our split-up, because you would do just fine not knowing. But you are a full-grown adult and were before me, so I felt you were entitled to the news, unhappy as it might be in the short run. There are evidences already that I am righting my life. What did Dad used to say? 'The important question, after every personal crisis, is not how did this happen, but what do I do next?'

I will call you, probably from Texas, in a few days, after I know you have received this to talk some more.

Love,
Dan

Chapter Nine
Sour Lake/ New Jersey

1. The Militia

J.D. had changed. Dressed in his Vietnam fatigues he spent most of his time in his trailer behind his house. After all, he had a lot to do.

J.D. oiled his guns every day after target practice at the militia range. His care was especially loving with the new semi-automatic attack rifle he had purchased in a gun shop in Dallas. He didn't do any hunting in this hot Texas summer season, but his attention to his guns gave him excitement.

Then there was the larger role he was playing in the Sour Lake militia cell. He had assumed an organizational role, keeping track of the training for their cache members, and making up the little weekly communication fact sheet on a Fed's abuse that week, taking the lead from Montana headquarters. J.D. had added in corporate abuses, and the small band of the militia members liked that just fine. They hated the big companies as much as the government. 'Shit, they're the same, aren't they?' J.D. argued at that morning's target practice.

The Sour Lake militia cell really liked J.D.'s intense involvement since he had summarily retired from the plant manager's job. Before that he had just been another guy –

often not showing up for shooting practice or drills. But, since he had retired, he was a great old guy giving them leadership, and the cell members knew it.

J.D.'s bitterness over Bonnie's lawsuit fueled his fury over everything else. He said to them he 'hated that cunt, Bonnie Sutherland.' She would get what she deserved, he darkly threatened. They laughed but loved the sense of danger and action in his anger.

While he made bullets in the trailer, he thought about that damn cunt. He knew what she was doing over at the plant. He had his spies. She was fucking everyone in sight. She gave her pussy out as a bonus, he laughed, particularly to that Jew, Straus, from New York.

His lawyer had advised him to apologize to her, as she wanted, and then the suit would be settled in a very nominal way, as she had suggested. He would be goddamned if he would do that! At that last meeting with her, she had worn that long skirt and long-sleeved blouse, but she didn't fool him. As sure as he made the best bullets in Texas, he was going to show her.

What he really should do, he thought, was catch Bonnie at night outside and fuck her till she apologized to him. She was the one who teased him into fucking with her at the plant. That was why he moved her up, goddamnit, but not even his freaken lawyer seemed to believe him. Fuckin' Jew. And that Straus guy, comin' down here and acting like he knows it all, you know. Goddamn Jews.

J.D. thought someone was opening his mail. Goddamn FBI probably. Well, the militia would be ready when we finally put down the government fascists, he thought. His guns were ready, goddamn it.

J.D. was in a fury, and he was in it all the time these days. Everything he did with the militia cell encouraged his paranoia, but to him everything pointed to Bonnie as at the root of his problems.

He had mounted a blow-up of a snapshot of her in the trailer and put below it cutouts of newspaper headline block letters which simply said CUNT.

He never let his wife in the trailer, indeed she seemed to want to have less and less to do with him. She argued that they had their retirement and should move to Tampa to be near her sister. The old battle ax, he thought, well, maybe, they would but not yet. What the hell do I want to be in Tampa, he thought. He had no definitive plan, but he was not through yet.

Since the Oklahoma City blast, the Beaumont paper and that Jew, Wiseman, had been poking around asking questions about their militia cell, he knew. 'How the fuck did he know about it, anyway?' one of his comrades asked him.

'They got a network, you know,' J.D. said. 'Goddamn Jew communists, you know.'

Anyway, the Sour Lake police had been in to see him recently about keeping the lid on his activities. 'Cut down the drinking and the temper,' old C.C. Terry, his police buddy for years, had said to him, 'or it's going to get you in trouble.'

C.C. had asked to see his gun collection, but he had gotten an emergency call on the cruiser radio before they entered the trailer. Since then J.D. kept the guns in a trunk in the trailer and he put a shade over Bonnie's picture, because he knew old C.C. would be back.

Meanwhile he made his bullets and kept cool. The militia absorbed him. Maybe this would all pass like his wife said, but he didn't know about that. One thing for sure, she wasn't putting out for him since the harassment suit came to light after his retirement. He had to go to a Mexican whore in Beaumont he knew, when he needed his pipes cleaned. She was okay, though. He called her Bonnie when he fucked her.

2. The Board Meeting

On recommendation of the Finance Committee, the Board of Directors had just doubled the chairman's salary from one and a half million to three million dollars a year, plus stock options and benefits for a package, it was emphasized, of about twenty million annually. Tony Casey had his whole court there, including H. Jeffrey Bush, Horace Carpenter, Paul Atkinson and Marv Friedman.

All would benefit substantially from the reward to Casey, albeit in smaller amounts – especially Friedman and the other operation presidents who would be millionaires – comfortable for life.

Their body language made it clear that they knew who was their sun king, Dan thought. He and Bonnie and Anne were in attendance to be presented to the Board as part of the new team direction. Dan knew that Bonnie would particularly knock them over, with her singular youthful radiance.

This presentation of them to the Board, along with the new refrigerant product and plan for co-plants in Texas, Mexico and San Jose had been Casey's idea. He told the fifteen outside board members that the management was proud that 'like Phoenix we have risen from the tragedy of fatalities at Sour Lake to seize the opportunity to bring our products and these young people along.' He stressed their accomplishment, how 'they had not only put Sour Lake in order and moved forward toward start up in Matamoros, but established a relationship with Governor Bush's office that assured the company would be in the forefront of development under NAFTA. We've just started to turn on the tap,' he said gleefully.

Marv Friedman announced, 'We have had our eyes on Ms. Sutherland, a chemist and an outstanding plant operator for a while. She will be named Sour Lake Plant Manager and Assistant Regional Manager at the Labor Day – Family Day event at the plant.'

The two women board members – a black woman who was president of a minor Midwestern state university and a magazine publisher who liked her scotch – broke into spontaneous applause. Casey laughed and joined them, as did all the Board members.

'Dan Straus,' Friedman continued, 'is Vice President of Environmental as of this date for my operation. Where I can keep an eye on him,' he joked. 'For now he will continue to focus on the new CFC alternative facilities.' Friedman then surprised them all by adding, 'but when the new plant in Matamoros is on line, we expect Ms. Sutherland to become Operations Manager for both of them and San Jose.'

The director who was an Editor of *The New York Times* asked where they found such talented and beautiful plant managers, and Friedman said, 'Why under the chairman's leadership we home grow them.'

The curmudgeon Columbia University professor, who had been a director for over ten years, sucked up to Casey's 'business savvy' as he put it. He had been on the Board for three terms, and was vying for a fourth.

He said he was proud of the development of the environmental audit process in the company, and pleased that it had produced such a fine talent as Mr. Straus. He added that he knew Mr. Straus had been mentored in the environmental business by Tom Foley at Michigan State, who was a pantheon in the field and a good friend for years.

Dan said, 'I was fortunate to attract Dr. Foley's attention.'

'We all know that luck follows those who take advantage of opportunities,' the chairman added.

At that the newly named board member, who was the University of Texas President, made the longhorn sign with his fingers at Bonnie, which she returned. Bonnie then turned and made the sign to Anne who also returned it. Everyone laughed.

The chairman then introduced Anne Hennessy, a newly appointed Director of Public Affairs, under H. Jeffrey Bush, with special assignment for the Texas-Mexico region, including the Governor's office. 'Anne, Dan and Bonnie are responsible for much of the good follow-through with the Governor's office,' Casey said. Casey seemed enchanted with her, saying, 'Anne has made a great impression on the Governor, which will be helpful to us in our Mexican relationships, including the long-term plan we have been discussing to move the North Carolina chemical complex in stages to the Matamoros site.' He turned toward Bonnie and Dan and said, 'Now that's still highly confidential.'

This was the first Dan, Bonnie or Anne had heard of this particular plan, but Anne didn't miss a beat, as she put her arm briefly through Casey's, as they stood there, and said, 'Public Relations is really quite easy when you have someone like the chairman leading. Besides,' Anne smiled, 'Bonnie and Dan make my job easy.'

The chairman then added, 'This Texas-Mexican project is a part of our long-term strategy, as you know, and will involve about six thousand employees at the Matamoros complex eventually, but it will be built up in stages, capitalizing on our wonderful, youthful talent.'

He scratched the back of his head. 'And we are going to continue to show the world – and the state of Texas – a dynamic company which is going to reposition itself and help Texas grow with NAFTA. This is a great team we have here.' He concluded, 'Say, let's take a break and enjoy some refreshments with these young people.'

The Board crowded around Bonnie and Anne, attracted and charmed by the novelty of meeting such beautiful young women moving up in their company. Dan knew he clearly was not meant to steal this scene, nor could he. Casey beamed. He was at his best as the benevolent dynamic schemer.

*

Anne, Bonnie and Dan celebrated that night on the chairman's tab, at the Four Seasons Restaurant, in New York City. They had not changed from the meeting, so they looked the part of corporate yuppies on the town. When each of the women was approached at the bar by an exec. who thought he would join the threesome, Anne asked Dan 'where that Mafia don from Padre Island was lurking to help them now when they needed him'.

Dan answered, 'There are too many of the real things here (generally motioning to the men at the bar), so they better keep that impersonation under wraps.' They laughed at the memory.

They sat first in the glittering bar and then in the fountain room, drinking and eating. Bonnie said, 'We both know it's really you that made this happen, Dan.' She looked at Anne wide-eyed and continued to Dan, 'From that day together at my mother's grave to now, you are my guardian angel – and the best of all that is possible for me.'

'Hey,' Anne said, 'I'll drink to that too, Padre.' And they laughed at the oblique reference to Padre Island.

'You know,' Dan said, as they ate the first of the desserts they shared, 'this exorbitant pay for the chairman is great for him and spills down on us, I guess, but my liberal Jewish bloodline still is disapproving.'

'It did seem awfully like a club, didn't it?' Anne said.

'When you put your arm through Casey's, I thought he was going to get a hard-on and stain his pants,' Bonnie said. Again they laughed. And then she added, 'But you can see why J.D. is so bitter since he was turned out of the club.'

'Hell, don't feel sorry for that turnip,' Anne answered. 'A man spurned can have as much fury as a woman, you know, you know.'

They smiled and Dan added soberly, 'Let's continue to be careful about him.'

★

Dan and Bonnie drove Anne back to her apartment. She kissed them both on each cheek, saying to each, 'I love you.'

'Do you want to stay with us tonight?' Bonnie said. 'I feel sorry leaving you alone.'

'Yeah, I would like that,' Anne answered. 'But no, I don't think I could repeat that and keep my perspective. We might become rivals in a way I couldn't control, so it's better to simply kiss goodnight.' This she did again sweetly on each cheek.

As she left the car she smiled at them and said, 'Quite a day.'

*

Dan always marveled at Bonnie's sexual ingenuity. He went along with her wherever she took him, but she also made their sex transcend their bodies and become an expression of their love.

'Tonight,' she said, as they approached the Hyatt New Brunswick, where she was staying, 'I want to do something really special for you, darling. I want to become a fantasy you will not forget.'

'Hey, that's easy, baby,' he responded.

'No,' she replied. 'Let me do this thing – you will like it, I promise.'

*

'This is our own time together,' Bonnie had said to Dan. He sat in his undershorts on a chair by the open curtains. Bonnie was in the bathroom preparing her surprise. Dan thought about their happiness and their sharing. He was basically both an optimist and a doubter – after all he was an auditor, he thought. How long could this bliss continue, he asked himself.

They were surrounded by such pain and loneliness, and some he knew he had caused. His older daughter frankly told him, on the beach, during a day's visit the last weekend, 'I miss you, Daddy. Why do you keep going away?' Dan thought he heard the hint of a stammer.

Gloria had expressed second thoughts and he had told her that he couldn't come back, he had met someone else. She was coldly silent and pained. Finally she said icily, 'You will pay, Prince Dan.'

Foley was increasingly forgetful and confused. He was sealed into the pain of awareness of early onset of Alzheimer's disease, recently diagnosed, he confessed to Dan.

His mother too was increasingly forgetful, living in the past of her memories of parents and husband. She sometimes called him by his father's name, although she still could connect herself more often than not.

How long could this bliss with Bonnie continue? Forever he hoped, but he knew better. The gods were just playing with them, he thought. Anyway, he would put all his energy into making their life sweet. There was no need to stimulate lust, she brought it out of him at every movement and at every turn.

Bonnie opened the bathroom door. She was dressed in a little nightdress of silk chemise that was all see-through lace at the scooped neckline in front and just reached to her upper thighs. Cut to the bias to show her form, the nightdress was bunched at the bodice by a ribbon that gave her beautiful breasts contour while allowing them to move freely. The back was bare, except for thin shoulder straps which reached to the silk at the curve in her spine, where the silk fell in the rear and contoured her youthful shape. She had a young, adolescent girl look, with her long, blonde hair flat against her back. She wore no make-up but highlights for her open, blue eyes and red, red lipstick. The effect was stunning, a grown up Lolita, who, on sight, encouraged passion in him.

She came over to him. She kissed him gently and then put her fingers to his lips to stop him from talking. She kissed his mouth persistently this time, tongue licking his lips. He stirred and again she placed her fingers to his lips. She kissed his ear, his neck, his forearms and both of his nipples, licking them while she kissed them. She lowered herself to the floor and removed his briefs. She took his bulging cock in her mouth and kissed, licked it, sucked it.

He tried to pull her up to him but she would not come. She sucked with a gusty sliding motion, while he exclaimed, 'Oh Bonnie, oh Bonnie, oh Bonnie,' with growing emotion. He tried again to pull her up but she wouldn't, rather holding the head of his penis in her mouth and licking and sucking on it with great pleasure of her own. 'Oh baby,' he said, as he came in her mouth. She held on for what seemed like minutes more.

Then they repaired to the bed. 'Kiss my breasts through this nightie, baby,' she said and he did, while his hand explored her wet vagina. He unbuttoned the nightdress lace at the top and bared her shapely and generous breasts. He kissed them and then he repeated her ritual of licking and sucking her nipples until they were excited and hard. He lowered his mouth to her cunt and licked, then sucked and then greedily devoured her. She was responding by writhing under his grip.

His prick once more bulged with blood and anticipation. She was wet, open and ready for him. He quickened the timing of his thrusts and their length. Their mouths and tongues were engaged.

The heart of their passion threatened to consume them. He could feel her contractions. He was surging with power.

'I love you, baby,' he said.

'Hold on a little longer for me,' she countered. He tried to think of Jackie Robinson (an old trick of his) but, in truth, he kept seeing her so beautiful and enticing, as she emerged from the bathroom. She was his fantasy, and thinking about that fantasy slowed him down enough for her to catch up.

Their passion united in a frenzy of movement between them, with great sliding and sucking sounds. 'I love you,' she said, dissolving in a series of climaxes, but he pushed her further. He had reached a level of maleness with her that he thought impossible. The climax coming for him was not only in his prick, but his heart and head.

Pushed on by him, she too reached further and deeper in her orgasms. 'Oh baby,' she said, kissing greedily at him, his hands now under thighs, kneading her as he thrust on. She reached a level of complete abandon and said, 'Now baby, now, now.' And it was now for him, too, with a release and series of involuntary motions inside her, responding to her continued tremors.

'Like an earthquake,' she said.

'You are my fantasy,' he answered.

★

As was their custom, they slept in a tangled mass, as if in sleep they could finally become the one being for which their sexual relationship strove. Arms and legs overlying in sleep, often grasping on to each other. Bonnie sometimes laughed with Dan. 'We really sleep together.'

Now Dan was on his side against her back, his one hand casually around her and cupping her breast. Her fingers touched his, her foot resting backward as if running on his leg.

Dan was dreaming a most troubling episode. He and Bonnie were driving in a traffic jam in New York City at night. It was a dangerous area and bands of young toughs repeatedly tried to enter the car. The doors were locked and they were safe. They became lost and Dan was insecure not knowing where he was in his own city. He parked and ran into a drugstore to gain his bearings. While in the store, he realized he had not taken the car keys, so he ran back out to tell Bonnie she had the keys and to lock the doors. The car was gone with Bonnie. At first he insisted to himself that he had not remembered where he had parked, but frantic searching did not turn up the car or Bonnie.

He woke himself up with a start, sweating. His agitation woke her, as he moved to wash his face in the bathroom.

'What's the matter, honey?' Bonnie said.

'Nothing,' he answered. 'Go back to sleep.'

'When you come back close, baby,' she answered, and, before she dozed off again, holding hands with him, she said, 'I need to know your cock's close.'

Bonnie went back to sleep quickly. Dan lay awake, his mind working, churning, worrying, remembering. He admired her ability to sleep so deeply and easily. He knew he was too often full of thoughts, ideas, contradictions, repetitions. He wished he could just go to sleep again, as she did, but he couldn't. So, holding her hand as if they were walking instead of lying flat on their backs in bed in the dark, his mind worked.

He thought about Gloria telling him he would pay for his flight from her. He guessed she had a point, but she had precipitated the break by going to Long Island and a lawyer friend told him he should continue to occupy the house as evidence of the fact that he had not abandoned them. He was generously putting money in her account, so she was under no financial pressure, and, although the same lawyer had advised against the arrangement, he would continue to do it. Yes, he guessed he would pay.

Dan thought about their wedding, an ugly day he held in low regard and often resented. It had been a large wedding, held in Teddy Roosevelt's estate house turned historical museum, on the North Shore of Long Island. No expense had been spared but the more elaborate it got, the more people Gloria invited from her family Dan didn't know, the more Dan became oppressed by the baroque setting and arrangements the more he resented the noisy day. He felt that his family's values had simply disappeared in the elaborateness of it. 'Good-bye Columbus' run rampant, he had said to her, in earnest confidence, while on their honeymoon. She had been white-hot angry at that and then sulked for a day.

Dan knew his father disapproved. He didn't say anything, just kept smiling and saying, 'Weddings are not the end but the beginning.'

Still, in some way, he thought, the trouble generated by the clash of his conservative personal and liberal political values with Gloria's affluence and dysfunctional stubbornness, as the wedding approached, should have been apparent to him. Dan knew why his father had gone along with all the nonsense, but he couldn't figure out why he had. In the environment, he thought, you look for early markers of trouble, so you can respond soon enough to turn the ship around. Why hadn't he recognized the signs of eventual catastrophe then?

He thought of a joke his father liked to tell – 'A Yankee to a South American is any American. To an American, a Yankee is someone north of the Mason-Dixon line. To someone North of the Mason-Dixon line, a Yankee is a New Englander. To a New Englander, a Yankee is someone from Vermont. And, in Vermont, a Yankee is someone from the Northern part of the state who eats his peas with a knife.'

His dad used to say that you had to look at the relative facts and the perspectives to understand where people were coming from. 'Open your mind up,' Dan's dad would say, when he was a child, 'and try to understand what's really going on, including in the other guy's shoes.'

Well, he thought, that didn't work with Gloria. She just kept coaxing, wheedling, demanding, but always diminishing his values.

He held Bonnie's hand lightly as she stirred. He should go to sleep, he thought.

★

A few mornings later, at the New Brunswick headquarters, at lunch in the cafeteria, with his environmental peers, the subject came up of whether to be an environmentalist, representing the public interest and get away from the industry pressures and positions. Dan finally chipped in, 'Well, I think it is easier to be an environmentalist with one of the big pressure groups – Sierra, Audubon – because you can be purer. In a sense you are not responsible for anything but your opinion. In industry, it is true you have the competition and job to consider, even if you don't care too much about profit. But, more important, in industry, you need to worry about how to get something done, not just how it should be done. You are an advocate for the environment, but within the context of other priorities and technological feasibility. On the other hand, I have a friend at one of the big environmental pressure groups,' Dan continued, 'who says the pressure to say the right or accepted thing and the attention to career, in terms of being politically correct, is as great a pressure as anything or anyone in industry faces.

'Careerism is rampant, I think, in the environmental community, because they have no hard product,' Dan continued. 'We don't always do the right thing as environmentalists in industry. God knows we cave in to the bottom line pressure and we have our ambition too,' he added, 'but, at least, we can see tangible results to our work in the plants and in products, and, of course, in protecting the employees in the plants – not just in some new set of regulations or a well-written argument that may or may not do any good, but in tangible processes and equipment, not to mention better health and safety.

'Bonnie Sutherland has told me,' Dan told the group at the luncheon table, 'that she loves her work in the Sour Lake plant, including the environmental progress she really is making happen, because it's so tangible and directly affects the people's lives in that little town. Now I don't even like most of the people in that town,' he continued, warming to talking about Bonnie in a permissible way to his mates, 'but I know what she means. Perhaps there are some leaders in the environmental movement who can feel the same satisfaction,' he said. 'No, I'm sure there are but the rank and file like us in those organizations do not have the same solid satisfaction we get. They have to keep the belief up that industry is the villain and source of evil to maintain their standing. My friend,' he concluded, 'tells me he has grown to hate the weekly bash industry sessions. So, no I have never been sorry for the path I took,' Dan added.

Later, sitting with Anne, while she ate, he recounted the conversation with his peers. 'And besides it led me to be able to talk about Bonnie.'

Anne loved Dan for that comment. He was so true to Bonnie, and, somehow, in his fealty to Bonnie's professionalism and her effect on him, to her too. She knew that she would always be their friend and that she would always desire much from Dan, but that Bonnie now stood permanently in the way. They went back a long way, she and Bonnie, but Dan was now beyond a simple fascination or even lover for her. Bonnie and Dan were a permanent number and she could only take pleasure in the fact that they shared so much of their love with her.

That night together – the three of them – on Padre Island was vivid and a repeated memory for her, but she knew also it was only that, a memory. She hoped to get herself a romantic life, but she also knew she would never get over Dan or that luscious, sweet, sexy night with Dan and Bonnie.

Did Dan read all this in her face? He is so goddamned intuitive, Anne thought. He seemed to react to her isolation with a sympathetic glance and touch of his hand. And then he said, 'Say, you are the greatest for us, Anne and we are going to have one helluva time being friends over the years.'

'Don't worry about me,' Anne responded. 'You and Bonnie are going to have me around your necks plenty,' she laughed.

'That's the way we want it,' he answered seriously. 'You know that.'

'How is she doing this week away from you?' Anne asked.

'She said this morning that the last touches were put on the Sour Lake Plant reconstruction, and that,' he emphasized, 'bids were in to review for environmental considerations for the first construction phase in Matamoros to begin when I get there.' Anne sweetly clapped and a few heads turned to look at her. 'The Labor Day Open House is fully planned?' he asked.

'It will be fun,' she nodded, 'but I'm leaving it mostly up to Bonnie – she has such great ideas and knows the people better.'

★

Dear Bonnie,

As we spoke last night, all seems settled now in New Brunswick toward the Labor Day festivities. The Chairman and Marv Friedman will attend, as I understand the Governor will too. Get set for it, because there will be great public recognition of you, as well as myself, and Anne too, I believe. But you will be the main course!

I know it will be a great day under your organization (so much better than mine!) and leadership. Now that we have secured the authorization for the Matamoros facility construction, it's good we decided to invite the officials from Brownsville and Matamoros to Sour Lake for the event. Construction is someone else's headache from Corporate, thank God.

Anne would like to have the three Mayors on the podium when the Governor speaks. Would you ask the Wisemans if they would like to join us for dinner afterward too, so we are sure Sarah and Joe come and not just to photograph.

But these details are not the reason for this note. With a little time here in New Brunswick with these corporate captains and pencil pushers, I have had more time to think about you.

Bonnie, you are exquisite. The greatest thing to ever enter my life. I won't deal with your professional abilities – you know them and they are capable of taking you anywhere you want to go, with the competence you inspire and the trust of those who work with and for you. Don't blush!

What I'm talking about is your effect on me, Bonnie. You know that I have opened up to your love, not to mention your fabulous and natural eroticism. I cannot conceive of living without you. But what I want to laud here is your complete receptivity to me, both just as I am and how I might become. I feel I can spend the rest of my life with you, as I said last night. I will profit from and love you every day.

To digress, the afternoon before last I went to a conference briefing on NAFTA in New York City. I stayed on in the evening and went to see The Heiress. *I know you read it because I saw it all marked up in your bookcase and you mentioned the Olivia de Haviland movie to me once. Remember?*

Well, this production gave me one of the greatest and most profound experiences of my life in the theater. The actress playing the lead role is unknown to me, Cherry Jones. She was more than sensational, she created a complete woman on stage, and totally suspended disbelief. From the shy, reluctant ambiguity at the start to the hardened determination to control events at the end, Cherry Jones, romantically and realistically, created a woman in the 1850s on that stage who no one in the audience will ever forget!

I had an absolute resolve on leaving the theater that we must never let our love and understanding together and the excitement we have slip away. We must never doubt each other, and not allow the outside to corrupt or embitter us, or interfere with the completion and extension of our great love.

Our love both consumes and enlarges me. When I think of the fact that this is my second chance and that I only found you through the happenstance of my work, I am truly shaken and thankful for your aggressiveness in the cemetery that first day together.

We must not become like the woman Cherry Jones plays in The Heiress – *bitterly disappointed and vengeful against the possibility of romance. I know that my mission is fulfillment for you, for that is how I will grow myself. And, Ms. Sweet Bonnie, that fulfillment, in case you worry, includes an entering into and sweet mixing with you by every opening, sexual or intellectual.*

I am not embarrassed by the physical nature of our relationship, or the fact that you hold my sexual appetite in your hands. Nor will I love you less if your incredible beauty and sexuality fade. Do not fear that aging process, my beautiful and wonderful Bonnie. I love you.

How to close this little letter which would seem so plebeian if the sentiments and desire were not so true. Last night I was feeling lonely and in need of you after we talked. I was roaming about my empty house and took a college book of Shakespeare's sonnets down from the bookcase, I think to reinforce the emotion of my most all-consuming romantic love for you. So here is the well-known Sonnet twenty-nine which expresses the depth, the continuity and the permanence of how I feel.

When, in disgrace with fortune and men's eyes,
I all alone beweep my outcast state,
And trouble deaf heaven with my bootless
    cries,
And look upon myself and curse my fate,
Wishing me like to one more rich in hope,

Featur'd like him, like him with friends
    possess'd,
Desiring this man's art and that man's scope,
With what I most enjoy contented least;
Yet in these thoughts myself almost despising,
Haply I think on thee, and then my state,
Like to the lark at break of day arising
From sullen earth, sings hymns at heaven's
    gate;
For thy sweet love remembered such wealth
    brings
That then I scorn to change my state with
    kings.

Chapter Ten

Key Biscayne, Florida

Dan drove his rented, new, white Pontiac Grand Am across the Richenbauer Causeway to Virginia Key and then Key Biscayne. He loved the view from atop the causeway on his left of the city of Miami rising from the waters.

Miami with its skyscrapers of steel and glass, its art deco style, its great tropical sky of fierce sun and fast moving clouds. Dan always felt good there, and he especially felt he needed this weekend break from the intensity of his job and parting from Gloria, but perhaps also from the heat of his relationship with Bonnie. I need time to consider, Dan thought.

Dan's mom lived in the Commodore, one of the big condos on the ocean by the beach on Key Biscayne. He was always caught up by the open sky and greenness of the sea for, at Key Biscayne, the warm gulf stream of the Caribbean almost came in to touch Cape Florida.

Dan's mother was something of a painter, and she kept a working canvas on her deck, off the sliding doors of her living room. She was as fascinated by the changing light over the sea and beach as Monet was in his gardens. Her technical painting skill had declined in the last few years, in keeping with her general decline in faculties, but her sense of light and color remained.

The pastoral quality of Dan's mother sitting on the deck, brush in hand, with canvas before her, in front of this beautiful vista of sky, clouds, sun, sea and palms below in the sand, made him wonder again about the relative quality of her life versus his. 'Gee, Mom, you have so much beauty here,' he said.

'Your father so loved the sky in Florida, Dan,' she replied. 'He said he felt it was the clearest expression of natural wonder. He said it was as close as he ever got to a sense of God.'

'We are so lucky to have our memories of him, Mom,' Dan answered.

'He was a special man, Dan,' she mused, and they sat in silence. 'Soon I'll be dead, Dan. No, don't interrupt, please. I'm not sad. I don't believe in an afterlife, but somehow I am comforted by the fact that I will be joining your father.' She paused, and then stirred, adding some yellow to the sky, saying, 'At least my ashes will be mixed with his. Remember, my darling son, I wish to be cremated, not put below the cold, dark ground but added to this beautiful sea.'

While his mother napped in mid-afternoon, Dan rode his fat-tired bicycle (his mother kept it in her apartment for him) south on Crandon Boulevard to Cape Florida. Past the last apartments he entered the state park.

It was different since Hurricane Andrew. No more Australian pines, willows or deep underbrush. Cape Florida was being regrown with native plants (mostly sea oaks) and palms. The cars shared the road to the lighthouse at the point with bikes, roller blades and joggers. Beautiful, Dan thought, simply beautiful.

From the island's southern tip, a winding path not large enough for cars traversed the western coast. On this path

Dan rode among the tropical beauty of a section of Cape Florida fully reborn with palms and flowers.

His thoughts had turned to Bonnie, as he knew they would.

His mother had told him just to do good and seek to be happy.

The family motto (do good and be happy) was also a heavy burden, but Dan's mom had said it in a kindly fashion, emphasizing that he should find personal happiness beyond his work contribution and career success.

'Do you love this Texas woman, Dan?' she asked. He said he thought he did. 'She makes me happy.' He showed her a picture. 'She *is* a beauty,' she said. 'You love her, she is obviously very sensual, she is available, so go after her, Danny boy.' He was amused, as he rode on past an inlet in the cape, with boats rocking in the gentle sea, that his mom used the appellation, Danny boy, much as Bonnie did – a term of personal endearment.

★

That Saturday night he took his mom to the fish house across the bridge on Virginia Key. They watched the Florida sunset as they ate. 'I can't get used to these old people here, who eat at five or five-thirty, or even earlier in some cases, to get the lower prices,' she said. 'The early bird special is no special, if dinner is over before the sun even starts to go down. The nights are made so long.'

'I haven't got that many dinner engagements,' she said, 'and I'm too frail now for Miami, but I would like to eat out on these islands once in a while, if I could get my women friends in the building to wait until a little later in the evening. They are so afraid of getting robbed or mugged that they turn their lives upside down. So mostly I eat by myself after the light fails and my poor attempts at painting are done for the day.'

'You are doing very well, Mom,' Dan replied. 'I never knew you and Dad would take to Florida so well.'

'We had the money and that's most of the battle,' she answered.

He silently remarked at her continuing mental acuity, within her lapses of forgetfulness. She was still strong-minded and her advice on Bonnie showed how much of a realist she remained.

'Dan,' she said, 'after your divorce, marry this girl if you want to and use my ring your father gave me when I was twenty and he swept me off my feet. But don't forget your children. They are so sweet. They are your responsibility, Dan. Don't become one of those modern men who think they are free to choose not to be good fathers. You are not free, Dan.' She become quite agitated. 'You are not free and your father will tell you so.'

Dan was taken back by her mental shift into the time and space his father still occupied. It sobered him. They had both loved his dad so much. 'I know, Mom, I know. I would never forget them or my love for them or my obligations,' he answered.

*

They sat in the dining alcove playing scrabble later that night. As always, his mom was winning because she knew more words.

Dan's mom and dad had played scrabble almost every night after they retired. They would usually follow the game with plates of ice cream, and that's what Dan and his mom did that night.

'I'm not long for this world, I know, Dan. My heart and pulse flutter too much and something in my brain is fluttering too.' She laughed and raised her hand to ward off his negation. 'But I have had a very good and happy day today. You are a good son. You have some of your dad's turmoil and capacity for self-punishment, but you also have his wisdom and balance. It makes me happy to think that we leave you and your daughters behind.'

★

Early the next morning, before his mom arose, he ate the honeybell orange she had sliced and wrapped in the refrigerator (like she did when he was ten or eleven and they first came to visit Florida) and drove back across the causeway in the beautiful Florida morning light to the Miami airport and his new life.

★

The *Beaumont Independent* ran the following article on Dan's presentation to the press club on August 15:

SOUR LAKE PLANT ENVIRONMENTALIST
REPORTS INDUSTRY MAKES GREAT STRIDES
By Independent Editor Joe Wiseman

On August 14, Dan Straus, an environmental auditor with the American Industrial Corporation, which operates a chemical plant in Sour Lake, frankly discussed the environmental movement within industry before the Beaumont press club at its annual summerfest. He reported that industry has made great strides in running environmentally acceptable operations, as he demonstrated with changes made at the Sour Lake plant where three fatalities occurred in a gas leak last year.

Mr. Straus announced that Ms. Bonnie Sutherland of Sour Lake, the plant chemist, would officially become the Sour Lake Plant Manager after the Labor Day maintenance was completed. A company spokesperson, Ms. Anne Hennessy, also originally from Sour Lake, invited the public to an Open House at the plant on August 29. Ms. Hennessy indicated that settlement was reached with the families of each of the fatalities, but no terms have been made public.

GOVERNOR ATTENDS

Governor Bush is expected to attend the Open House, according to Ms. Hennessy, to help launch American Industrial as a partner in developing the enlarging Texas relationship with Mequiladora business in Mexico. Mr. Straus indicated that Sour Lake, Brownsville and Matamoros would be sister cities for American in developing the economy and good environmental picture on both sides of the border. Mr. Straus indicated that 'improved environmental conditions were spurred by prosperity.' He referenced the Rio

Conference on Environment and Development in 1992, which he attended, at which the UN or Rio Charter was signed for 'sustainable development', coupling economic and environmental advancement. The Governor's father, then President Bush, attended the Rio Conference and signed the charter on behalf of the United States.

EQUIVALENT ENVIRONMENTAL STANDARDS

Mr. Straus announced that as Ms. Sutherland took full control of the Sour Lake operation, which produces HF chemical product, including fluorocarbon substitutes, and a companion operation in San Jose, California, he would be focusing his attention on the Matamoros, Mexico, operation, where another sister plant to Sour Lake is being built. The State of Texas and Mexico are encouraging with tax incentives a cross-border, free import-export business with its Mexican neighbors on chemical products 'with equivalent environmental standards in both regions,' Mr. Straus said. He said he felt he 'was at the real birth of the Rio agreements, where the economy and environment are cosupportive.' He noted the Mayor of Matamoros would attend the Sour Lake plant Open House over the Labor Day weekend.

A Houston Greenpeace representative in attendance asked Mr. Straus if he 'weren't being too rhapsodic about the industry role in the environment, since thousands of people in

Matamoros were dying from industry's pollution of the water and air.' Mr. Straus responded that he 'didn't feel informed enough to be drawn into that controversy, and no one knows the cause of the problem in Matamoros. But', he said, 'certainly, prosperity in Mexico will help buy the expensive plumbing and water treatment to make the drinking water acceptable there. Continued poverty is not going to help them,' Straus added, 'nor condemning the Mexicans to less development because people north of the border think that that is really better for them.'

HITTING THE GREEN WALL

In response to questions, Mr. Straus was particularly candid when he questioned whether industry could sustain its environmental momentum, saying, 'It is not only poorer economic times that could sabotage our environmental progress in industry but what we call hitting the green wall.

'That is,' Mr. Straus explained, 'the expression which has come to represent for industry environmental people the threat of so integrating their activities into the business decision process as to lose their distinctiveness or special clout of representing society's need for a decent environment long term whatever the short-term profit pressures.' Mr. Straus strongly maintained that he believed that that would not happen at American or other environmentally-minded companies because the leadership understood the contribution protecting the environment made to the employees and the public, as well as profits long term. Mr. Straus said, the company was 'particularly proud of the job Ms. Sutherland had performed in turning around the Sour Lake plant both economically and environmentally.' He said that that was a perfect example of environment benefiting from profits and long-term profits benefiting from responsible environmental management.

ENVIRONMENTAL PROFESSIONALISM

Mr. Straus did admit upon a question from Sol Abrams, Chairman of the Texas Chemical Industry Council and a well-known Houston and Beaumont industrialist, that vigilance and commitment were necessary to maintain the environmental momentum. He joked that his profession as an environmental auditor made him constantly question whether a good environmental system was in place and would stay in place in industry, but he said colleagues like Ms. Sutherland and Ms. Hennessy prodded him as peers to do his job. 'As a matter of fact,' Mr. Straus concluded, 'the greatest safeguard in industry of environmental progress is that there are literally thousands of environmental advocates now drawing their pay to be environmental advocates within their companies. I don't see how that will change,' he said, 'unless we go into really bad economic times or those advocates get so fully absorbed into the competitiveness of the business as to be seduced away from their environmental professions.'

Editor's Note

Those who have visited the Sour Lake plant report marked progress there. A brief article by Mr. Straus that appeared on *Greenlife Wire* is found elsewhere on this page.

ENVIRONMENT AND DEVELOPMENT
By Dan Straus

The Cairo Conference on population issues last summer reached a stunning conclusion. After considerable bickering over abortion and like issues, the conference got down to business and based on good data nearly unanimously affirmed the key part which the advancement of women's lives plays in affecting birth rate decline. Poor women's lives are most often improved: by alleviating poverty; by their having greater control; by education and by the raising of status through an enlarging viewpoint.

Once again, the data affirm that the restrictive, 'doom and gloom' outlook of 'smaller is better' that pervaded in the Seventies, at the time of the First Stockholm Conference, has been repudiated. It is not by restricting the lives of poor women or imposing on them limited roles or duties or codes of conduct that the population tide may be affected, but rather by developing and enlarging their lives through activity and education.

Why should we be surprised? A John Hopkins University study in the Eighties reported that quality of life indices for the urban poor in Baltimore were more favorable when employment improved and declined when unemployment gained. I do not believe that anyone really doubts, on a personal basis, that, when resources and alternatives are available, awareness and quality of life behaviors, including those which affect the environment, improve. The harmony at Cairo on the necessity of attacking population concerns through the expansion of the role of women is directly affirming and supportive of the conceptual shift in environmental thought adopted at the United Nations' Rio conference earlier in this decade. In the Rio declaration and throughout Agenda 21 (the work plan adopted at Rio) are the affirmation that a responsible approach to the environment *and* development are mutually supportive, not in opposition. Of course, the marriage of the two requires responsible conduct in both arenas, but neither environmental protection nor economic development can be successful for any sustained time without the other. Again, there are few in the general population who do not intuitively understand that link.

The positive and important link between environmental protection and prosperity is now to be determined under NAFTA. As the Mexican economy, and the USA's and Canada's, too, grow, more resources will be available in North America to finance the environmental steps that must be taken to meet the needs on which attention will be focused.

As in the rest of the world, the twenty-first century environmental focus in North America may well be centered on good water for drinking and agriculture. It is probably not an exaggeration to say that whereas wars in the nineteenth century were fought over land and in the twentieth century over oil, the twenty-first century will be most vulnerable to conflict over available water resource for a growing population to consume and for the products to feed it. Technology to purify water and treat waste, which contaminates water, will be available, but costly. With prosperity, there is the hope that the technology can be available and affordable to developing countries to meet their growing water needs, whether it be in Mexico or China, for example.

A diminishing perspective, à la the Club of Rome, would doom those 'have nots' on both sides of the US-Mexican border to lives of desperation. Conversely, with the growth of the economic base under NAFTA and the contexts of separate environmental agreements and programs, governments and, more importantly, the people in North America will continue to seek an enlarging commitment to improving the quality of life. As economic opportunity and environmental awareness increase, there will be the will and the means to realize such improvement.

Biography

Dan Straus, an engineer, is an Environmental Auditor with American Industrial, Inc. of New Brunswick, New Jersey.

Chapter Eleven

Sour Lake

The Friday morning of Labor Day weekend had bloomed cool and clear. By ten, when the townsfolk started arriving, the sun had heated the air up as might be expected in East Texas, Labor Day weekend, but the humidity remained low.

The plant looked just great, as the chairman had told Bonnie Sutherland, when he had arrived from Houston at around 9.00 AM. All painted up and grassed, with benches and balloons. Bonnie was very proud. Tents for eating and for the special events were set up and gaily decorated. During the morning, happy events spun out – a fashion show, Dixieland and mariachi bands, a basketball exhibition by two pro players from the Houston team, and the Dallas cheerleaders, when the Governor arrived.

The production processes were railed off, but there were walkways around them and poster boards to explain what they produced and their operation. The plant personnel, wearing straw bowlers with American flag bandannas spelled each other showing their plant to the community.

There was a feeling of camaraderie and excitement among them.

A special exhibit on the pilot facility and NAFTA were surrounded by Mexican, Canadian and US flags, to be noted at the formal ceremony, and the Mayor of

Matamoros, the Brownsville Mayor and the Sour Lake Mayor, and their wives, as well as the Governor and his guests, would be presented by Bonnie, after she was introduced by the chairman. The chairman would announce Bonnie's promotion and then Dan's, when he introduced her.

Marv Friedman was there, of course, paying special attention with Anne to Joe Wiseman, as they had agreed he would. Sarah Wiseman told Marv that 'it is a miracle how this junk pile of a plant has been transformed by Dan and Bonnie.'

'They have done a great job for us, along with all the good folk down here,' Marv answered.

'Well,' Joe joined in, tartly, 'I'd like a picture of you, Mr. Friedman, Mr. Casey, the Governor, Mr. Straus and Ms. Sutherland, if we could get you all standing still long enough to take it.'

'You know, Sarah and Joe,' Anne countered, 'we're going to announce Bonnie's becoming manager of the plant for the company in a few minutes in the chairman's remarks, after the Governor speaks, so there will be a good opportunity for all the pictures we all want.'

Bonnie stopped and said, 'hi,' to Sarah and they chatted for a moment like two schoolgirls.

Sarah asked, 'Are you staying around this hot place all weekend? I know in the old days no one would have caught you and Anne here in this sultry Labor Day heat.'

'Actually,' Bonnie said, 'Dan, Anne and I are going on a little business planning retreat to South Padre tomorrow morning, to return after four or five days there. After all the work of putting this together,' she said, 'we are giving the plant the weekend off and then some for routine process maintenance, and we are just going to go somewhere quiet to draw up strategies.'

Sarah knew she was telling only half the story. She had heard the rumors about Dan and Bonnie, but she only smiled and cheerfully responded, 'Well, have some fun, too.'

Bonnie was in her glory. She looked beautiful, Dan thought, in play clothes and her loose, blond hair. Happy, she led by example. It was clear to Dan and Casey, in a chat they had while eating hot dogs, that Bonnie was a positive, moving force at the plant and had given it a new spirit.

'You've done a great job here, Dan,' Casey said.

'It's really Bonnie, you know, Mr. Casey,' Dan replied.

'I know,' the chairman answered, scratching the back of his head, 'but we can share some of the credit with that beautiful creature, can't we?' They both laughed.

Dr. Foley was there chatting with the Mexican lawyer, Dr. Orantes, when Dan brought him over to meet the chairman. 'I know this great educator from Michigan State,' Casey said. (He had been primed as to the guests.) 'We are pleased to have you here, sir.'

'I am pleased to be here, sir,' Foley replied.

'You have some friends on our Board,' Casey said, to which Foley responded, gesturing to Dan, 'Yes, but it's this fellow of whom I am most proud.'

Dan thought that slightly inappropriate, but the chairman laughed good-naturedly saying, 'How's the football team going to be this season?'

'Should be great,' Foley answered, amiably. 'But Texas will be good this year, too,' apparently confusing Casey with a Texas official.

Dan's eye caught sight of J.D. sitting on a bench, lazily talking to a couple of other men from the town. He didn't like seeing J.D. there, but the day was open to the town and any other visitor who happened in, so they had little choice.

He did say to Anne at the next opportunity, 'We ought to keep an eye on J.D. – nodding toward him – we sure don't want any trouble.'

'Yes,' she replied. 'I asked security to keep an eye on him, but he seems well-behaved. I told Bonnie he was here,' she continued, 'and she only responded that Mr. You Know must be chock-full of envy for what's happened to this plant since he left.'

Late morning the ceremonies began as the Texas heat started to build. They would be finished with formal festivities by noon, have a tailgate lunch for everyone, and people could then hang around as long as they liked.

Tony Casey introduced the Governor as a man of the people. Governor Bush spoke about the Texas economy and how proud he was of its rebirth. The Governor asked Bonnie to come up to the rostrum and he spoke of 'this beautiful woman's tragic loss at the plant and the way she had led to it being rebuilt and reborn since that day.' He said he had visited the little park under construction named after her mother, Beatrice Sutherland, that morning, on his way to the plant, and he 'was inspired by this tale of family dedication and economic growth' in Sour Lake. He was absolutely rhapsodic, Dan thought, as he and Anne exchanged smiles of recognition at the simultaneous corniness and truthfulness of this politician's words.

The chairman then announced Bonnie's promotion, to her dazzling smile and asked Dan and Anne to join them, along with Marv Friedman and the Governor on the little platform stage.

Friedman announced that the business had made new record profits in the last quarter at the plant. He announced the plant was expanding into new products and would be expanding its payroll. He briefly reviewed Dan and Anne's new assignments as well.

Tony Casey asked the Mayors of Sour Lake, Matamoros and Brownsville to join them, symbolic of Texas-Mexican-American unity. The little band then struck up the Mexican and US National anthems, each played in a shortened version, in view of the heat, Bonnie had commented to Dan in their run-through.

The chairman then wished them all a happy day and 'please stay and enjoy the Texas and Mexican lunch of barbecue and tacos. The plant facilities are open for your inspection as long as you like.' He and the Governor walked together from the stage to the Governor's limo, which had been brought up nearby, while the others stood on the stage and chatted.

Dan turned to Bonnie and said, 'Well, you are the champ.'

She leaned up close to him and answered only for his hearing, 'No, the champ belongs to you – I just get to use it sometimes.'

'That's not for publication, is it Ms. Sutherland?' he joked.

She answered, 'I'd shout it to the hills if you like, or whisper it to you, only, if you'd rather.' A plant photographer took a picture of the group. It was the last thought she expressed to him.

★

There was no time to do anything. The instant of the ending for Bonnie occurred before she clearly saw what happened and could react to ward it off. Anne, to one side, raised her arm in fear, and perhaps to push Bonnie away, but it was too late. Dan could remember nothing to have given them a warning.

As they happily stood there, on the little stage in the tent in Sour Lake, murmuring to each other about the day and the weekend to come at South Padre, J.D. was upon them shouting something incoherent, which Dan later recalled as, 'Die fucking corporate bitch.'

He had his semiautomatic rifle in one hand and was waving the other arm about wildly, as if leading a charge on to an island being taken from the enemy. He had put on a fatigue cap from Vietnam. His weight propelled him forward.

Someone said he yelled, 'We're liberating this plant.' He was not followed on to the stage by anyone. Several cracker comrades, as Anne would call them later, in their fatigues and similar caps, were letting out rebel yells at the edge of the crowd just a few steps from the platform.

In the instant J.D. advanced on the platform, he fired the polished semiautomatic weapon point blank at Bonnie. The soft bullets, each lovingly prepared by J.D. in his trailer, took her life away, ugly and immediate. Her face contorted in a scream, but there was no time for even that. She had reached up and grabbed Dan's arm as she hit the floor, ripped in her chest and midsection by the destructive bullets. Dead when she hit the deck, her hand, reaching up on her extended arm from the lifeless body, continued to grasp Dan's arm.

A bullet struck Anne in the thigh and she crumpled to the floor screaming. 'No, no, my God, Bonnie, no, no, Dan, no, no, no.'

Dan, too, was struck in the lower arm. Although the wound was superficial, it bled profusely and his blood mixed with Bonnie's on the floor, as he fell atop of her yelling, 'Bonnie, Bonnie, Bonnie,' cradling her lifeless head, with their staring eyes, in his arm. She was still grasping on to him. He would never forget that final embrace.

J.D. stumbled and then hit the platform, the gun carried beneath him. A security guard, who was in fact a Texas teenager, jumped forward and wrestled with J.D. for possession of the gun. J.D. got an arm free and raised the gun from a prone position on the platform, aimed generally at the grouping of Dan and Anne, and the dead Bonnie, only a few inches from them and the grappling guard, who J.D. was overpowering. People were screaming and running from the tent now, or ducking down on the ground. The Governor's security guards were running toward the tent, weapons in hand, while the Governor and Tony Casey were pushed out of danger into the limousine.

Dan reached over wildly now with his bloodied arm, Bonnie still grasped on to his other arm with her death grip, and struck J.D. a blow, which felled the vigilante and knocked the gun across the platform.

The force of the impact of Dan's hand and arm on J.D.'s head not only incapacitated J.D., but broke Dan's bleeding arm, and he fell back on Bonnie, wailing at J.D., 'You son of a bitch. You killed her.' Tears were now flowing down his face from pain and the growing realization of the horror.

Dan then lay there on top of the lifeless Bonnie, blood oozing about them yelling, 'Please, sweet Bonnie, do not die, please do not die, do not die, sweet Bonnie.'

Anne was screaming, 'My God.' And she threw herself on both Dan and Bonnie weeping, 'No, no, no.'

By then Sarah Wiseman was on the platform and reached them and began yelling too, but coherently, 'Someone help them.' She turned to look for her husband. 'Joe,' she said, 'help them,' as she stood above the mêlée.

As Joe reached them, a great deal of reactive help arrived. Joe began untangling Anne and Dan from Bonnie. A nurse they had hired for the day to attend to headaches or upset stomachs reached the platform and called for a doctor to assist, if one was present. A graying gentlemen sprang forward and knelt over Anne and Dan, who were still screaming and crying. He ordered someone to call hospital emergency. The Governor's security were now on J.D. and holding him down, one with a pistol to J.D.'s head.

Dan was sitting up now. Anne, who was hysterically weeping, leaned against him, while the nurse applied pressure to her leg. The doctor asked Dan if he knew where he was and Dan simply said, 'Yes, Doc, Sour Lake.' The doctor said he would loosen Bonnie's death grip on him and Dan said, 'Not yet, doc.' While the doctor focused on Dan's bloodied and broken arm, he leaned toward Bonnie next to him and kissed her hand clutched on to him. Eventually he said, 'Okay, Doc,' real calm and resigned the Doc would later say. And Bonnie was loosened from Dan.

Two stretchers were brought and Anne and Dan put on them. An emergency vehicle came to the site, siren blowing and lights flashing.

Marv Friedman bent down over them saying only, 'Take it easy, Take it easy, Take it easy,' in a calm voice. Dan thought Friedman was cool and supportive under pressure.

The Governor and Casey were whisked away for the Governor's safety. Police were now on the scene and order was restored. Procedures were being followed in taking a cooler Dan and an hysterical Anne to the hospital, leading a wildly vengeful looking J.D. away and dealing with a dead Bonnie. All this was duly recorded in what would prove to be great detail by the photographer, whom Joe Wiseman had brought along to record the happy Labor Day event, in a special family page of the paper. An editorial in the newspaper would state that the militia was feared in Texas for reprisals and military actions ever since Waco.

Chapter Twelve
Epilogue

Two years had passed. Summer had descended into winter and then to summer again, and then the cycle repeated.

Dan had stayed in control. He had turned down the vice president job, when he returned to the company, a month after the killing, and asked to be assigned straight environmental auditing work.

He mourned Bonnie and testified against J.D. at the grand jury indictment. Dan insisted on being allowed to do that, although he was assured that his evidence was not needed. J.D. pleaded not guilty by reason of temporary insanity. He said he was avenging the conspiracy of government and corporations and the media. He faced execution or jail for life.

Dan went to Sour Lake each of the first six weekends to settle Bonnie's affairs as best he could, and just to be there. He got himself declared her administrator on Joe and Sarah Wiseman's intervention with the local bank. He tended her grave, weeding the lawn about her mother's tombstone, where they had first embraced and felt their passion, and spent time in the little park she had created. He couldn't reconcile her death and get over his shock and grief.

After that he returned monthly, with no real reason except to be near her. She left no will. He set up a trust for the little park she had established and arranged for the rest of her money to be given to the few cousins he could find after the state took its share. He had also collected all the photos from the last day at the plant into a scrap book, which he searched for clues or signs of warning he had missed and the whereabouts of a God who cared. He felt he shared responsibility for her death with that God. He added the photo of her, which they had had taken together in Austin at the airport. He felt it was his most precious possession of her.

Anne took longer to heal from the shattering injury and walked permanently with a stiff leggedness, where a pin supported her upper leg. Her red hair developed and took on streaks of white from the trauma. She made a number of attempts to console Dan or seek consolation from him, but he seemed unable to be more than polite. She left the company after a few months and eventually took a job with a small electronics firm in San Jose she had been introduced to when they were working the pilot plant there.

The company absorbed the shock, shrugged and went on without a hitch and little institutional memory, except of what became increasingly known as the Sour Lake Affair. Casey forced Friedman and most of his cohorts within the year to retire in what was applauded and referred to by the New York Stock investment community as long overdue delayering to move the company's operations closer to the customer.

A new environmental VP had been hired after an extensive search to replace O'Reilly, who had retired. It was a woman, Johanna Shields, from a small company that was less aggressive in its environmental practice and had had more regulatory difficulties than American. Johanna was among that new group of younger, more conservative women, who were rising in corporations. They were more business-oriented than their predecessors, more interested in showing they directly contributed to profits. They emphasized their dedication to full environmental integration, and they fulfilled their personal and career promotion, as compared to those pioneers who came before them. Perhaps it was to be expected that the women who broke the glass ceiling in the corporate environmental arena would make their Faustian pact for corporate success through toeing the business line and bringing the green movement within companies back to more classic capitalistic goals. It remained to be seen whether environmental affairs within companies would be managed as aggressively by these more financially-oriented, more frankly ambitious, career-oriented trendsetters.

Dr. Foley retired in the full, rapid decline of Alzheimer's disease.

Dan's mother died during the first winter after Bonnie's murder.

Gloria remarried and kept custody of their growing daughters. She felt Dan had betrayed them and had paid for it.

The Beaumont paper won the Pulitzer prize for its photo essay on the sensational murder. The TV networks news programs each featured the issue of home-grown gun violence by local Texas vigilantes, but the story passed quickly. *The New York Times* did a feature on women managers under the glass ceiling, referring to Bonnie and Anne, with relation to machismo justice. Tabloids briefly highlighted the luridness of the killings and Bonnie's beautiful body crumpled on the stage platform floor in her own blood.

The momentum for the future in the company passed from Sour Lake to the new growing Mexican operation, where NAFTA was flourishing, despite the ongoing peso difficulty.

Governor Bush prepared for a Presidential campaign in the footsteps of his father. The publicity in Austin and Dallas said it was a near miss for him, and that did him some good as a local hero. He called for guns to continue to be available to law-abiding citizens, but to be taken from criminals. He expressed shock over the life sentence instead of death penalty for J.D.

*

In August, two summers following Bonnie's death, Dan was in California auditing the small CFC replacement plant that was operating in San Jose. His heart was no longer with industry or his job, but his environmental intellect was returning. He was tired of Corporate Environmental.

He had begun thinking about the future – his future. He hoped for enough peace of mind to allow him to focus on his daughters. He was interviewed to take a teaching job offered him with the Stanford University Environmental Institute in a program aimed at developing environmental awareness and programs in Third World countries.

He knew Anne was living nearby and called her from his Marriott Hotel room. He gazed out at the California mountains while her phone rang. On the fourth ring he almost hung up, not wanting to leave a message on the voice mail.

After the fourth ring, Anne answered, with a drowsy, voiced, 'Hello.' She had been sleeping in the early evening.

'It's Dan,' he said. 'I hope I didn't wake you. I'm in Palo Alto.'

There was a pause and then she answered in a voice that painfully recalled for him the Sour Lake directness. 'Oh, Dan, it's you – thank God. Oh Dan.' She started to cry. 'How are you?' she said. 'Are you okay? I miss you so much, Dan.' It spilled out.

'I'm different than I was, Anne,' he said. 'I don't want to make you sad. I'm afraid I've become a bore socially. I don't have much left. I'm grayer.' He paused and confessed what was very painful for him, 'I seem to have lost everything with Bonnie.' He sobbed now, too.

'Oh, Dan,' she replied, 'that makes no difference to me. I walk with a limp and use a cane because I fall if I don't. I go to bed early most nights because I'm afraid. I'm much older, too, Dan.'

'Yes,' he said. There was a long pause.

Neither spoke. Then she said, 'Don't go away without us talking, Dan. Please may we see each other?'

'Yes,' he said. 'I would like that. Can you come here to the Marriott and have dinner with me?' he asked.

'Oh yes, yes, my precious Dan. We need for our lives to start again. I will be there in an hour.'

'I will meet you in the lobby,' he said. 'I'm glad I called. See you soon. Come quickly.'